STELLA FORELOVE

Shot Down Love

First edition

ISBN: 979-8-9929196-0-8

This book was professionally typeset on Reedsy.
Find out more at reedsy.com

For anyone who loves the idea of love, but hasn't found the real thing.
Here's something to dream about.

Playlist

How Much Do You Love Me - Kelsea Ballerini
Jealous - Nick Jonas
How Would You Feel - Ed Sheeran
I Like Me Better - Lauv
Pocketful of Sunshine - Natasha Bedingfield
There She Goes - The La's
Jump Then Fall - Taylor Swift
Never Be The Same - Camila Cabello
Miss Independent - Ne-Yo
Dandelions - Ruth B.
Touch - Little Mix
Work Song - Hozier
I Wanna Be Yours - Arctic Monkeys
Look After You - The Fray

One

⁓◦⦿◦⁓

Summer

"Shit." I mutter, shoving my bag to the ground, the noise of my water bottle clattering pushing me closer to my breaking point. The Kronos machine blinks back at me: 'Format Not Recognized'. I try another angle, digging my nails into my palms. *One more try. One more, or I'm quitting.*

'Out Punch Created', it reads, and a relieved breath rushes out of me.

Finally free, I reach the elevators, the weight of five lives lifted. Someone waves at me as I walk to my car. I don't bother waving back. After being a Med-Surg nurse for 9 months, I already consider myself seasoned. My back is constantly aching, my positive attitude diminished, and my sleep schedule? Nonexistent.

I unlock my Toyota Camry—Chuck, my high school relic—and hop in the front seat. I slam the door shut, leaning my head on the steering wheel. *Is this what my life has come to?* I thought that becoming a nurse would mean saving lives every day. Instead, it's arguing with family members, hiding in the nutrition room, and fighting with middle-aged nurses who think the profession is "not like it used to be".

I whisper a prayer, before shoving my key into the ignition. I wait in suspense as he sputters, patting the wheel softly when the engine hums to life. He was the first thing I ever bought for myself, and there's no way in hell that I can afford a new car at my current stage of life. I can't remember who lied and told me nursing is where the money's at, but clearly they never lived in a big city. I can't imagine splurging on name brand Oreos, let alone a new car.

On the drive home, I snack on sour candy, my trick to not falling asleep behind the wheel after working a twelve-hour night shift. I dream of the smell of coffee as I walk through the door, my warm bed calling for me. After a long shower to erase the smells of the night, of course. My scrubs are lucky that they were a gift from Eliana—my one, and only, childhood friend—because after what they've seen, they deserve a proper burial.

But her love language is gifting and mine is nonexistent so I try to avoid any conflict. Having someone like Eliana Jacobs as a constant in my life is something I'll always cherish. After having her as a friend for ten years, she's like a sister to me. Being an only child, I needed someone to fill that role, and as a 5'11" raven-haired badass, she does.

Walking into the apartment complex, I opt for the elevator, bypassing the stairs completely. I pay $1600 a month and will use every amenity available. When I open the door, an eerie feeling sets in. The lights are off, despite Eliana's typical arrival time.

Weird.

Normally, our living situation could not be more perfect. With me as a nurse and her as a flight attendant, our flexible schedules merge flawlessly. By the time I get home, she's leaning on the kitchen counter, mug in hand. My post-shift rant is the only thing that keeps my sanity, and my bank account, within normal limits.

I flip the kitchen light on, calling out for her, with no response. She must be out early—or staying somewhere late. I shrug, dropping my stuff to the floor and head towards our shared bathroom. I turn the shower on full heat and jump in, humming gratefully at the feeling.

After more than a few minutes of steamy bliss, I wrap myself in a towel and walk into my room. I rake a hairbrush through my hair and read through some emails. Most of them are from my manager, asking if I can pick up a few extra shifts. To which my answer is, hell no.

I snag my TV remote and flip to YouTube, then pick a random video to have for background noise as I drift off to sleep. I turn on both of my fans—because sleeping in a room that isn't below freezing would be a crime—and throw my phone on the charger.

My hand reaches for my favorite pajama pants, making me curse when I remember they're still in the dryer. I leave my room, stepping into the bathroom to grab my dirty scrubs, and begin to walk that way when I immediately stop myself.

There is a man. Sitting on my couch. I stare at the back of his head, eyes wide. Is this what perverts do now? Get comfortable in your space and strike when you least expect it? A minute passes as I contemplate my options. I could run out the front door, though he'd surely be able to catch up before I made it. I'm not exactly athletic. Or I know! I could jump out of my bedroom window! But he would hear me open it, and even if he didn't, I would probably end up snapping my neck. Which leaves me with one option.

"MURDERER!" I scream, launching an empty Starbucks cup that had somehow ended up in my hand at the creep.

He goes stills, then turns his head in my direction.

"Did you just throw your fucking trash at me?"

Two

Summer

I gape at the man side-eyeing me from the couch, my discarded Starbucks cup lying six feet away. *How did I miss?* I recognize his face instantly, and stomp towards him until we're facing each other.

He gives me a pointed look. "If I truly was a murderer, that was an unfortunate attempt at saving yourself. Zero survival instinct, sunshine."

My surprise quickly morphs into a scowl at the nickname. Sean Jacobs. My best friend's brother. My enemy. The hottest man I have ever seen-

Okay. That last part was intrusive.

But the rest still stands.

Practically growing up at the Jacobs house, it was clear Eliana's older brother couldn't hide his distaste for me. Whether it was my loud demeanor or childish behavior, he never let me get a word in without scoffing or rolling his eyes. So I, naturally, returned his attitude with one of my own. Being four years younger, my insults never landed, but it didn't stop me from trying.

Aside from the way he's currently glaring at me, I can see that he's changed. My eyes drift down his large frame. He shares the same dark hair, excessive height, and green eyes as Eliana, but that's about it. Sean has a sharp jawline, a perfectly manly nose, and soft, angled lips. Not that I stare at his mouth.

And that body. Before he left for the army seven years ago, he was scrawny with long straggly limbs. Still attractive, but underdeveloped, even at twenty years old. He's always been undeniably nice to look at, but insufferable enough to ruin any appeal.

Sean has always been as tough as he looks. As a teenager, he was moody and kept to himself, which made him all the more mysterious. It made him desirable to the girls at our school, and he took advantage, meanwhile Eliana and I had to swear off men by graduation. I was always jealous of that. The ease he had being liked by others without putting any effort in whatsoever. If we're being honest, he's an asshole. Always has been. But men can get away with that. The only time his exterior broke was with his mom and sister, him being their main protector after their father passed when they were young.

He clears his throat. "If you're finally done staring, I'd like to get some sleep."

"I WAS NOT!" The words burst out of me.

"Why are you yelling at me?"

"WHY ARE YOU IN MY HOUSE? Okay, I hear it now and I'm gonna lower the volume," I reply, backing down.

"Glad we fixed that." His gaze becomes calculated, eyes trailing down my body. "Could you maybe put on some clothes?"

I look down, staring at my towel, that's getting dangerously close to falling. *Oops*.

"Seriously? You're telling me what to wear in MY house? That YOU broke into? You have some nerve, asshole."

He smirks. "Or don't. But I'm having a real hard time focusing on your face."

I blink. "I was trying to get dressed, until I saw you sitting here, and thought the weird cook from dietary had finally followed me home."

"Well, aren't you glad it's me instead?"

"No. I'd take him over you any day."

He frowns, giving me a one-over. His eyes stop at the blood on the balled-up scrubs in my hand. "Who'd you kill?"

"More like who'd I save." I give him a smug smile. No one in this case, I fell victim to an exploding fat roll abscess.

"Can't imagine that," he mocks.

"I WILL HAVE YOU KNO-" I start.

"You're yelling again."

I let out an irritated breath, stepping closer to him. "Why are you even here? Aren't you supposed to be out saving the world or something?"

"Not exactly. I'm only back because-" he begins.

The door flies open with a cheerful Eliana stepping inside, arms full of groceries.

Sean gets up with a groan, attempting to help his sister out.

She drops the groceries with a huff. "SEAN! What are you doing? Sit down before you pull something."

I scoff at her motherly attempt. "Um, he's a big boy. I think he can stand without hurting himself."

"You're right, S. He would be able to normally, but apparently he can't stand without getting a bullet through his abdomen."

"Eli, I'm fine. It's been a few weeks, I'm healing great, and I already apologized for not calling you sooner," he says softly.

I gape at him. "I didn't know you were shot."

"Medically discharged." He grumbles. "Can you guys finish this elsewhere? I need rest."

My eye twitches, and I latch onto Eliana's arm. Hard.

Three

Sean

"He needs to go!" I hear Summer whisper-shout, shoving Eli into her room.

So much for getting some sleep.

It's honestly ironic she has a name accompanied by ideas of sunshine and warmth when almost everything about her resembles pure ice. Her name fits her appearance. With golden blonde hair and honey-brown eyes, she looks like she hangs out in bookstores. Her 5'6" frame is more filled out than I remember, more soft and huggable. She looks different. Not as youthful, which makes sense, being that she was all but a child the last time I saw her.

Aside from that, her personality is still rotten. With the way she passes out scowls like candy, it's a shock that her career revolves around caring for others. While it's not a surprise that she went into medicine—she's always been sharp and reactive—I think if I had her as a caregiver, I'd rather drift into the light.

9

Maybe staying here wasn't my best move. But when I called Eliana and told her about my accident, she insisted, and promised she would warn Summer before I got here. Based on the blonde's reaction, I'm guessing that didn't happen.

Aside from her roommate situation, Eli is the perfect sister. She has always supported every decision I made and never questioned my reasoning. She trusts me. So, when I needed a place to stay, I called her first.

I guess I could have gotten an apartment. I have a steady income from my time in the military and didn't spend much, aside from sending money home every month. It just seemed dumb to reach for my savings while I didn't have another job lined up. The second I do, I'll be out of Summer's wrath for good.

I run a hand down my face, thoughts racing around in my head. It's weird being back, talking to people other than the men from my crew. I was used to a strict schedule with someone always telling me where to be and when. Now, I have complete freedom. And I hate it.

I try to sit up, my stomach lighting on fire. I lift my shirt to peek at it, the wound looking as nasty as ever. Sighing, I grab a few pills from my duffle, downing them, and snag my phone to make a call. It's time to get my life on track again.

Summer

"Come on, Summer," Eliana whines, "I know you guys have some weird juvenile feud, but this is the only time he's come to me for anything. I have to take care of him like he has for me."

I can already see this whole situation unfolding. It wouldn't start out bad. He'd feel the need to be neat since it's not his home. Then, when he gets comfortable, the man in him comes out. He'll leave dishes in the sink, and when questioned about it, will say, "I'll get it later, don't worry. I'm just letting them soak." Spoiler alert: he never gets it later. He'll see laundry in the dryer and instead of leaving it, or taking it to the owner, he'll throw them on the ground to put his own in.

And then you add his personality into the mix. He's a grouchy, Negative Nelly who likes to judge every little thing that I do. There's no way he can stay here. So I'll have to just annoy him until he leaves.

I flop backward onto my bed dramatically. "That's what I don't understand! Why can't he stay with Caroline?"

"Because you know how my mom is. She'll worry, and he doesn't want to upset her after everything that happened with Dad. He barely even told her about his accident and she was ready to drive three hours to our doorstep. I had to promise her daily FaceTimes for a month to talk her down."

I sit up, setting a pillow over my lap with a pout. "What I don't understand is why you didn't tell me. He said he's been recovering for weeks."

Her eyes lower to the ground. "I've only known for a week. He said he couldn't explain the details, and they only transferred him to the hospital in the city a few days ago. The second they mentioned discharge last night, he was out."

"Eliana! He was at the hospital I work at and you still said nothing!? I could've checked on him."

"He wouldn't even let me visit him. You know how he is, never wanting to make a fuss. It's only gotten worse since he was deployed." She shrugs. "Plus, you hate him. I didn't think you would care."

"You're my family. So I obviously care by default."

"Great! So you won't mind if he stays here, just until he figures everything out?" She asks, her eyes shining.

"You sneaky bitch. Fine." I say, rolling my eyes.

She beams, walking over to give my head a soft pat. "Yay! We're all going to get along great. I can feel it."

Four

Sean

Stepping onto the loud streets of Chicago, I reconsider my choice of residence. After seven years away from civilization, my distaste for people has only gotten stronger. I distanced myself from nearly everyone during my twenties, finding it easier that way. I still called home to make sure the girls knew I was okay, but made every excuse possible to avoid coming back. Every time I did, my mom pleaded for me to stay, and eventually, I couldn't take the guilt.

I hop in a cab and give them the address of my buddy's construction site. We grew up together, and he was the only friend I really paid attention to. Ethan has always been supportive, and when he heard about my accident, he reached out to help.

Not that I want the charity. But I'm also not gonna sit at home and wallow. I need to get a job, temporary or not, and try to rebuild a life for myself. I felt like being in the military was an easy escape. If I kept re-enlisting, I could keep hiding from the world outside of it. Since that is no longer an option, I have some catching up to do.

Ethan is waiting outside the office, beaming, when my car pulls up. "Seany boy! You sure grew up."

Unlike me, Ethan looks exactly the same—5'8" with short, ginger hair. Back in high school, it drove girls away. But now, after bulking up on the job, I can tell he no longer struggles. "Hey E, thanks for giving me a shot."

I go for a handshake, but he pulls me in for a hug instead. "Of course, man. You know I got you. Look, just check out the site and meet the guys. I'll have you start in the office while you're recovering, and when you're ready, we'll get you out on some jobs."

"Sounds good, man. How's your mom and dad?" I ask. Ethan's family was a huge support base for me when my dad passed. I felt inclined to hide the pain from my family. They needed my strength and guidance. Ethan gave me a place to process everything, but we lost touch when I left.

"They're great. Thanks for asking! So, I heard you're staying with your sister and the she-devil. That's gotta be interesting."

I sigh at the mention of her. We all grew up in a smaller suburb of the city, so everyone at school knew how much Summer and I fought. They always said we had the normal sibling dynamic compared to me and Eli, but I never saw it that way. "Yeah, she doesn't seem very pleased by it."

He opens the office door, gesturing for me to go inside. "I can imagine. I mean think how you would feel if you had a routine in your life and then suddenly some guy who you absolutely despise and think is the scum of the earth-"

I clear my throat. "Careful."

He nods. "Right, you get the point. Anyway, someone who

you don't get along with is just constantly there. In your space. I'm surprised she didn't kick you to the curb."

"I think it has a whole lot less to do with me and a whole lot more to do with Eliana."

"Makes sense. Well, if you want to come stay with me instead, my couch is open. We could even carpool!" My eyes widen at his enthusiasm. "No? Okay. Rude."

"Nothing to do with you. Honestly, if it means I can spend a little more time with my sister, I'm willing to deal with Summer."

"I get it. You've been away a while." He walks me to what I assume is to be my desk. "This is all you."

"I even have my own desk? You certainly know how to treat a man."

He winks, gesturing for me to sit. "Well, if living there becomes too much, let me know. I'd be happy to have you stay."

"Thanks. I'll keep that in mind." I say, ready for the conversation to shift. "So, meeting the guys?"

"Right this way," he says, leading me to them. As I get up to follow, my phone vibrates.

"Dinner is at seven. Make sure you're here. BOTH of you."
It's a text that Eli sent to me.
And her.

Summer

After the delay in my sleep yesterday, hiding in my room was a simple task since I'm awake when no one else is. I slept until I knew he was out cold. And I stayed up until I heard the door slam this morning, signaling that he was gone. I then ran to the kitchen and grabbed enough food to last me a few days, shoving it under my bed. Now, the only reason I have to leave the room is to get to work and the bathroom, both things that I can do quietly.

It's the perfect plan! If I camp out in my room until he finds another place, I won't have to see him! Once I had all my supplies, I fell asleep calmly, proud of my ingenuity.

That is, until a text jolted me out of my blissful slumber. I let out a groan and snatch my phone, ready to rain hell on whoever pulled me from a dream that I've already forgotten. What I read only darkens my mood further. Dinner. With him.

Well, there goes my plan.

Flashbacks immediately hit my mind, us bickering at the table, young Eliana eating unaware, and Caroline grinning at us. My family didn't eat together unless it was a holiday, so I spent a lot of dinners with the Jacobs family. I'd never met their dad. He had passed before Eliana and I met, so I think having a fourth person at the table was a comfort for them as well. Well, for two of them.

Eliana likes to plan her schedule so that she has flights back to back for a few weeks and then gets a few weeks off. She just started her off-week, and that's how I know she's already bored because there's no way in hell she would sit through the dinner that's to come on a normal day.

I mean seriously. Am I the only one seeing the problem here? He probably eats like a caveman now and forgets to chew with his mouth closed. If he smacks his lips even once, I am grabbing my fork and stabbing it right into his thigh.

I drag my tired body out of bed, and change into a real pair of clothes, instead of my 3XL T-shirt that says "kind people are my kind of people" on it. I think it's perfectly appropriate, and outstandingly cringy, but I could at least put on some pants. After combing through my hair and wiping off yesterday's mascara, I do a one-over in the mirror. I look atrocious, I think, making my way towards the door.

* * *

The silence is suffocating.

I assumed that dinner was going to be interesting at the very least, but I never could've guessed how awkward it would be. The only sound being the scratching of forks against plates and an occasional sigh on my part.

Eliana clears her throat. "So, I heard Frozen on Broadway is coming in a few weeks."

"I LOVE Frozen!" I announce, "We should get tickets." A scoff follows and my smile immediately drops as I turn towards the culprit.

"Do you have something to say?"

"Nothing. It just that it makes total sense that you love that movie," Sean says casually, moving his peas away from the mashed potatoes with his fork, before taking a long gulp of water.

"And why is that?" I ask, my tone turning deadly.

He sets his glass down, wiping his mouth with the back of his hand. "Because you're like an ice princess. Literally. The glare you're giving me right now could turn a man's blood cold."

"If I'm so icy, why do you call me sunshine?"

"Maybe I like irony." He smirks.

"Maybe you should just," my voice trails off, and I'm unable to think of a comeback. "Die or something."

I mentally facepalm while Eliana's eyebrows furrow.

His deep eyes snap to mine. "Tried that. Didn't love it. Would rather avoid it if possible."

"How is it that you guys turned a perfectly normal conversation so dark?" Eliana ponders out loud.

"I don't know what you're referring to. Eliana, this chicken is delicious," I say innocently.

"It really is, sis, thank you." He smiles warmly at her.

"Did you guys just agree on something?" She asks, her smile widening.

"I'm a very agreeable person. His opinions are just wrong."

He throws his fork down in frustration. "And here I thought you had changed. Still the same spoiled brat from before."

Any amusement I had leaves my body. I push out from the table, dropping my plate in the dishwasher, and slamming my door shut, all in a matter of seconds.

Five

❧

Sean

I stare at the space she occupied mere seconds ago. "Just to be clear, she did tell me to die before that, right?"

"You hit a nerve, Sean. I don't know how much you remember about her family, but things got a little more complicated after you left," Eli explains.

"I thought her family was practically perfect. I remember being jealous of her when we were younger," I say. And it's true. Everyone knew who Summer was—including me—even if she was a lot younger.

Her family was notoriously rich. Their house was huge, the kind people point at as they drive by. They all rode in expensive cars, wore recognizable brands, went on expensive vacations. Just knowing Summer, you wouldn't be able to guess how fortunate she was. She was humble about it, never bragged. But her parents? The complete opposite. They knew they were wealthy. And they wanted everyone else to know it, too.

I always found it weird that she went to the same school as me and Eliana. Apparently, they originally wanted her in private school, but the ones in our area had bad reps. They assumed that once she got to a certain age, she would go to boarding school, but it never ended up happening.

I wasn't jealous that she was privileged. Well, maybe a little. But mostly, I was jealous because she had everything I lost. She had two loving and involved parents. She had a whole life being practically handed to her. Meanwhile, I was doing everything I could just to keep our lights on.

I remember being so excited when Eliana started talking about her new friend. Before, she didn't let anyone get close to her. I knew it was because of Dad. She was worried that letting people in meant feeling the pain that's caused when they leave. But Summer weaseled her way into all our lives without objection.

When I finally met her and realized who she was, I couldn't help but hold a grudge. I tried to be civil for Eliana's sake, but she was everywhere. With her loud laugh and snarky comments, she was a constant thorn in my side. When I ended up leaving for the army, I remember smiling on the bus ride out just because I wouldn't hear her voice for months. I would finally have some peace and quiet.

But here I am, sleeping with one wall between us. And if anything, her laugh has only gotten louder.

"That's what her parents wanted everyone to think. They raised her to be successful and marry someone to take over the tech business that her father runs. Her mom wanted her to be perfect, always counting her calories and tracking her grades, things like that." She says, eyeing Summer's door. "I mean, do you really think a girl with a perfect family would eat dinner with us every night?"

"I guess I didn't think about it." I give her a confused look. "Why couldn't she take over the business instead of her husband?"

"They're old fashioned, for one. Don't think a woman could run a company and be respected. But either way, she wasn't interested in business. Medicine is the only thing that makes sense for her," Eli finishes.

I rub a thumb across my jaw. Was I really so involved in my own shit that I couldn't pay attention to the things going on in her life? I knew that she didn't have siblings. I assumed that she was just lonely or that her parents worked a lot. It never occurred to me that her home life wasn't as perfect as she let everyone believe. "I didn't know."

"It's fine. She prefers it that way. She's not traumatized or anything, but it made her act out a little in her teenage years."

"I still don't get why what I said was so wrong. It's not like I haven't resorted to name-calling before."

"She spent a lot of time fixing some mistakes she made around the time when you first left. She's proud of her progress. I guess she just can be a little insecure about her past still," Eliana says, rubbing my shoulder in comfort.

I grunt out a response, grabbing our plates.

Summer

I throw myself on my bed, face down, with a groan. I admit, that was a little childish of me. But the only person in my life who knows what my family—what I—was like during high school, is Eliana. Hearing her brother say I hadn't changed took me back.

My parents wanted a boy. After they had me, they tried for

years to have another child, but it never happened. I know they blame me for it. They wanted a perfect son to take over the company and look good in front of their friends. Instead, they got me.

For a while, I tried to be perfect for them. I wanted their life, surrounded by high-class friends and expensive business trips. They were also the only family I had, I couldn't imagine disappointing them. I hadn't known any of my grandparents, I assumed they were all dead. Both of my parents were only children, like me. I wanted to make them proud. But it didn't matter how much I tried, it was never enough.

So naturally, I stopped trying. I thought that if they would never be satisfied, I wouldn't waste my time. I kept my grades up, but that's about it. I stopped putting effort into extracurriculars, was constantly partying, and slept with too many guys who were too many years older. I thought that by making them mad, I would at least be getting a reaction from them.

But they didn't care. They'd given up. The second I left for college, they moved away from the city, and we haven't spoken since. Eliana is the only person who put up with my shit, and she's the only person who truly knows the extent of everything I did. Having Sean belittle everything I've made for myself without them annoyed me, even if he meant nothing by it.

My door swings open to my best friend holding a bottle in the doorframe. "Wanna get wine drunk?" She asks cheekily.

"Immediately yes."

Eliana and I had our fair share of hard liquor in college. I was through with my party phase, I had more than enough during high school. Instead of going to the bars, we sat in our dorm and drank cheap tequila until we passed out. Being a nursing student was hard enough, I needed a break every once in a while.

Now, after one too many drunken mistakes, we've become distinguished women who only keep wine in the house. Anything stronger is strictly for special occasions, and must be finished or thrown out before the night ends.

She smiles, stepping into the room. "Wanna talk about it?"

"Not really," I murmur. "Distract me. How's work?"

"The same I guess." She sits down, sighing. "I love my job, don't get me wrong, but I'm worried about my next rotation. They put me with the pilot who is known for making attendants' lives miserable. Entitled, young, and handsome. The worst kind." She says, taking a swig straight out of the bottle before passing it to me.

"Sounds like you're the perfect wake-up call for him. He's handsome, you're hot…" I say, wiggling my eyebrows and taking a large gulp. Eliana is cautious of all relationships. She rarely dates anyone casually, or at all. She claims that love is out of the agenda for the time being. Instead, she'd rather focus on writing and traveling the world.

"You wish. Pilots are notorious for having secret wives. I'd prefer to get through my twenties without being a home-wrecker." She throws me a pointed look. "And some of us like to keep work relationships professional."

"I'm gonna pretend I didn't hear that personal attack. Wanna watch a movie?"

"God yes. To All the Boys?"

"Que it," I order, giving her a salute. We get comfortable on my bed, take a few more sips, and turn on Netflix. After a few seconds, we hear a soft pounding on the door.

Sean eases the door open, stepping into the frame. He takes in the view for a second before asking, "Is there room for one more?"

I say nothing, patting the spot next to me. He crosses the room in a few strides and sits down, his large body taking up more space than predicted. I pretend not to notice the way his thigh shoves against mine.

"What the hell is this?" He asks, pointing to the screen, then lets his hands fall behind his head. The movement showcases his arms and lifts his shirt up so that a sliver of skin is showing. His sweats sit low enough that the waistband of his boxers is exposed. I snap my eyes back to the screen, thankful for his inattention.

Eliana smiles youthfully. "A rom-com!"

He lets out a groan. "I might want to revoke my attendance."

"What's wrong with rom-coms?" I ask, trying to ignore how his deep voice rattles near my ear and the way his leg pushes further into mine with every word. A shiver rolls down my spine. *Focus.*

Eliana and I love rom-coms, like most girls our age. It's a way to see love that plays out almost perfectly every time. They're funny. They're light. They're an escape from real life. But if anything, they give me hope that there's true love out there for some people, even if I've never seen it.

"They're a way to give people unrealistically high expectations. They make a perfect relationship with characters who dance the line but never make big enough mistakes to be deal breakers. They make love seem real," he says casually.

Eliana and I stare at him, shocked. "You don't think love is real?"

He shrugs. "Why would I? It's human nature for us to

connect with each other. No reason to romanticize it when, in most cases, it ends with heartbreak."

"But it doesn't always end in heartbreak."

He wets his lips. "Give me a real-life example."

I think for a minute before realizing that I can't. We sit in silence for the rest of the film.

Six

Sean

I wake up bright and early for work. I borrow Eli's beat-up Ford, promising to take good care of "her baby". It already makes me embarrassed enough to know that my baby sister, who I am supposed to be taking care of, has to drive something so unreliable.

On the ride over, I turn on an audiobook and let myself stare at the sunrise for a little while. I've always liked sunrises, mostly because I could look up and know that my father is watching over me. When I was a kid, I thought that he'd made the sky colorful just for me. Now, I just think they're pretty.

When I arrive, I park next to Ethan's pickup, the only other car in the lot. I walk inside and Ethan greets me with a hug. "Hey man, good to see you." He keeps a hand on my shoulder, steering me towards a cluttered desk. "I thought I could start you looking over the books, answering phones, setting up potential jobs, etc."

I nod. "Definitely, I just appreciate you giving me a job like this. I know most people wouldn't take the chance, with my health stuff and lack of experience."

He mumbles out a response, pulling a chair over to my desk. "So tell me more about this living situation," he says cheekily.

"It's… interesting. I'm glad I get to spend some extra time with my sister. I didn't realize how much I missed her, being gone for so long. And Summer is Summer." I pause. "It's complicated. We fight like we always have, but it feels different. Like before, it was like fighting with a little kid. Now, she's not a kid anymore. She's a full-on woman."

He barks out a laugh. "She sure is. I saw her for the first time in a while the other day. I almost didn't recognize her."

For some reason, hearing him talk about her like that makes my palms sweat. "Right, well, what's going on with you? Anyone occupying your love life?"

He holds his left hand, and I notice a gold ring settled on his finger. "I'm married, actually. Two years next month."

"What?! Congrats, bro! Sorry I couldn't be there."

Even though I personally don't believe in love, I never would pray on the downfall of a relationship, especially not someone like Ethan's.

He shrugs. "Not a problem. You had bigger things going on."

"So what's she like? Do I know her?"

He pauses for a minute, contemplating his words. "No, her mom is friends with mine. They introduced us. We dated for a few years, then decided to tie the knot. It's…calm."

"I could never imagine a relationship being calm."

He snickers. "That's because calm isn't your vibe. You need someone to keep you on your toes. Someone who's not afraid to fight you on things."

I shiver. "Sounds miserable. I don't need someone constantly questioning my every move."

"You'll get it one day."

Preferably not.

I frown. "Aren't you supposed to be introducing me to the crew?"

"Right." He jumps from his seat, waving me along. "Follow me."

Summer

I wake up around 5 PM and drag myself out of bed to start getting ready for work. The one thing that I haven't stopped doing is trying to look presentable for my shifts. Even though my body should be used to the schedule by now, when 3 AM hits, I start to shut down. So by putting on some light makeup and making my hair look somewhat purposeful, I go into the shift feeling more put together.

I fill my Stanley with water, another gift from Eliana, because she needs me to look like a basic new grad. I throw on my navy scrubs and grab my work bag, mentally praying for good patients.

I check the time, smiling when I see that I have ten minutes to spare. Perfect. Just enough to start phase one of my plan: scaring Sean out of the apartment. If he thinks that we're living in a complete dump, he won't want to stay a second longer than he needs to. Man, I thank God every day for making me pretty AND a total genius.

I giggle to myself, walking back to my room and grabbing the supplies. After I found out he was staying with us, I knew I needed to find a way to get him out faster. So, I Postmated some rat traps and a mouse from the pet store named 'Gouda'.

The laziness of America has seriously gotten out of hand. Since when could you get animals delivered to you?

I walk out to the living room with Gouda, setting his box on the table. I shut my and Eliana's bedroom doors, along with the bathroom, so that the rat doesn't get any ideas.

I set the traps in the corners of the room, not adding any bait, so Gouda can't actually get hurt. They are just a prop. After securing all the cabinets, I let him out with an evil laugh.

Have fun chasing him for the next hour, Sean!

I leave the apartment, walking towards the elevator. To my dismay, a scowling face greets me when the doors open. "Hey honey, good day at work?" I ask cheerfully.

"You mock but pet names turn me on, sunshine." Sean says with a wink.

My mouth downturns in disgust. "I think I just threw up a little," I say, my eyes sweeping over his body.

His work boots are caked in mud, but the rest of him remains untouched. His baggy jeans falling at the V of his waist, with a light blue button-up sitting completely open, exposing the white wife beater tank underneath.

He looks good.

When he notices my dazed expression, he gives me a lazy smirk. "Did you? Because it looks like you're drooling instead."

Not having anything to respond with, I flip him off as the elevator doors close, my cheeks turning bright red.

I finally get to work, my mood shooting up when I find Jonah sitting at the nurses' station. Jonah is my official work bestie. When it's us on the schedule, I know the shift will run smoothly because we work perfectly in tandem.

"There's my girl! Ready to run this shitshow?" He asks,

jumping up to give me a hug.

I lean into him, patting his back with an eye roll. "So ready."

The shift goes as expected, eventful but controlled. Working Med-Surg is like putting out endless dumpster fires. Nothing is ever perfect, all we do is make sure something's good enough so that we can move on and put out the next fire. That's why the amount of DAISY awards—nominated to nurses by patients—is so low on the unit. We have less than the ICU, and most of their patients can't even talk. I envy every single one of them, traipsing around with the pins on their badges. Egotistical show-offs.

"I don't know how you do that." Jonah says as we walk out of his patient's room.

"Do what?" I ask, grabbing a handful of sanitizer.

He does the same. "He yells at you for twenty minutes about his meds, you yell back, and now he likes you more than me?"

"You gotta stop being so polite all the time. We're all adults here. They can handle it. If you keep talking to them like they're children, it'll just piss them off more." I say, plopping down in front of my computer.

He follows, snatching the chair next to me. "You know, when I first met you, I thought you would be this sweet suck-up that takes everyone's shit. Then you opened your mouth."

"Looks can be deceiving." I grumble, wrapping myself in a warm blanket.

"Okay, so what's new? I feel like I haven't seen you in years."

"We worked together last week, but sure," I murmur. "Eliana's older brother just started staying with us."

He scans his badge into the computer, types his password in, and starts charting. "I didn't know she had a brother."

"He's just been away for a while. He's in the army, but was

in an accident and now he's back," I explain.

He gives me a filthy smile. "Soldier. That's hot. He'd be a great third."

Jonah sleeps with anyone that has a pulse, men included. And because of his looks and lighthearted personality, he gets away with it. Jonah is a year older and precepted me when I was new. At first, I had a huge crush on him.

I admired how easy he made everything look, how calm he was in every scenario. Male nurses are just wired differently, they don't let anything throw them off balance. It's enchanting to watch.

Being half Korean, he has an innocent look about him. Only that's where it stops, his looks. He has short black hair, a jawline that could cut a steak, and a smile that could turn anyone's limbs into jelly. His physique is near perfection, with broad shoulders, thick thighs, and his height of 6'4".

We always joked that our sex life would be explosive until it wasn't a joke anymore. It's the perfect arrangement. We're both young and single, with jobs that cause a lot of pent-up frustration. So we are the perfect friends with benefits, because there are absolutely no strings attached to either of us.

I cringe internally. "God, no. He probably sticks with missionary because it's 'classic.'"

"Damn. Maybe you could bring out his adventurous side." He says, wiggling his eyebrows.

"No, I think he'd rather get shot again than be within five feet of me."

He lets out a low whistle. "And he's got a gunshot scar? This mental image keeps getting better."

In an instant, Tammy, our new manager, jumps between

us. "Maybe you guys could stock something instead of sitting here gossiping."

"Why is she even here?" I grumble, logging out of the computer and walking away from the station. "One of the only perks of nights is no management. I hate people looking over my shoulder."

"Apparently, she wants to get to know everyone on the unit, and this is her plan to do it. Maybe I could sleep with her to loosen her up?" He plots.

I gasp in horror. "Ew. She's like fifty."

"Never stopped me before," he flaunts, strolling towards the linen cart while I gag.

By the end of the night, I'm ready to jump straight into my bed. After giving report, and getting in my daily fight with the Kronos machine, I practically skip to my car to book it out of the hospital.

When I get home, the siblings must be out because I find myself alone. I take the opportunity to play music full blast in the shower and even use Eliana's expensive soap. Wrapped in a warm towel, I skip into my room, jumping at the squeaking sound coming from my dresser. I flip the light on and groan.

Gouda is in my room.

I walk towards his new habitat. He's sitting in a large cage, filled with bedding, food, water, and hidey-holes. On the front of his cage is a post-it note. I snatch it, reading what it says.

"Nice try, sunshine ;)"

Damn it. Well played, Sean.

I only get a few minutes of sleep when I'm interrupted by the sound of stomping around the apartment. I rub my eyes, confused why Sean isn't at work before remembering it's the weekend. I peek my head out the door and see a him shirtless, grabbing a fresh set of clothes.

I have the full intention of confronting him about my new roommate, but when I look at him, no words come out.

His biceps flex as he moves, and my eyes trail down his scarred back, glittered with tattoos. The lighting is off just enough that I can't make them out, but I can somehow still tell they could make me weak in the knees. I stare in awe at his physique, gasping when he turns slightly, giving me an eyeful of his hard chest and tight abs. His eyes shoot up to mine, but he says nothing, cocking an eyebrow with a smirk.

I slam my door shut and don't come back out for the rest of the day.

Seven

Summer

I wake up in an awful mood. Gouda was sprinting a marathon on his wheel and I've snoozed the alarm five times already, so I have to actually get up or I'll be late for work. I fling my legs out of bed, silently cursing myself for scheduling two shifts in a row. Grabbing a fresh set of clothes, I put my hair in a curled, slick-back pony, and grab my stuff. I make a B-line for the door, ignoring Sean's eyes on my back.

When I arrive on the unit, Jonah is working again, so we fall into the same pattern as the night before, chatting about little things along the way.

After a few hours, the munchies hit, so we DoorDash McDonald's and snag blankets from the warmer, ready to get comfortable. We always try to get everything our patients could possibly need into their rooms before they go to sleep so that they leave us alone and we can relax.

We sit in the same spots as always, in the corner of the nurse's station, far away from everyone else. We always joke that we should switch to the ICU so that we can sit on our stations. Not that it matters much, anyway. Sometimes we catch the other nurses charting everything in their favorite patient's room, just so they can avoid us. We take no offense, of course. Their presence isn't welcome either way. The techs usually like us, but still keep their distance, almost out of fear.

"What would you do first if you became a man for a day?" Jonah asks, falling into our routine of random questions to pass the time.

"Take a piss. Or maybe jerk off? I don't know, whichever is more urgent. Then I'd walk around Sephora and see how many numbers I could pick up just for an ego boost."

He laughs. "Why haven't I tried that?"

"Because you have an easy enough time getting girls' numbers anywhere you go."

He flicks his hair back dramatically. "So true."

"Well, what would you do first if you were a girl for a day?"

"I'd probably put on the sluttiest outfit ever and go to a club. Dancing with long hair and practically no clothes just looks so freeing."

I nod, munching on a nugget. "It so is. Kinda shocked none of your answer included something dirty."

"I was trying to be wholesome, but the truth is most of my thoughts are not appropriate."

"Oh, I know."

He rolls his eyes. "Shut up. You love it."

"Something like that. Did you know that I'm a mother now?"

His face goes white as a ghost. "Please say it's not mine. I'm supposed to be the hot uncle, NOT the father."

"Unless you have whiskers and beady red eyes, you're safe."

He gives me a disgusted look. "Ew, Summer. Your taste has

gotten seriously out of hand."

"It's a mouse. Named Gouda. I am mothering a mouse."

"Do I even want to know?"

"Nope."

We continue talking about nothing and everything, answering call lights when they go off. We turn everything into a two-person job. It just makes everything more fun that way.

The night was going by seamlessly.

Sean

I sort through the fridge and try to find something to cook. Half of it is full of Eliana's weird health food that I immediately pass on. The other half is random ingredients that Summer snacks on through the night since her schedule is flipped.

I tried to ignore the way she looked in her scrubs as she averted my eyes leaving for work earlier. She really does look different in her nursing attire. Hair flat on her head, framing her face and soft jawline. The way she did her makeup made her brown eyes pop, something I didn't even know was possible.

And those scrubs. Summer isn't incredibly thin, but if anything, it dulls down the edginess in her face. Her scrubs hang tight in all the right places, making her plump ass be on full display.

What am I doing? She clearly doesn't want me here, based on her sad attempt of scaring me yesterday.

Technically, it's completely normal to think about her in that way. I haven't seen her in a while and it's been too long since I've been with someone. I may not like her, but I still have hormones.

And she would agree, wouldn't she? I saw the way she

looked at me when I was changing the other night—eyes wide, lips swollen, cheeks flushed. Her breathing even picked up. She still hates me, that much is clear. Maybe it wasn't about me at all. She could've been exercising in her room or something. Yeah, that's probably it.

"What's got you so lost in thought?" Eliana appears beside me, making me jump.

"Nothing, just the Super Bowl and everything," I lie. I don't even watch football, it just seemed believable.

"It's literally August. Men are so weird." She mumbles, jumping to sit on the kitchen island. "What're you making?"

"Vodka pasta. I'm using spaghetti squash instead of noodles, so it's almost healthy, if you want a bowl."

"Yes, please. When did you learn how to cook? Before you left, you could find a way to burn cereal." She says in a playful tone.

"Had to get resourceful. We didn't have ingredients or utensils like this, obviously, but I learned a lot from some of the guys I was with," I explain, putting the squash in the oven and throwing my diced onions in a pan. "When you all come from different places, the only thing you really can do is get to know everything about each other."

She nods, passing me the garlic mincer. "You don't talk about it much."

"Partially because I genuinely can't talk about it. But mostly because I don't want to. I loved serving. It was the only consistency I've ever had. It gave me a way to provide for you and mom, and I'll always be grateful for that." I give her a small smile before continuing.

"But that aside, it was the worst few years of my life. It's almost like an addiction. I kept going back because I didn't know what else to do, but I was miserable while I was there. I liked knowing that I could help my country, but sometimes the lines got blurry, and I couldn't even remember what I was fighting for."

I thought basic training was impossible. I hated being told where to go, how to live, what to eat. I didn't like the men I was training alongside. It's like they thought everything was one big joke. They constantly got us in trouble through stupid pranks or the inability to show up on time.

I felt entirely alone. I spent most of my free time training. Since my genetics were against me, I had to work twice as hard as the rest of them. I was slow, a horrible shot, scrawny, and too lengthy. But my hard work paid off. By the time I graduated from basic, I had a spot at one of the most intense bases in the country for more training.

People were more like me there. They were serious when they needed to be, but could joke around to inspire hope in us. I first learned what being bonded to other people in the military meant. It's unlike anything else in the world.

We spent every minute of every day with one another. We worked through all the shit they gave us together. And we leaned on one another, just to stay alive. I tried to stay in contact with some of them—even after I got deployed—but quickly learned that having people as disposable as me in my life would only make things harder. Loss became the expected. The only thing that made it easier was the fact that I was already familiar with it.

She stays silent for a moment, eyes getting moist.

"Oh shit. Don't do that. Why are you doing that?" I ask frantically, pulling her against my chest.

"This is all my fault. I made you feel like you had to be there instead of getting off my ass and helping provide for Mom. I'm just so sorry, Seany." She says between sobs.

"Look at me right now," I say, grabbing a hold of her chin. "You and Mom are the best part of my life. I went because I wanted to take care of you both. You were a child. You owed me nothing. You still don't."

"Then why did you stay away from us? I thought for sure it was because you blamed me," her chin wobbles. "That's why I was so excited when you came to me instead of Mom. It made me feel like I could pay you back for everything you've done."

I am an asshole. Everything I've done has been for her. Ever since my dad died, she became my number one priority. I wanted to protect her from everything bad in the world. I never wanted her to struggle the same way I did after it happened. That's the real reason I left. For her.

My mom played a role in it too, but it was mostly Eliana. She was who I thought about when the accident happened. I saw her face in my head when the bullet made contact with my skin. She wasn't old enough to fully process the feeling of grief when our father died. But now? It would be exemplified. I am the closest person to her other than Summer. I knew I couldn't leave her.

When I woke up in that hospital bed, my commanding officer was at my side. He told me I had two options. Rehab, retraining, and reenlisting, or leaving for good. I was terrified. The plan I had for my life was drifting from my grasp, all that I had worked for fizzling away. But I knew I couldn't do it.

I couldn't risk my life for her sake. So I signed the medical discharge papers and said goodbye. To the man who had held my life in his hands for seven years. To the life that I had learned to yearn for. To the person I had become.

I just don't know if I can admit that.

"You don't need to pay me back for any of it," I say, rubbing circles on her shoulder. "I didn't come back because every time I did, I had to say goodbye again. I didn't want to see the look on your or mom's faces as I walked away. I could see your thoughts, how you were silently praying you would see me alive again. I was just trying to avoid hurting you and myself."

"You promise?"

I hold up my pinky, interlocking it with hers. "Promise. Now, can I finish this without any more tears?" I ask, wiping the moisture off her cheeks.

"That's probably a good idea because I think your onion is burning."

"Shit!" I run towards the pan, sighing when I see that the onions have turned completely black. I dump them into the trash, roll up my sleeves, and start chopping a new one. Eliana turns on some music and I finish cooking with the sound of my sister horribly belting along to her playlist.

Eight

Sean

I wake up to the front door slamming shut. I run a hand over my face, willing myself to look that way. When I turn, I see Summer stalking toward her room.

I sit up, slowly making my way to my feet, and walk after her. "Hey if this is about the other day.."

I can't even finish my sentence before she slips into her room, interrupting me by slamming her door shut. I stare at the wood in front of me, shocked for a moment, before barging in. "Okay, I know we don't exactly get along, but there's no need to be hostile".

When I get a glimpse of her face, I shut up immediately, my blood running cold. Her mascara had smudged from tears, leaving dry streaks down her cheeks. Even with messy hair and makeup, she looks beautiful.

What is in the air today? First Eli and now Summer? Is my presence really throwing the balance off this much?

She sits down on the floor, facing away from me. "I would

like to be alone."

"Sunshine, please. Talk to me. Did someone say something to you?" My hands ball at my sides. "Did someone touch you?" I ask, my tone turning deadly.

"One, like you would care-"

"I'm gonna stop you right there. You know I would kill anyone that laid a hand on you."

Summer

I look at him, fully expecting him to be making a joke, but he stares back, fire burning behind his eyes. My heart rate picks up and I force myself to look away, averting his gaze. "No one touched me. Either way, I can handle myself. I just had a rough shift, is all. I'm fine. Seriously, you should go."

He stares blankly at me for a moment before plopping down in the space in front of me. He grunts when he makes contact with the floor, long legs laid out in front of him, feet getting dangerously close to my own. His arms cross over his chest, and he stares at me expectantly.

"Did you not hear what I just said? Or did that bullet somehow damage your ears?"

"My ears work perfectly fine, among other things." He winks. *He actually winks.* "Seriously, what happened?"

I sit quietly for a few seconds, deciding if I am truly going to confide in Sean Jacobs. Eliana has locked herself in her room writing, and I would feel bad about disturbing her. I look at him again, sighing. "There's a patient that's become almost a regular on my unit. She's a middle-aged oncology patient".

I look up at him and he sits patiently, eyes encouraging me to continue. "I can't say much, but over time I really grew an attachment to her. I don't get cancer patients often, our floor isn't really built for it. But because of some complications, our doctors work alongside her oncologists. She came in late last night in rough shape." I pause, her tired face popping up in my head. "She should've been in the ICU. It just happened so fast that we didn't have time to transfer her. She ended up coding and we couldn't get her back." My voice cracks, salt coating my tongue from the tears. "You'd think I'd be used to it by now. Death. It's a part of my job. Pathetic, right?"

His jaw tenses as he looks at me. "Don't say that. I would've loved to know that my dad's nurses felt that way about him." He says, eyes widening before dropping. Like the words coming out of his mouth almost surprised him.

I follow his gaze. "He was sick?" I ask softly.

He nods, scratching the back of his head.

"What happened?"

And just like that, the spell breaks. His walls go back up, hard expression falling into place. He looks like a different person than the one who had listened to me mere seconds ago.

He stands up, making his way towards the door. He pauses for a second, turning back to look at me.

"Maybe some other time." He says, tightly. And then he's gone.

Nine

Summer

I get up in the afternoon feeling weird about last night, and the morning that followed. I decide to grab my sneakers and go for a run to clear my head. Putting on my headphones, I play a workout playlist and opt for the stairs. Because that's what fit people do.

Walking out of the apartment complex, I look around at the busy streets of Chicago. The sun is blaring down on my back, but there's a nice breeze keeping me from overheating. I weave through people, making my way to a calmer block. I stare at cars around me, wondering where everyone is driving to.

Some people assume big city equates to a high crime rate, which is generally true, but I've never felt anything but safe. Its almost like there's a code in the city, and everyone knows who's local and who isn't. I've never even been pickpocketed, let alone anything worse.

The large buildings make the city feel almost dystopian,

and the constant buzz of people talking on the phone or cars honking fills the silence. People don't stare as I pass them, it's what I like about the city. Everyone minds their own business, entirely suffocated by their own problems. They're selfish. They make me feel validated, because I'm selfish too.

Two minutes into my run, I am reminded of why I avoid exercise. I slow my pace, choosing to do a thinking walk instead. Memories from this morning flood my mind. The way Sean listened and comforted me, it was totally weird and out of character. I'd never seen him so gentle. I didn't like it.

Our dynamic works. Everyone needs to be humbled every once in a while, and we do that for each other. I don't need any more friends. I have Jonah and Eliana. That's enough. I do need someone to keep me in check. Although my friends keep things real, they care about my feelings. Sean doesn't, meaning everything that comes out of his mouth about me is honest.

The one thing I don't understand is why he followed me to my room. Was he just trying to pay a favor to Eliana? Or maybe actually has a conscience? Or maybe he was trying to gain material that he could use against me later?!

Okay, that one might be a tad unrealistic. But at this point, it makes the most sense out of the three. It was nice though, to talk to someone who gets loss in the same way I do. Jonah sees it all the time, like me, but he handles it better. He somehow always finds a positive and meaningful way to explain it. Eliana has only ever seen it with her dad and hasn't spoken to me about it once. But Sean, he saw it all the time in the military. I can tell that he carries it with him, his eyes speaking to the guilt he feels. I know he would get it if he would just open up.

But I don't need him to. I can deal with it by myself, like I always do. Checking the time, I realize I've walked 40 minutes away from the apartment. I turn around and crank the music up, deciding that thinking is overrated.

Sean

I step into the steam-filled shower, hot water gliding down my back, hissing when it makes contact with my wound. The apartment only has one bathroom, so I try to time my showers for when no one's home. Eliana is at a meeting for work and Summer is somewhere, probably hiding from me. I grab a handful of soap, lathering it down my body. I try not to think of this morning, but her sad eyes keep making their way into my head.

I truly don't know what came over me. I normally wouldn't care about what Summer is feeling, but I'm a gentleman. I'm not just going to leave a woman crying in her room alone. Grabbing a shampoo bottle, I flip the cap open, and immediately am hit with sweet citrus. Like grapefruit or maybe orange and lime and—why exactly am I smelling her shampoo?

I hear the front door open, so I finish washing quickly and shut the water off. I grab a towel off the rack, wrapping it around my waist, and open the door. For a minute I'm blinded by the steam filing out, but when it passes, I am met with a wide-eyed Summer. Her hair is in a tight ponytail, sweat dripping down her forehead. She's wearing a sports bra with tight, matching leggings.

I flex my abs unintentionally and give my hair a small shake, letting water droplets roll down my stomach and arms. I make sure to adjust the towel so my scar is hidden underneath it.

"Like what you see?"

She scoffs, arms folding over her chest defensively. "In your dreams, Jacobs."

I let out a low chuckle. "Oh, you're in them." *Why am I flirting with her?*

She pauses for a moment, eyes warm, dodging mine completely. Her eyebrows furrow, gaze hardening. "Well, I'm glad you're never in mine. I have a distaste for nightmares."

"You have a distaste for everything, it seems." She's negative. The glass is always half empty with her, probably a result of her uppity childhood.

Her arms fly to her sides, the corners of her mouth turned downwards. "Maybe you only think that because I distaste everything that involves you."

"Careful sunshine, I think that's called an obsession," I tort.

"Impossible. You are obsessed with yourself enough for the both of us."

I raise my hand to the doorframe, letting my biceps flex a little, the corner of my towel lowering. "And you aren't? I see you check yourself out in the reflection on elevator doors."

"You'd only notice that if you were checking me out first."

My voice drops an octave. "Can't argue with that."

Summer

My mouth goes dry at the sight of him. His dark hair dripping water down his face, abs and arms on full display. His bright eyes pouring into mine at the admission. He doesn't find me completely repulsive, so what? I can admit that he is conventionally attractive while also hating his guts. "Uhm, I'm kinda busy. Bye."

I practically run towards my room, shutting the door before

he can worm his way in. I drop to the floor, my comfort spot, and yank the elastic out of my head, letting my hair fall down my back.

"UGH." I let out a childish groan. He is doing it on purpose, making my mind go all blank. Well, two can play that game.

Ten

Summer

I unlock the door, letting a smiling Jonah inside.

He gives me a hug, throwing his coat on a hook. He raises his arms in a stretch, gray sweater riding up and exposing his white T-shirt underneath. His baggy black jeans are practically falling down, completely covering his New Balances.

"You're wearing a sweater and a jacket in August?"

"What can I say? Style overcomes all discomfort," he says with a shrug. "Thank God we're doing this. I haven't had sex in a week."

"Oh my god, what will you ever do?" I say sarcastically, dragging him towards my room.

"Right? Where is that hot soldier? I could use some new inspiration."

I shove him playfully. "Are you saying I'm not attractive enough anymore?"

He pulls his sweater off, shoving me onto the bed. "It's okay,

I can close my eyes."

I flip our position, pushing him down. I grab a pillow, smacking him across the head before he snatches it and chucks it at the floor. "You're gonna regret that."

The corner of his mouth lifts into a smirk. "Alright, make me regret it."

And I do.

Sean

I walk towards the apartment building, ready to crash on the couch. Work has been exhaustingly boring. Don't get me wrong, I'm grateful Ethan found a spot for me, but I'm ready to get some actual work done instead of sitting on a computer all day.

After being challenged physically every day in the military for seven years, I want a little more excitement in my job. Maybe I'll talk to him tomorrow and see if we can get me on the schedule sooner.

I open the apartment door and throw my keys on a hook. My eyes are caught by the jacket hanging next to them. A man's jacket. Right on cue, Summer's door opens, and some guy slips out.

His eyes flick to mine, and he looks me up and down, nodding with approval. "That bitch has been holding out on me."

My eyebrows burrow in confusion. "Who the fuck are you?"

My response makes his smile widen, and he lets out a small tsk. He mumbles something, clearly proud of himself. When I look closer, it all makes sense. His hair is disheveled, his shoes untied, and his undershirt peeking out halfway.

I storm towards him, grabbing a fistful of his sweater. "The fuck do you think you're doing?!" I say with a growl.

"This is just turning me on more." He says, eyes wild.

"Get the fuck out!" I yell, shoving him towards the door.

Once he's successfully locked out, I stomp towards her room, barreling the door open. "Who is that guy, Summer?"

She looks up from her bed, as if she was expecting my outburst. "That's Jonah. He's a friend of mine."

"A fr-" I pinch the skin between my eyebrows. I can feel my blood pressure rising with every word she mutters. I know that she's had…relations with people. But do I want to actively think about it? No. "A friend? What kind of friend? The kind of friend that sleeps with you and just leaves?"

She scoffs, throwing her hair into a bun. "Trust me, I am nowhere near offended."

"He can't just, like, do that." I sputter, pacing. "You're too young for this."

Her eyes narrow. "One, I've been 'doing this' since I was a lot younger. And two, I'm gonna assume you 'did this' when you were a lot younger, too."

"It's different. You're you."

It is different. I was fourteen when I lost my virginity, and it was a mistake. I never had an issue picking up girls, and I liked the ease of it all. They didn't ask for anything more than sex, nor did I want them to.

Then, when I was in the military, relationships weren't as common as I expected. When I was stationed in America, it was normal for people to have a family at home. But as my missions started getting more and more dangerous, the number of married soldiers was slim.

We all were aware what having a family meant. Leaving them for months on end. Not being able to communicate for long stretches of time. And most importantly, letting people in meant causing them pain when the mission goes wrong. And they did. All the time.

I wouldn't want that for her. She deserves someone who's a constant in her life, not some bum to hookup with. I know she believes in love, even if I don't. I just never thought she'd be the type of person to avoid it.

She stands up, walking towards me. "What, because I'm a woman I should be waiting for marriage? Didn't think you were the sexist type. Or is it because you think I'm so atrocious that no one would want to have sex with me?"

I throw my hands behind my head, letting out a groan. "God. No. I just meant- Well he's- Is he even educated? He doesn't look very smart."

"You aren't educated. And he has the same degree as me. Are you calling me stupid?"

"WHAT? NO! No. I-" I pause for a second, trying to control my breathing. "Just don't bring him back here." I say, before walking out.

Summer

That went even better than expected. It's not like I'm using Jonah. If he knew what I was plotting, he would completely understand, encourage it even. And after my failed attempt at having him leave of his own free will ended in me gaining responsibility for a rodent, I needed an alternative approach. I am just tired of Sean messing with me. It was time I did the same. So what better way than to make him jealous?

Honestly, I'm surprised he got as angry as he did. For someone who's usually pretty composed and always knows exactly what to say, he was at a loss for words. I think it has more to do with the fact that he's known me since I was a gangly pre-teen, and still sees me that way, than him having any sort of attraction for me. But either way, it felt great to see the look on his face.

I open my bedroom door slowly, scanning the room for any sight of him. When it looks empty, I tiptoe out, checking for his keys on the hook. Gone. I must've really annoyed him, so much so that he couldn't be in the apartment anymore. Good, maybe it'll be permanent.

I cross the living room and throw Eliana's bedroom door open, flopping onto her bed. I turn on her TV and watch some *Gilmore Girls* while I wait for her to get back from her meeting.

After about twenty minutes, she walks into the room, sighing, and landing next to me. "How was the meeting?"

"Boring. Some people must be hooking up or something. It was all about workplace harassment. Hey, was Jonah here? I feel like I can still smell YSL Myself."

"Yeah, we both needed some fun. Life is boring. Work is work. I really need to get a hobby or something."

She hums. "Oh, I know!" She says, sitting up. "Let's do something together! I feel like I've barely seen you lately."

I sit up, matching her excitement. "Yes! What should we do? Cooking?"

"I don't think we have any hope there. But maybe baking?"

"That sounds harder. Maybe crochet?"

She scrunches her nose. "What are we, 50? What about wine tasting?"

"I prefer to chug rather than savor."

"Book club?"

"Bleh."

We sit in silence for a minute, pondering other ideas. "What about pottery?"

She claps her hands in delight. "Yes! Pottery." I can see the gears turning in her head. "I'm going to make a jewelry dish. And maybe a new bowl for Sean."

I shiver at his name. "I will make a mug."

We go to Google, find a shop near us that isn't run by a hippie, and watch more of the show. I order us takeout while she opens a bottle of red and I crash in her room, like a sleepover. It was exactly what we both needed, each other.

Eleven

Sean

A few days go by and the environment has been somewhat awkward. Neither of us have spoken about her playdate with Jonah. We've mostly been avoiding each other completely. Well, that ends now.

I am almost certain that part of that situation was to upset me. The whole thing seemed a little planned, but the worst part about it was that it worked. I haven't felt that much rage in a while, and I didn't like it. So if she wants to play games with me, I'm going to return the favor.

Summer worked a double last night, which means she'll be home around lunchtime. I told Eliana I'd cook for us all and started prepping a few minutes ago, so she'll be home for the show.

Right on cue, she walks through the door, dropping her stuff and moaning at the smell of my cooking. The noise goes straight to my dick. I recover quickly, throwing a plain white apron around my waist for added effect. I roll my sleeves up, showing off my forearms, and start chopping some celery, biceps flexed.

Summer

I walk into the kitchen smelling something absolutely delicious. After a 16-hour shift, I'm ready for some comfort food, and as much as I hate to admit it, Sean is a fantastic cook.

Not only is his food amazing, but he looks great throughout the whole process. I take the time while he's distracted to let my eyes roam over his body. His hair is mostly neat, with a few defiant strands settling on his forehead. His arms are almost bursting out of the tight black long-sleeve he has on, and his hands...

As a nurse, I find it perfectly understandable to find hands and arms attractive, and boy are his. His arms are covered with deep veins that are exposed all the time, popping out more on exertion. They trail up, hiding beneath the sleeves of his shirt that are almost ripping from how tight they squeeze his biceps.

His eyes snap up, catching me ogling him. "You really have got to stop looking at me like that."

I hide my surprise with a cough, looking down to take off my shoes. "You are too conceited. I wasn't looking at you in any kind of way."

"Oh, there was a look."

I throw my shoes towards the door and drop my Stanley in the sink. "Maybe I'm just hungry. Did you think of that?"

He moves an inch closer, hovering over me completely. "You look starved," he says in a husky voice.

I look up at him for a minute, at a loss for words. Recovering quickly, I turn on my heel and sulk towards my room without a word. I do a quick body shower and change into sweats and a hoodie, walking out right as Sean is spooning soup into bowls.

"That looks great!" Eliana praises, snatching a bowl for herself before settling in her unspoken assigned seat.

Sean and I follow without a word, weirdness settling around us. "It does. Thanks, Sean."

Sean

"Anytime," I say, worried by how much I mean it. I can't tell if I actually rattled her earlier or if she just wanted to shower, but I pulled out all the stops.

I take a seat across from her, letting my legs stretch out into her space. "Agh!" I yelp, in response to her kicking me as a warning. I glare at her.

She lets out a sweet smile. "What's wrong Sean?"

I grunt. "Nothing, just need some water."

She takes a sip of hers, eyeing me, then drops the glass by my plate. "Here. Take mine."

Eliana's eyes dart between us, clearly confused. "Am I missing something here?"

"No." "Nothing!" We both respond quickly.

"Oh-kayy, that was weird, but whatever. Sean, did you know that me and Summer are picking up pottery?"

My eyebrows shoot up in surprise. "Summer, you do know that pottery requires patience, right?"

She drops her spoon, curling her hand into a fist. "I will have you know, I am a very patient person."

I scoff. "I'll believe that when I see it, sunshine."

"Too bad. I don't remember inviting you."

"It's quite a shame. I tend to be great with my hands," I say with a smirk.

Eliana takes a big gulp of water, forehead wrinkling. "That was pretty gross and I'm gonna ignore what was just said."

Summer nods in agreement. "I would like to do the same."

"Can we not get through one meal without the two of you bickering?"

"Yes." She says at the same time I respond with "No."

She points to me enthusiastically. "See! It's him, not me. I would like to be civil, but he's annoying me on purpose."

I shrug. "I don't think I can be civil with you."

She scowls, grabbing her empty dish and dropping it in the sink. "Whatever. I just spent sixteen hours fighting with patients. I don't need to fight at home too. MY home. Goodnight."

I smile at her back as she leaves. Victory.

Twelve

Summer

Eliana and I were talking and decided it was time for a night out. Even though we're both in our early twenties, we've been acting pretty geriatric lately, so it's time for a little fun. I texted Jonah and invited him along, to which he enthusiastically accepted. As much as I hate to admit it, being an adult sucks, and I'm excited to get drunk like a teenager with my friends.

The only problem with this whole plan—I have no clothes. And I mean none. My clubbing clothes from college no longer fit, being that I've gained 20 pounds in the past two years. Not that it really bothers me. I like my body; I think the weight makes me look mature. So, I'm currently scrambling to pull myself together for a mini-shopping trip before it's time to pregame.

I throw on shorts and a hoodie, grab my purse, and make my way towards the car. I sigh at who I see walking out of Eliana's Ford, walking straight to me.

"Why are you everywhere?" I huff, still heading towards my

car.

He follows. "I don't know. We do live together. Could that possibly be a reason?"

I unlock the car and climb in. "You're an asshole, you know that?"

"Keep yelling at me. Please."

I reach for the door, but he holds it open. "Will you stop flirting with me? It's weird. And a little gross."

"Honestly, it's not even intentional."

A laugh bubbles out of me. "Are you saying I'm irresistible? Is someone in love?"

"Don't get excited, Ms. Romantic. I don't believe in love, remember? But I don't mind casual fun."

"I normally don't either, but here we are." I end with, finally taking control of the door and speeding away, leaving him standing in my wake.

I arrive at the mall a few minutes later, hurrying out of my car and into my favorite store. I immediately start grabbing things off the rack, ignoring price tags. I work hard and deserve a treat.

A nice worker named Kelly assists me, finding items she thinks I'll like, and helps me get a dressing room. I try out a few outfits, none of them really looking right.

Kelly analyzes me in the mirror. "Look, honey, you're one of the most gorgeous girls I've ever seen. Seriously. And these pieces are just dulling you down."

I sigh, feeling defeated. The outfit shapes the whole vibe of the night. If I don't feel confident, I know I won't be able to have fun. I look back to see her running towards a rack, grabbing a sparkly gold bodycon dress.

She sprints back to me, smiling happily. "We just got it in. I completely forgot! This is it. Put it on."

"It's beautiful, but I think a bit much." The straps are thin, leading down to a drastic V neckline. It's mostly backless, and is entirely too short, but pretty nonetheless.

"We live in Chicago, babe. If this is too much, you just need to find a better club."

I cough out a laugh and go back in to change, mostly just to humor her. But when I put the dress on, I shock myself. I haven't seen myself out of scrubs or baggie clothes in forever, and the girl smiling back at me looked, well, happy.

I walk out, and Kelly giggles, clapping her hands. "I knew it! I knew it. He is going to love it, girl!"

I make eye contact with her through the mirror. "Oh, there is no he. This is for me and me only."

"Trust me, it may be for you, but there's always a he."

I ponder her words. The thing is, there truly isn't a he. The only new guy who's been new in my life is Sean, and it isn't like that. To be honest, I hadn't thought about him once since I got here. This dress truly is for me. Making him drool is just an added bonus.

* * *

Me and Eliana take our time getting ready. I play some 2010s hype music, while she keeps a steady flow of seltzers running through us. Jonah didn't feel like watching us put on makeup and do our hair for two hours, so he's meeting us in a few, and made us promise to wait for him to do shots.

I finish straightening the last strand of hair, satisfied with the girl staring back in the mirror.

Eliana decided to wear her hair unstyled since it's naturally pin-straight. "I love this hair on you. The waves are very you, but straight feels so powerful."

"Right? We look hot. Like seriously hot."

At that moment, Jonah bursts through the door, cackling. "What's up bitches? You guys look so sexy!"

I squeal, pulling him to the ground that's become our makeshift vanity. "What's got you laughing so hard?"

He smiles, recalling the memory. "Oh, just the look on Sean's face when he saw me walk in. I swear to God, I thought he was gonna choke me out right there. Kinda mad he didn't." He says with a wink.

Eliana slaps him on the shoulder. "Ew! Please, give me a warning so I can cover my ears."

"Sorry, Ana, but your brother is fucking hot." He looks to me, waiting for my agreement, which I don't give him the pleasure of.

She shivers, grabbing her outfit to go change. She walks back out in a black miniskirt, thigh-high boots, and a revealing silver top. Eliana doesn't have much curve to her, but her tiny frame and height would make her a perfect model if only she would go for it.

"Oh my God!" I yell while Jonah whistles.

"Yeah, yeah. Go get dressed, S. I can't wait to see what you bought!"

I nod, stepping towards my walk-in closet and shutting the door. I pull the dress on and pair it with some matching gold heels. They're taller than what I'm used to, and I'll regret it in an hour, but might as well go all out, right? I run my hands along my hair and walk out to an empty room.

"Where the hell are you guys?!" I yell and hear their response from the kitchen.

"We are so late and we forgot about shots! Pouring now, get out here!"

I sigh, stepping out into the open layout. I see my friends taking a shot, Jonah choking when he sees me. When I look over more, I see Sean glaring harder than he ever has at Jonah, then at me.

"We might need to stay in," Jonah says with a wink, unaware of the murderous stare being thrown at him.

Eliana runs towards me, jumping up and down. I join her, then throw back a shot, grabbing my purse.

Sean remains scarily silent, and I can't say I'm not a tiny bit disappointed. Maybe he doesn't actually think I'm attractive. Am I really that delusional? I don't let the thoughts bother me. I know I look good, and even Sean Jacobs can't ruin my mood tonight.

I steer them towards the door, side-stepping him. "Let's roll."

They cheer, walking out when I remember something. "Shit! I forgot to unplug the straightener! I'll be right back!"

They wait outside as I run back to the room, eyes sweeping over it. I unplug the iron and do one last look in the mirror. Satisfied, I run out, dodging Sean's stare. Right as I'm about to be in the clear, my heel catches on something and I stumble.

A calloused hand grabs me at the waist, pulling me back. His mouth gets close to my ear, so much so that I can feel his hot breath against my skin. "I don't need to tell you that you look good. You know that already. But be safe tonight, got it?"

I stand there for a moment, savoring the way he feels behind me. I make no effort to talk, stepping out of his embrace. When I reach for the door, his hand snakes around and latches onto my arm.

"One more thing. You don't have to try to make me jealous. I already want to fucking kill Jonah, let alone any other guy that sees you tonight. Go."

I pause, still unsure of what to say. So I say nothing, slipping out to join my friends.

Thirteen

Summer

We step into the club, taking in the surrounding atmosphere. "Fireball" by Pitbull blasts from the speakers, people screaming along to the lyrics everywhere. We head straight for the bar and order two rounds of shots, downing them both immediately.

"THIS PLACE IS AWESOME!" Jonah screams. His black hair is a complete mess, pieces sticking up in all directions. I can tell he put on some sort of shimmer spray because his exposed chest is glittering against the lights. His black button-up is mostly open, and tucked into a pair of gray trousers, completed with an expensive-looking belt. How he affords his clothes will always be a mystery to me.

Eliana flinches at his volume. "Agreed, but we're right next to you. We can hear you just fine, babe."

"OH, OKAY!" He yells, not lowering the volume at all.

We giggle at his hysterics, him completely unaware. I wink at the bartender, who won't stop staring, and turn towards my friends. Staying quiet for a moment, I let the liquid heat warm my body. I can already feel the shots mixing with everything we drank at home, slowly helping me relax.

Jonah orders us another round before yelling that we need to dance. We agree and run towards the floor, mixing in with the sea of bodies. We coast into the middle, where Jonah gets snagged right away by a pretty redhead and what seems to be her boyfriend.

Eliana and I roll our eyes at his ease, before grabbing each other's hips and grinding to the beat. Pretty soon, we also get snagged by men of our own. She wanders off with some guy that I barely get a look at, mumbling something about her dickhead boss.

I let myself get pulled into the arms of a gorgeous brunette. He looks young, probably mid twenties. He has a soft look to him, almost like a puppy dog. It's extremely cute. I back my ass up right against him and sway to the beat. His hands settle on my waist and venture lower with every song.

We sing along to the music, hips matching every note. At one point, he turns me around, pulling me tight against his chest as we sway, palming my ass completely. We stay like that for a while, sneaking kisses in between songs.

"What's your name, beautiful?"

"How'd you know?"

"Huh?"

Okay, so clearly not the brightest. But that's fine. "Summer."

"Cool. I'm Stone."

Stone? Like a fucking rock? I mean, I guess I can't blame him for his parents' mistakes, but you'd think he'd go by something else.

"Wanna get a drink?"

Wonderful, something I can't make fun of. See? I knew this would turn around. "Please."

He grabs my hand, pulling me through the crowd. I walk up to the bar and he settles behind me, caging me in. "So what'll it be?"

"Tequila, just one, please." I'm a lightweight and was already feeling it until this point. I'm not a messy drunk, I normally get more calm and loose. I just prefer not to black out. I have a problem with losing control. I've lost it enough in the past.

"Two shots of tequila on my tab, please."

The bartender nods, looking at me sideways. "You got it, bro."

We take the shots, laughing at the drop that escaped from the corner of my mouth. He lifts a finger to it, wiping it, and licks the pad of his thumb. He moves next to me and turns us so that we're facing each other.

"So what's Summer like?"

"Hot and miserable."

He frowns. "You don't seem miserable."

"I'm not. I was talking about the season."

He cracks a smile. "You're funny. I like that."

I cringe internally, knowing I can't say the same back. "Thanks. What do you do?"

"I'm an accountant. Nothing exciting, but it pays the bills. How about you?"

"I'm a nurse. Definitely exciting and barely pays the bills."

"That's okay, I could support you."

I roll my eyes at his lame attempt at flirting. I look to my right and see Jonah being dragged out of the door by the same pair from earlier. He catches my eye and winks, smiling shamelessly. I scan the room and find Eliana, now alone, but dancing her heart out happily. I smile at the state of my friends and give my attention back to the guy beside me. "Are you here with friends? Or alone?"

He shakes his head. "Alone today. My friend was supposed to come, but he has work this week and doesn't want to be hungover."

"Nothing wrong with responsibility."

"More like boring."

I ignore his comment, slowly losing interest. Normally, I wouldn't have even engaged in conversation this long. We would have gone straight to a hotel room after a few minutes of dancing. But right now, I'm enjoying myself and am not really feeling up for it.

As if sensing my thoughts, he asks, "so, you wanna get out of here?"

I sigh, turning to him. "Not today."

He's quiet for a minute, as if confused at my rejection. Once he realizes I'm serious, his face morphs into an ugly snarl. "Are you kidding me? You fucking tease! If I knew you weren't gonna sleep with me, I would've found some other bitch."

Sean

I tried keeping my distance. I really did. But when I heard the first angry word come out of that guy's mouth, my legs had a mind of their own. One minute, I was by the door, scanning the club for any sign of Summer or Eliana. The next, I had one hand snatching the dickhead's jacket, the other curled in a fist, slamming into his jaw.

He immediately falls back against the bar, and I step towards him, making sure Summer is safely out of the way, before repeating the action.

Blood spurts out of his face as he whines like a baby, limbs flailing. I get one more good punch in before I'm pulled away by security. Out of the corner of my eye, I see Summer snatch Eliana from the dance floor before following.

Once I'm outside, Summer rushes towards me. "Are you okay? What are you doing here?"

I take Eliana from her, letting her tired body lean against me. She mumbles something, then drops her head to my chest, leaving a trail of drool. "You forgot your phone at home. Eliana wasn't answering hers, and I was worried. This is the third club I've been to."

I tried to have a relaxing evening, but something was nagging me the entire time. I texted Eliana first, just wanting to check in, but she yielded no response. When I called Summer and heard it ring from the other room, I decided to trust my gut.

"Shit, I'm so sorry! I didn't realize. And oh my gosh! Your hand!"

I look down to see my knuckles already bruising, blood trailing down my arm.

"I think most of it is his. Are you okay?"

She nods. "I'm fine. Just glad you came. I didn't feel like punching anyone today."

"Apparently I did. You're not mad?"

"For the first time in a while, no, I'm not mad at you, Sean."

I nod, dragging Eliana towards the car and settling her in before opening the door for Summer. I get into the driver's seat and start the car, pulling away from the club. We sit in silence for a few minutes, her sleepily resting her head against the glass.

"Did your friend get home okay?"

She looks at me curiously. "Jonah? You hate him. Why do you care?"

I shrug, keeping my eyes in front of me. "Doesn't mean I want something to happen to him."

"He's fine. Not home, but fine. I guess he texted a little while back."

I let out a hum in response. She falls asleep for the rest of the short ride, and I take turns taking them up to the apartment and settling them in their beds. I drop a glass of water and some Advil at both of their bedsides, along with a trash can.

I fall onto the couch, checking the time. 4 AM. It's fine. I can run just fine on two hours of sleep. No biggie.

Fourteen

Sean

Running on two hours of sleep is in fact not "no biggie". As if I wasn't feeling the lack of sleep enough, I was greeted at work by a cheerful Ethan.

"Hey, man! You look like absolute shit!"

I shoot him a glare, walking past him to my desk without a word. He doesn't take the hint, and rolls towards me in his office chair, stopping at the other side of my desk.

"I don't know if you've noticed, but I'm not really in the mood to gossip."

He smiles. "Oh, I noticed, but when have you ever been in the mood to gossip?"

I roll my eyes, logging onto my computer. "Is there a point to your imposition of my space?"

He nods. "There is, in fact. I know you've been dying to get on the site, which, by the way, I think is a bad idea being that you wince every time you get up,"

"I don't remember you becoming a doctor, but continue."

He leans back in his chair, setting his feet on my desk. "I have a proposition for you. I'll let you work on the site three days a week, and for the other two, you stay in the office."

I ponder his offer, shoving his feet back to the floor. If it's my only chance to get some action, I want to take it, but I seriously don't know how much more bookwork I can do.

He continues before I can say anything. "I can see the negativity flowing through your brain. The office work won't be the same as before. I've got a new project that's going to require a lot of my attention, so I need you to take on some of my duties. Like a manager."

"A manager?"

"A manager. Think of me as the boss, and you as a helping hand. You'll have more responsibility than my other guys, but still will feel like part of the team."

"Does it come with a pay raise?"

"No. I'm going to give you a crap ton of more work and pay you the same rate," he says sarcastically.

"No need for the sass. Fine. I'll do it."

He shakes my hand. "Only you would make a promotion sound like a chore."

Summer

I spend the day feeling like I got continuously run over by a semi. I tried resting, but was interrupted every hour to puke my guts out, and heard Eliana doing the same. Poor Gouda has witnessed too much today. By about 6 PM I can finally stand without running back to the trash can, which I take as a win.

I decide to shower, mostly to wash away all the horrors of last night. After washing up, I go to Eliana's room to make sure she didn't choke on her puke during the day. I walk in to see her face-down, groaning into the pillow. I launch myself on her bed, mirroring her position.

She turns her head towards me, looking like a complete mess. "I fucking hate Jonah."

"Are we blaming him for how we're feeling right now?"

She grunts. "Yes. You know that bitch is probably running a marathon somewhere completely unaffected."

I shake my head. "I have a feeling he ran the equivalent of a marathon last night."

She turns her head back into the pillow, letting out a small scream. "I am never drinking again."

"Preach it. We're too old for this shit."

"I want donuts. Call Sean to bring us donuts."

With my head spinning, I was in no mood to argue. I snatch my phone, dialing his number. He picks up immediately.

"*Summer? Is everything okay?*"

I grunt. "Donuts."

"*Can we try explaining with our words instead of talking like a caveman?*"

"You're making my head hurt," I whine. "We need donuts. Please bring us donuts."

"*Did you just ask me for something with a please, sunshine? Maybe I need to get you guys drunk more often.*"

I hang up the phone, tired of hearing his voice. I chuck it away from me, and it hits the wall with a smack. Eliana's head jolts up at the noise, looking like a meerkat. "GET DOWN!"

I slap my hands over my ears at her volume. "It was my phone, you idiot. I think you just gave me a noise-induced concussion."

She slumps back down, drool hanging from her mouth.

"I can't work tomorrow. I'm quitting my job. I can just be homeless. Like Sean!"

"Same, let's just freeload for the rest of our lives."

As if we summoned him, the door flies open, and he steps inside, walking towards the bed. "Are you guys talking shit about me after I brought you donuts?"

"Yes. You can go now. Leave the donuts."

He rolls his eyes, walking towards the window. He throws the curtains open right as Eliana pokes her head up. "AGHHA. IT BURNS! It burns."

He turns around, giving her a pointed look. "Are you serious right now? Get up. You look like shit. At least your friend had the decency to shower." He says, turning his nose up.

"He's right. You smell really bad, babe."

She gets up and stomps towards the bathroom, giving us the bird. I giggle at her antics and sit up, grabbing a donut from the box.

I moan from the taste of real food without being tainted by nausea, and do a little dance. He shakes his head at me, sitting down at the edge of the bed.

"Thanks again for showing up last night," I say, mouth full of food.

He snatches the rest of my donut, downing it. "No problem."

I grab a pillow and smack him as hard as possible. "Just because you helped me doesn't mean I like you now."

"Clearly. What's with you and hitting people? It's quite violent."

I shrug, grabbing another donut. Eliana comes back in record time and snatches the box, setting in on her lap. She looks between me and him. "Thanks for the donuts. You're dismissed."

I nod in agreement as he shakes his head, making his way towards the door. He gives us one last look before stepping out, shutting the door behind him.

She turns to me. "I know you don't like having him here, but he's practically our personal assistant. He can cook for us, clean, and go on errands."

"True. It really does feel great bossing him around. Maybe we could call Ethan and tell him Sean quit? Then he would have no choice but to be our permanent servant."

She squeals with delight. "Yes! Let me grab my phone."

"I heard that! And I already told Ethan to not trust a word either of you say to him," he yells from the kitchen.

We pout at the door. "Stop eavesdropping, asshole."

"Yeah!" She cheers in agreement, chucking our last donut at the door. It hits the wood and leaves a trail of goo on the way down. We stare at the disheveled donut before shrugging, picking it up, and splitting it.

Fifteen

❧❦❧

Summer

It's been a few days since our outing and I'd be lying if I said the atmosphere hadn't changed between me and Sean. We still talk in our normal manner, but it has less hatred behind it. It's become almost playful. Like when I left for work a few hours ago.

"Going to save some lives?" He asked, walking with me to my car.

"Something like that."

"Right, I forgot. Real nurses are in the ED."

I shot him a glare, ready to bite his head off.

He threw his hands up in defense, laughing at my expression. "Joking! You know I think your work is amazing."

I gave him a confused look, climbing through the driver's door he had opened for me. "Actually, I didn't know you thought anything was amazing about me."

"I think your roommate is pretty amazing."

"You're right. Eliana is pretty great."

He rolled his eyes. "Wasn't talking about her." He shut my door and walked away.

Jonah whacks me with a purewick, pulling me out of my thoughts. I narrow my eyes at him. "You better pray for your sake that it's unused."

"The good old cooter canoe." He cackles. "I guess we'll never know. What are you daydreaming about? Or night dreaming? Ha."

I shiver in disgust at his lame attempt at a joke. "Ignoring that. Just thinking about what I could do to get you fired."

He gasps dramatically, clutching imaginary pearls. "Rude! You would die without me. We hide in the corner from the other nurses for a reason."

"True. They're so judgy for what? If I wanted to go back to high school, I would just—actually, I would rather die."

"Agreed. Hey," He says, punching my arm. "Eliana said that you guys ended up getting taken home by Sean the other night? What the hell happened?"

"Oh my god! I can't believe I forgot to tell you! This guy was being a jerk to me and Sean showed up out of nowhere and beat the shit out of him."

He stares at me with a blank expression before smirking at the ground, mumbling "Figures".

"What was that?"

He laughs, looking at me sideways. "So you mean to tell me he just showed up? Right when a guy was hitting on you?"

"I mean, the guy and I had been together the whole night before that, but sure. Why? What are you getting at?"

"Nothing. He just seems a little protective, is all."

"Well, obviously. Eliana and I have been best friends since we were thirteen. He still sees me as a kid he needs to protect."

"Sure. That's the reason."

My patient hits their call light, so I get up. "You're being weirdly cryptic today and I'm not liking it. I expect a full report on your night when I get back."

And boy, do I get one. I was right about the two people he left with being a couple. Apparently, they've been married for three years and like to find a third every once in a while to spice things up. Jonah says he "performed so well" that they asked him out again, but he refused. Said he prefers to not repeat hookups, with me as the exception, of course.

A nurse huffs from behind her computer, turning towards us. "Is this a work-appropriate conversation?"

Jonah snaps his head towards her. "Is your wedding ring off because it's getting cleaned, or have you already moved on to finding husband number five?"

I cackle at his response as she gives him a dirty look and walks away. "And we wonder why all our coworkers hate us."

He shrugs. "It's not our fault that they're hormonal—emphasis on the whore."

I gasp. "You are ridiculous."

He winks. "You love it."

"I do."

Sean

My first day doing actual construction goes better than expected. The guys are cool and very understanding. They are patient, taking time to show me how to do certain builds, and they say nothing when I have to stop for a minute, holding my side.

Now at home, I stare at the scar in the mirror. It looks rough. Too much time has passed since the accident. It should be fully healed by now. I try to clean part of it, throwing a bandage on similarly to how the nurses did at the hospital. Satisfied with my work, I put on some sweats and walk out to the couch, seeing I have a missed call from Ethan. I hit him back, and he asks if I want to grab a drink.

I accept his invitation and change into something a little more appropriate. I can't lie and say I'm not a little excited. Even though I've been back for a while, Ethan and I have acted more as coworkers than friends, and this is the first time we really crossed the line. I found myself missing the crew from when I was stationed a lot, and the idea of having some friends again intrigued me.

I spray some cologne and head out, typing the address into my Maps. I listen to my audiobook on the way over and park next to him when I arrive. He's not in his truck, so I walk inside and find him saving a spot for me at the bar.

I smack a hand on his back, sliding into the seat next to him. "Hey E, good to see you outside of work."

"Yeah buddy, thanks for meeting me. I feel like we used to be so close. I want you as my best friend again."

I let out a breath I didn't know I was holding in. Why am I twenty-seven acting like a five-year-old? I've fought in wars and been less nervous. What is my problem?

"Same man. Is everything okay?"

He looks down at his glass, rubbing a hand across the back of his neck. "I think I'm getting divorced? I don't know, actually."

I stare at him for a moment before grabbing the bartender. "Whiskey on the rocks, make it a double. And fill my friend up too."

"You got it, boss."

"What is it with people calling each other boss? Where did

that come from? I mean, you're clearly not his boss." I let Ethan ramble for a few minutes, noticing his clear distress. "And what happens if someone calls their employee boss? Are they both the boss now?"

"Do you seriously want to talk about the slang word 'boss' or do you want to tell me what's going on?"

He grabs his new drink, downing it, and I follow. "The second option, if you don't mind."

"I'd prefer it, actually."

He sighs. "I don't actually know if I ever loved her." He pauses, as if gauging for my reaction. I don't give him one. "My wife, I mean. We got married pretty young. We met when I was twenty, she was nineteen. Our moms worked together and knew they had kids in the same age range."

I nod, urging him to continue.

He flags the bartender down, ordering us another round, and asks to keep them coming.

"She was pretty. Very polite, always knew exactly what to say. She was funny enough, kind, comforting, and warm. Everything you want in a person. But there was never a spark. For a while, I didn't mind it. I had just taken over the business and had a lot on my plate. It was easy with her. She took care of me, I provided for her. I took her to business dinners and everyone loved her. They would always pull me aside and tell me what a catch she was, how sweet and witty she was, the works."

He drops his head in his hands, and I pat him on the back, giving him a minute.

"I thought, 'What am I missing?'. If everyone else loves her so much, then I must love her too. So I told her I did. She said she was surprised I felt that way, and that it didn't seem like I liked her at all. I got upset. I didn't know that she could tell how much my head wasn't in it. So I started doing better. I got her flowers constantly, surprised her with lunch, took her on cute dates, made love to her."

He sits up straighter. "The whole time it felt fake. Like I wasn't doing it for the right reasons, but every time I thought about breaking up with her, I wanted to throw up. She was my first girlfriend, I was comfortable with her. So I asked her to marry me. She said yes, of course, and we tied the knot the following year. We were just too young. I was twenty-three, had finally gotten my business where I wanted it, and was kind of riding that high.

"I felt unstoppable. But after about a year, I was tired of putting effort into the relationship. It was shitty, but being with her felt like a chore," he lets out another sigh. "She never put in any effort of her own. Said it was a man's job to make a woman feel loved and wanted. That I should be happy from her happiness."

I shake my head. "That's shitty, and pretty stupid, if you ask me. Even if you weren't being a good husband, she wasn't being a great wife."

He shrugs. "Maybe. Maybe not. Doesn't matter. We pretended nothing was wrong until this month. Always avoided each other. The only time we interacted was when we were having sex, and after, she would leave to sleep in the guest room.

"Recently, though, it's been different. Like we're in a competition to see who can be the shittier spouse. I'll leave dishes in the sink, she'll leave a trail of shoes in front of the door. Anything to get any sort of emotion out of each other. And it worked. Last week, she came into our bedroom and yelled at me. 'Why are men so stupid?' she asked. And I laughed. In her face." He smiles for a moment. "She got so angry, and then she paused, dropped onto the bed next to me, and laughed too."

I smile too, at the sound of the memory.

"We laughed for so long, but it fizzled out. She turned to me, and said 'Ethan, I want a divorce'. And I agreed. She told me I never loved her. But that's the thing, I think I did love her. I just wasn't IN love with her."

Why did that sentence make it feel like I was being punched? I mean seriously. I have been against the idea of love for as long as I can remember. But hearing his story? It was heartbreaking. "God. I'm so sorry, E."

He nods. "I think it's okay. It's just scary. I've been with her for five years. In a way, she filled the role of best friend after you left. And not having both of you was just something I knew I couldn't handle."

"So that's why you called?"

"Mhm. I don't want to deal with this shit alone. And based on the way you're looking at me, it looks like you've got some shit of your own."

I crack a goofy smile. "Ethan Carter, will you be my friend?"

He smacks me across the back of my head, a matching smile of his own. "If you insist."

Sixteen

Sean

I am drunk. I can't remember the last time I got drunk. All I know is that right now, I'm nowhere near sober. Ethan and I stayed at the bar for a while, reminiscing about old memories. I even told him about my time in the military, something I hadn't done with anyone else. It felt good to open up a little, and he made it easy.

Or at least the alcohol did. But now I'm facing the consequences. We stumble into the parking lot, hanging onto each other, laughing at nothing. We make the obvious choice of not driving, so I call us an Uber.

"Wait, no need! I'll call my wife! Or ex-wife? Almost ex-wife?"

"Yeah, I'm going to say Uber is better."

He laughs for no reason. "I love you, man."

I let out a giggle. *Why did I just giggle?* Like a literal teenage girl giggle. "I need tacos."

He throws his hands up, smiling brightly. "OH MY GOD.

Let's get tacos!"

We hop in the Uber, ordering him to take us to the nearest taco shop. We rattle off our cravings at the speaker box, where an angry employee asks us to stop yelling. After begging the driver to pay, we somehow end up with thirty tacos and decide the only logical choice is to have a taco-eating competition.

The Uber driver, Mohammed, not appreciating that choice, kicks us out for getting taco shells and lettuce all over his car. Ethan, not liking his attitude, jumps on the hood.

"YOU CAN'T LEAVE US! I AM ONE WITH THE CAR!"

I try to jump on too, but Mohammed sees my approach and starts driving. Ethan gets scared and slides off, rolling in the dirt.

He lets out a scream that makes my blood turn cold. "HOLY SHIT! ARE YOU GOOD, E?"

He looks up at me like a sad puppy. "He crushed my tacos!"

I sit down next to him, shoveling crushed taco pieces into my mouth while he mourns his taco. "STOP! WE MUST BURY IT!"

I spit some of the taco back into the wrapping. "Shit, man, you're right!"

We dig a small hole in the ground, place the taco in, and cover it. "Say grace please, Sean."

"Why do I have to do it?"

He punches me in the arm. "I don't know, maybe because you ate half of it? Honor our fallen brother!"

"I'll miss you, man," I say, giving the taco a final salute. Ethan leans down, kissing the dirt.

"I have a question."

"Okay."

"How are we getting home?"

The question sobers me a little as I think about our options. I could call an Uber, but at this point, I think Mohammed has gotten us banned from the app. I could call Eliana, but she's sleeping and I don't want to worry her. Which is why I am left with one option. Summer. Because she works night shift, she's the only person awake that will answer, and she worked yesterday so she should be home.

"I'll call that sunshine girl."

Ethan looks at me thoughtfully. "I just love the earth, man."

I dial her number, watching it ring. She picks up quickly, her voice sounding raspy and low.

"Sean? Where are you?"

"I don't know sunshine. Your voice sounds very crispy, I'm liking it."

She lets out a small laugh. *"Great, glad we cleared that up. You're drunk. Send me a pin and I'll come get you."*

"Thank you, Mother Sunshine!" Ethan screams from beside me.

"Why do I do this to myself? I'm on the way. DON'T MOVE."

"I love it when you get all bossy."

Click. "Aw. She hung up on me."

We wait for a few minutes, kicking rocks and seeing who can jump the furthest when her car pulls up.

She rolls down the window. "Get in, please."

Ethan stares at her before running in the opposite direction. "RUN SEAN RUN. MOHAMMED SENT HER, I KNOW IT!"

"GET BACK HERE… DAMN IT! Go get your friend, Sean. And who the hell is Mohammed?"

I cringe. "Not important. Help me?"

She lets out an annoyed groan, putting the car in park, and gets out. "Remember how easy it was to get me home when

I was drunk? What is it with men turning into children the second they have a sip of tequila?"

"Whiskey actually. A real man's drink."

"Are you seriously calling yourself a real man right now? Really?"

I ignore her, jogging towards Ethan. "If you come with me, I'll bring tacos for lunch next week."

He nods, slumping against me. Summer rounds his other side, hoisting one of his arms around her shoulder as I do the same. We trudge back to the car; him whining the whole way. When we finally shove him in the back, I open her door for her and hop into the passenger's seat.

She starts the car, pulling back onto a main road. "Why on earth are you this drunk on a Thursday?"

"Ethan has some stuff going on and I wouldn't pass up a chance to get drunk."

"Oh, are you an alcoholic now?"

I laugh. "Alcoholic. Such a silly word, right? There are so many addictions out there. Like that lady on that show who ate couch."

Summer sighs from beside me, letting me ramble on the way to Ethan's. His wife meets us outside the house and I help her get him to the couch where he knocks out. She thanks me, and tells me to get home safely.

She's very pretty, in a sweet kind of way. Dark chocolate hair and tanned skin, with a smile so bright it could blind someone. If I'm being honest, she doesn't seem like someone Ethan would go for. She seems nice, to be sure, but is just too quiet for a guy like him.

I get back in the car with Summer, resting my head on the back of my seat. I choose silence for this ride, and let her help me get out and walk towards the elevator.

We continue to sit in silence on the ride up, and she fumbles with her keys when opening the door. I pull her to my side for a hug.

"You're so soft."

She shoves me away, clearly annoyed. "Not exactly what a girl wants to hear."

I yank her back into my chest, wrapping my arms around her. "I like it. You feel homey. You're perfect."

She lets out a long breath and pulls away again, dragging me towards my couch. I sit down, and she shoves me until I'm lying, pulling a blanket down on top of me. She drops a trash can at my side and places a cup of water with some Advil on the table, similar to how I did for her. She starts walking away before I stop her.

"Wait!"

She turns back, unamused. "Yes, Sean?"

"I'm drunk."

"I can see that."

"Wanna fuck?"

Seventeen

Summer

I let his words process before I can't help myself. A loud laugh bursts out of me. The only problem is, it doesn't stop. I laugh until there are tears in my eyes, and I'm doubling over.

He folds his arms over his chest and turns away, looking like a five-year-old. "Why are you laughing at me?!" He whines.

My laughter calms into a giggle. "I'm just thinking about how embarrassed you're going to be tomorrow."

"Fine, just say I'm ugly."

"You're not ugly, Sean, and you know it. Go to sleep. I'll see you tomorrow." I say, another laugh escaping.

He flips me off as I leave. God, he looked so cute. I had never in my life seen Sean act that way. Around me, he was usually more serious and composed. I had seen him act pretty goofy with his friends, but nothing like this. He's acting like an insecure teenage girl. And I'm loving every minute of it.

I skip happily back into my room, putting on some music, and go back to my coloring. Working night shift can be hard when everyone is asleep while I'm awake. It also makes it so that I'm usually averaging six hours of sleep, but the pay makes it worth it.

I grab my phone and text Jonah to see how his shift is going. It's a full moon tonight, meaning the patients are all going to be on one, especially the ones with dementia.

He ignores my text and FaceTimes me instead, popping in his earbuds. "It's a complete shit show. Bed alarms going off every five minutes, and patients talking all kinds of crazy. How does this always happen to me? I'm going to start scheduling off every full moon. I can't take this, especially not without you here."

"Aw, you love me?"

"No. I tolerate you. And you're the only person here that gets my humor. Everyone else is so judgy. What happened to night shift being filled with cool twenty-year-olds, and dayshift being full of moms who shop at Trader Joe's and say 'I'm so bad' after eating a chocolate-covered almond?"

"It's all a myth. Not the age part, that's usually true. But the rest of it. Majority of the people in nursing are stuck-up assholes who hate the world because they never went back for NP or CRNA."

He groans. "You're so right. But where are our people? The ones that are fun and hot and can actually take a joke?"

"Oh, they're out there. They've just escaped the hospitals. Soft nursing is where it's at. When I am finally financially stable, we're busting it out of this hellhole and going straight to plastics."

"Yes! But the sexy kind, not the burn kind. That stuff makes me sad. I just want to give some granola moms some Botox and make their lips the size of a balloon."

I nod in agreement, as he shoves me into his pocket, running towards another bed alarm. "No! Stop! Get out of the ceiling now! Your daughter is NOT in the ceiling to pick you up… dammit! LIZ! GET THE LADDER!"

I listen to their struggle from my phone, cackling at his commentary. After it goes on for about twenty minutes, he leaves the room, coming back into view.

"What the fuck is my life?"

"Sometimes I miss full moon shifts. Never boring. Always ends with a good story. They're classic."

He clicks his tongue. "That's easy to say when your patients always listen to you. Why do people with dementia bond with you so easily?"

"I just roll with whatever they're saying. One time, Dr. Peters walked in on me fighting the imaginary squirrels that were coming from my patient's ceiling. He put in a psych consult. For me."

He barks out a laugh. "See! The best stuff always happens to you. It's like you've been blessed by the Med-Surg gods."

"Something like that." My mouth morphs into a smile at the memory of mere minutes ago. "You will not believe what just happened. Sean tried to sleep with me."

Suddenly I'm flying towards the ground. Jonah snatches me back up, wiping the dust off his phone. "SHUT UP! How big?" He starts his hands in a praying motion and slowly backs them away from each other. "We're still going? Damn girl! Are you walking okay?"

"Ew, stop! I didn't do it!"

His hands drop along with his smile. "And why not? He is seriously hot. Like movie-star-level hot. You don't see men like that every day."

"Because I don't see him in that way. And besides, he didn't actually mean it. He was drunk."

"Drunk words are sober thoughts."

"Oh, so you actually think the movie E.T. is based on a true story?"

He shivers. "Alright, there are certain exceptions. But still, how do you know he didn't mean it?"

"Because he was seriously drunk. Dancing naked on the table, drunk. Sucking off your English teacher level drunk-"

"It was one time!" He shrieks. "And I get your point, no need to continue. So he didn't mean it. Does that disappoint you?"

I gag. "Hell no. I'm glad. It would be too awkward. And if something went wrong, which it would, I wouldn't want Eliana to feel like she needed to pick sides."

"You know she wouldn't do that."

"Maybe not. But either way, it doesn't matter. He's not even a friend, let alone something more. Let's drop it."

"Whatever you say." A loud crash echoes through the microphone. "Aw shit. Gotta go, he's back in the ceiling. Bye!"

I hang up, dropping my phone. For the rest of the night, I try to stay busy, but can't help feeling like a kid on Christmas. I have never seen him hungover before, and I seriously want to see how he's going to face me tomorrow.

Sean

I wake up feeling like complete shit. My head is pounding, my body aches for some reason, and I have little to no recollection of the events of last night. I grab my phone, wincing at the brightness, and read a text Ethan had left.

"I think I tried to sleep with my wife–almost–ex-wife last night."

I laugh at the mental image, groaning at the movement. I text him back right away. *"I am banned from Uber. Any idea how that happened?"*

I'm trying to make my way to my feet when Eliana runs into the room, snatching the curtains open.

"Payback's a bitch!" She yells, leaving the apartment.

I cover my eyes like a vampire, regretting every drink that caused the feeling. I take a small whiff of my shirt, gagging at the smell of old tacos and cheap whiskey. Letting out one last breath, I wander towards the shower, stripping completely, and hop in.

I spend a good thirty minutes in there, then get dressed, flinching at the sight of myself. I look like shit. I run a hand through my hair, scrunching to add some volume. When I'm satisfied with the look of it, I walk out to see Summer sitting on the couch, sipping her coffee.

She smiles as she sees me. "Morning sunshine!"

My eyebrow raises at her cheerfulness. "That's my line."

She ignores my comment. "How are you feeling? Weird in any way?"

"Not exactly, just like my head's been shoved against a brick wall. Why? What did I do?"

She kicks her feet up onto the table, enjoying this too much. "Oh, think hard. Think long and hard."

I roll my eyes, dropping onto the seat next to her. "I seriously have nothing. All I know is that tacos were involved based on the smell of my shirt."

"And that's all?"

"Out with it. Now. What'd I do?"

She smirks, hopping up from her seat. "Let me jog your memory." She states, grabbing my feet so that I'm lying on the couch. "You were lying just like this. Then I covered you up with this blankie here. Now close your eyes. Think Sean. What did you do-"

My eyes shoot open, my hand smacking over my mouth in horror. "I didn't."

She giggles evilly. "Oh, you did."

"I. Did. Not."

"Oh, but you did!"

I groan, pulling at the strands of my hair. "I'm gonna throw up."

"Oh, don't take it back now! You think I'm sexy and hot and you want to have my babies. Or at least do the baby making action-"

I cut her off. "Don't you dare finish that sentence."

She shrugs. "Don't need to. We both know how it ends."

I sit up, dropping my head in my hands. "Are you ever going to let me live this down?"

"Absolutely not. But stop sweating. I know you didn't mean it. We all say stupid things when we're drunk."

"You didn't."

She smirks. "Well, that's because I'm perfect, like you so obviously think."

I groan again. "Lord, give me strength."

"Oh, you need him. Especially with all of the dirty thoughts floating around in that head of yours. Maybe about a certain beautiful blonde?"

"I have always had a thing for Ellen DeGeneres."

She looks at me in disgust. "Seriously?"

"Oh yeah. Her pixie cut turns me on."

"I'd prefer if you'd stop telling me what 'turns you on'."

"Fair enough," I say, running a hand through my hair. "Thank you though for, well, putting up with me."

"No problem. I don't like being indebted to people, I was just returning the favor. But I'm not buying you donuts. It will take years for me to erase the emotional scarring of last night. You don't deserve them."

"I understand."

She pats me on the head. "Good boy." She says cheerfully, before skipping back to her room.

Eighteen

Summer

I steer into the lines, parking the car to my best ability. After Sean decided to get completely plastered at the bar, he needed to get the Ford back, so Eliana and I dropped him off on the way to our first pottery class. Now that we're here, I check my backup camera and see that my parking is actually atrocious.

"Think I can get away with this one?"

She opens her door, checking for a line. "Nothing. Take two!"

I throw the car in reverse, practicing my maneuverability. Once I'm in a more acceptable spot, I put the car in park, snatching Eliana's hand as she reaches for the door. "Wait! We need a game plan."

"You want to make a game plan for a pottery class?"

"Um, obviously. What if we step inside and the whole place is filled with people who try to get us to join their cult? The pieces we make are all just sacrifices to be made to their weird God."

95

"I think you've been watching too much Riverdale. And by too much, I mean one episode is already enough."

"Rude. You never got fully into it. That's not my fault! The musical episodes make me want to crawl out of my skin and join a caroling group all at the same time."

She shakes her head. "Nothing you're saying is convincing me to watch in any way."

"Fine. Be that way. But on a serious note, what's the plan?"

"What plan?" She says with a laugh. "Are you maybe just nervous that we'll finally find something you aren't good at?"

"Nonsense. Let's go. And don't look at me if they start singing some witch song because I'll already be far gone."

We walk into the store and are immediately greeted by an older lady with a clay-covered apron. "Hi, guys! Did you have a reservation?"

I step up to her desk. "Yes we did, it should be under Summer."

She checks her computer before confirming some of my information. "Perfect, Summer! We will have you in our beginner's class, second door to your right."

The class started pretty simple. The instructor, Pam, taught us how to spin the wheel, what movements cause what shapes, how to hold our hands, and how to sit. After getting a hang of the basics, she finally trusted us with clay. I plop it on my wheel, ready to make a beautiful mug.

Pam sits at her wheel, angled towards us all, there for us to copy her movements. "Alright everyone, we are going to start very simple with a small pot."

I frown at Eliana. "Excuse me, ma'am, I was hoping that I could make a mug."

She looks at me, annoyed at my outburst. "That's very well,

Miss, but before we move on to more advanced projects, we must learn the basics."

"But I don't really like plants. I can't keep them alive. And fake ones are too expensive. Like it's not even real, why does it cost $50?"

"You can use it as a pencil holder. Now, everyone, I'd like you to place your foot on the pedal, slowly adding pressure. The further down you go, the faster it will turn. We want to start slow and increase the speed over time."

I try following her instructions, but my wheel turns faster than expected, my ball of clay flying off and smacking against the ground.

Eliana slaps a hand over her mouth, trying to hold her laughter in. Seeing her laugh makes my body recoil, and I frown to try to keep the giggles in, pulling my lips into my mouth.

"Ladies and gentlemen, that is an example of what happens when you don't follow directions in this class. You see, I'm all about artistic individuality, but at this point in your journey, you should have none. You will make a pot. A boring, simple pot."

I nod, still trying not to laugh. I get up from my seat, and walking to where my clay has splat on the floor. I grab it, picking out some of the hair sticking off of it. Satisfied, I make my way back to my wheel and sit down. I mold my clay to the wheel, making sure it sticks this time, and slowly get it to spin. This time, it stays put, swiveling in uneven circles.

"Great! Now that we're back on track, I want you to grab a small amount of water and rub it into your hands. This will make it so that the clay won't stick to you and break from resistance. You will be able to mold it easier, and the water will smooth it as you work."

I follow her instructions, watching Eliana begin to make her pot with ease. I follow her movements, but my thumb cuts too far in, and a large dent forms in my clay.

"Now, if your clay gets dented like this young lady's, no need to give up, it can be fixed. Clay is very forgiving. Mistakes can be fixed easily, but they escalate quickly, so always proceed with caution. Now Miss, I want you to skim some clay off of the top, and fill the dent."

I do as she says, my pot coming back to life. I continue to work it when I feel a spray of water hit me in the face. I turn towards the direction it came from, screeching when I see a clay-covered Eliana, mouth hanging wide open.

A laugh bursts out of me, with her following. I wipe a hand down my cheek, murky sludge finding its way onto my hands. I gag at the smell and the feeling of clay drying under my fingernails.

Pam sighs, standing up from her chair. She walks over to us, handing us each a wet rag and aprons. "Usually I only keep aprons for kids. Most adults can handle themselves without making a mess, but I see now that you two are an exception."

A young kid laughs at us, looking backward from his chair. I stick my tongue out at him, ignoring the fact that his pot looks effortlessly perfect.

Pam walks back to her seat and continues working. I follow her movements, making a tall column. It's uneven and chunky looking, and there's a black spot in it from when it catapulted to the floor, but it resembles her example to an extent.

"Alright, now that we have an outline, I want you to stick your thumb down through the top of it so we can make the opening. But don't do it yet!"

I stare at her, thumb deep into my clay. I look to my right and see Elaina looking guilty, thumb in hers as well.

We cringe at each other as Pam closes her eyes for a minute, counting to ten. "The reason I said DO NOT do it yet is because if your thumb is dry, it won't come out of the clay easily, and you will have to pry it out. By doing this, it will make more dents in the outside of your pot."

I smile at her. "Perfect! My edges were already ruined!" I rip my thumb out, checking the damage. "Oh."

I stare at the two fingerprints stamped into my pot. Eliana attempts to do it more gracefully but gets the same results.

Pam gives us a cocky smirk. "Hm."

She then shows the rest of the class how to do it the right way while we try to smooth out our mess. When everyone has caught up to us, we make the opening larger so that it actually resembles a pot.

"Alright everyone, now that we have the basic shape, we can start adding carvings. I will pass out some tools and extra clay to cover any mistakes. You can use the tools to make a design, and in a few weeks, we will paint them."

Eliana grabs a tool, stating that she is going to carve tulips into her pot. I smile at mine, opting for a different design.

We spend around twenty minutes designing our pots and wait for Pam to collect them and place them in the kiln. When she grabs Eliana's, she tries to look encouraging.

"Well, it's very artistic and special. Good work Eliana."

It looks like she drew vaginas all over it. We are all very aware that it is covered in female genitalia, but she pretends to like it anyway.

When she reaches mine, she frowns. "You made a mug."

I look at the handle that I attached to the side of my pot.

"No. It's a pot that can be held."

"You made a mug."

"No, it's portable and innovative."

She sighs. "You made a mug."

I nod proudly. "I made a mug."

She grabs it, placing it in the kiln room to dry before it can be fired. I know she is silently praying it will explode, but I skip away anyway. We wash our hands and return the aprons, leaving the classroom.

"How'd it go, girls?" Asks the front desk lady, whose name tag reads 'Shelly'.

"Oh fantastic!" I say cheerfully. "I think we have a real talent! I might even want to work in ceramics. Are you guys hiring?"

Shelly beams. "Wonderful! I can grab you an application. I'm sure there's something you can do around here."

"There's no need for that." Pam says from behind me, making us all jump.

Me and Eliana look at each other, before booking it out the door and towards the car. We hop in, laughing at the interaction.

"Did you see her face?!" Eliana says, tears coming out of her eyes.

"I think she made it so many times it'll stick."

We laugh some more as I back out of the parking spot, leaving our new place behind us.

* * *

I crash the second we get home, not used to being awake in the day. It was my full intention to just take a small nap so that my sleep schedule stays somewhat normal, but I find myself waking up at midnight instead. I sit up, having that post-nap confusion, feeling insanely groggy. I smack my lips a few times, craving water like I never have before.

I grab the Stanley from my bedside table, taking a huge swig. The water comes spraying out of my mouth.

"That water is very old and tastes very wrong." I say to no one. I force myself out of bed, grabbing it so that it can have a proper cleaning.

When I step out of my room, I almost jump at the sight of a figure standing in the kitchen. My heart drops, before I remember that there's a man living with me now. I'm about to make a sassy remark when I step closer, seeing the sweat beaded on his forehead.

He's hunched over, hands flat on the counter, fingers spread. He's facing away from me, and I can see the shadow of his tattoo illuminated in the moonlight, covering his entire back, but it's too dark to make out a shape. His chest is rising and falling hard, breaths unsteady. His eyes are scrunched shut, eyebrows drawn.

I stand in my doorway, contemplating whether I want to approach or not. I start backing away—assuming he wouldn't want me bothering him—when I hear a choked sound come from his throat. Unable to stop myself, I walk towards him, placing my hand on his bare back.

He flinches at my touch. "Hey, you're okay. Breathe for me, Sean."

His breathing continues at the same pace, chest falling harder. I continue to rub his back, trying to think of a way to help him. I hesitate, before wrapping my arms around him from behind, squeezing him. He melts into my touch on instinct. "You're safe. Come back to me."

He nods against me, trying to calm himself. I stand with him for what feels like forever, reaching up to run my hands through his hair. He lets me massage his head, keeping his eyes closed.

Once he's calm, he notices our position, and steps away. He stays turned away from me, dropping his head in his hands. I walk up to him again, rubbing his back in comfort. "Hey. It's fine. There's no reason to be embarrassed."

He shakes his head. "I'm pathetic."

"Don't say that. You've been through hell and back."

"Exactly. I've been through hell, and I can't be happy at a safe apartment in Chicago? What sense does that make?"

"It makes perfect sense. You went from constant stress for seven years to none. It'd be weird if you didn't struggle with the adjustment."

He says nothing. I walk around so that we're facing each other. "How long have you been having panic attacks?"

He shakes his head, leaning back against the counter. "I don't have panic attacks. I just get stressed sometimes."

"You don't have them? Or you don't want to admit that you do?"

He gives me a glare. "Why do you even care, Summer?"

"Don't start that shit with me. We've known each other too long to not care about each other's well being. How long?"

"Since I was shot."

I nod. "How often?"

He hesitates, deciding what to say. "A few times a week? Usually during the night, when I have nothing to distract my thoughts."

"Why didn't you say anything? I could've helped."

"It's embarrassing. I didn't want anyone to know. I'm a man.

I shouldn't be freaking out at nothing like that."

I roll my eyes. "Because that's 'too feminine'?"

"Come on sunshine, you know I didn't mean it that way."

"I know. You think that people finding out that you struggle with mental health or that you have feelings at all will make you less of a man."

He rubs his abdomen where the scar must be, currently covered by a dressing. "Something like that."

"Let me help."

He turns away, giving me an annoyed grunt. "You can't help. No one can."

"Let me try."

He looks back at me. "What would trying even look like?"

I think for a moment, ideas bouncing around in my head. "What causes them to start? What thoughts are there when they happen?"

"Sometimes they start because of a nightmare, other times not. It always circles back to the accident."

"Tell me about it."

He scoffs. "No."

I look at him, my eyes pleading. "Tell me about it. Please. I want to help you. I hate seeing you like this."

He bites the inside of his cheek, willing himself to talk. "It was my fault."

"What was?" I ask.

"The accident."

I tilt my head. "It wasn't your fault. The only person to blame is the idiot that pointed a gun at you."

"He wasn't an idiot. It's something you realize while you're away. Everyone is just fighting for their side. We're all people. Most of the time, we don't even know what the fights are about. They point and we go. The people fighting on the opposing side are no different from me, just born in a different place."

"Where did it happen?"

"I can't say. We were overseas, on a pretty high-profile mission. I was with a new crew, but I liked them a lot. They were smart, quick on their feet, they had critical thinking for the job. They also were just good men. Some had families at home, they cared about me and each other, we just wanted to make it out alive.

"The day it happened, they wanted to stay at base. I had a weird feeling and urged them to leave with me. We trusted each other, and if there's one thing you learn in the military, it's to always trust your gut."

He sits with his eyes closed for a moment, replaying the memory. "We made it out of the camp, and as we were leaving, the bombs went off. I turned around to see all the other crews blow up. It happened so fast. One minute, hundreds of guys were sitting around talking, and the next they were all gone."

I see his eyes getting damp. He blinks the tears away before they can form. "I knew something was going to happen, and I left them there. I told them why we were leaving, but they didn't know me, and had no reason to trust me. So I left them there. I left them for dead."

"You couldn't have known what was going to happen."

"I should've tried harder anyway. I felt so guilty after, I knew I couldn't just leave their bodies there. So I went back. Another guy went with me, not wanting me to go alone. It was surreal. Everything was black, completely unrecognizable.

"Every once in a while we would see a limb, and I would stop, saying words of respect and praying for their families.

I was so focused on what was in front of me that I didn't see him." He lets out a ragged breath. "It was a guy from the crew that set off the bombs. He had been there, alone. I still don't know why. I saw him once it was too late, the bullet already going through my stomach, right below where my gear had been sitting. The guy I was with shot him, killing him instantly, but it had been too late.

"He carried me back to our make-shift base, contacting the medics that were a few miles out. My crew kept me alive while we waited, and the medics did a few measures to limit bleeding until I was airlifted out. I passed out on the helicopter, and then I woke up in a hospital. I had surgery there to get the bullet out and repair the damage. Stayed for a few weeks and then I was transferred here."

I stay silent, trying to imagine how scared he must've been. "It's not your fault. You saved yourself and your entire crew. You tried to save them and had the decency to go back and honor their passing. You're a good man Sean."

"That's not all." He admits.

"Oh?"

He chews on his cheek. "You can't tell anyone."

"I won't. Promise."

He nods. "I had a choice. I could've gone back to the military, but I chickened out. I said no."

"That's completely reasonable. I think it would be more concerning if you went back, knowing you were struggling."

"You don't get it. I quit." His gaze lowers. "I'm a quitter."

"You aren't a quitter. You spent seven years serving, it's admirable."

He stares at me for a moment. "You don't think I'm pathetic?"

"Nowhere near it. It's clear that you have some pretty serious PTSD, you shouldn't keep going like this."

"I don't know what else to do."

I brainstorm for a few seconds. "Maybe I have an idea."

Nineteen

Sean

She can't be serious. I just dropped everything that has been keeping me up at night onto her shoulders, and she seems completely unfazed? I gape at her position, hand on her chin, eyes facing the ceiling. She's completely lost in thought, trying to fix the mess that is my brain.

"Hear me out. We could do some desensitization therapy."

I cock an eyebrow. "You want to shoot guns at me or reenact a war scene to try and fix my…problem? No offense, but I think that might give me more things to stress about."

She rolls her eyes. *She does that a lot, doesn't she?* "No, you asshole. We'll do activities that are normal for most people but have similarities to the things you experienced in war. That way, you can attach good memories to the bad ones."

"I mean, it sounds logical, but what do you have in mind?"

"Well, I don't want to give all of my ideas away now. I think it'd be better if you didn't know what you were walking into."

I take a step back from her. "Okay, you're starting to sound really creepy."

"I heard that, could have phrased it better. What I mean is, if you go in with an open mind, it might be easier for the sessions to actually work."

"How often are we talking?"

"I'm thinking once a week. How about Tuesdays? We could go after you get home from work. Five PM?"

I nod. "I could make that work."

"I'm actually shocked at how open you are to this plan. I was fully expecting you to call me crazy and laugh in my face."

I scoff. "I'm not a total asshole."

"Debatable."

I hide a smile, leaning against the counter. "At least I'm not a pervert."

Her brows knit together. "Well, I sure hope not."

"Oh, you would?"

She recoils, staring up at me in confusion. "What are you on about now?"

"I'm just saying." I motion from my chest to my face. "My eyes are up here, sunshine."

Her mouth drops open. "Are you for real right now? Can we not have one serious moment without you ruining it?"

"Its not my fault. You were staring at my man boobs."

"I was not!"

"You definitely were."

She crosses her arms over her chest. "Maybe I wouldn't stare at them if you would actually put a shirt on instead of traipsing around here naked all of the time."

"Oh, so I deserve to be objectified because of my choice of outfit? Real feminist of you."

She lets out a giggle, slapping my chest. "You are ridiculous."

I walk closer to her, catching her hand. "Maybe."

We stand there for a minute, staring at each other. Have her eyes always had specks of yellow mixed in? And since when were her lips this full?

"Go to bed, Summer."

"I don't sleep at night."

I tilt my head. "Then go to your room."

She stands on her heels for a moment, contemplating her options. "Goodnight Sean."

"Goodnight, Summer."

She pulls her hand away and walks back to her room.

* * *

I grab some coffee from the fridge, praying it does something to make me feel a little less dead. I stayed up for hours, tossing and turning last night after my conversation with Summer. Honestly, I can't help but feel a little excited about our weekly outings. Living with Summer has made me see her in a different light, and I wouldn't mind spending some extra time with her. As a friend, of course.

I look at myself in the mirror, pulling at the dark eye bags that have formed. I call Ethan up, asking if he wants to grab breakfast. He agrees and we decide to meet at a diner we used to go to as kids.

When I walk through the front doors, the familiar smell of syrup and bacon hits me. "Just one today?" The young hostess asks.

It's exactly the same. Primarily run by kids from the local high school, constant revolving door of managers. The uniforms have changed a little, looking more modernized, but the decorations are nostalgic.

"No, I'm meeting a friend."

She nods, urging me into the dining room. I see Ethan right away and walk up to him, sliding into the booth. "Hey man, long time no see."

His hand clasps mine. "Actually, it hasn't been that long. We both just called out of work on Friday because we needed some recovery time."

I scratch the back of my neck. "Yeah. We should probably never get drunk together again. It wasn't a good look for either of us."

"True. But there was a good reason behind it."

I suddenly remember the conversation we had at the bar. "Shit man, I'm already a horrible friend. How is all that going?"

"It's…weird. We both agreed that getting divorced was the best option. But since then, nothing. Radio silence. I expected her to move out, I mean she didn't even want to be in the same room as me for a while there. But she hasn't made any attempt to, and I don't want to kick her out like some asshole. I made it so that she wouldn't have to work, and now she has to figure out a plan to take care of herself since I can't anymore."

A server comes to greet us, grabbing our order. "It's pretty nice of you to let her stay, all things considered."

"Not really. I was a shitty husband. The least I could do is help her get back on her feet. Last time we talked, she mentioned going back to school for cosmetology. But how long does that take? At least a year, right?"

"Honestly, I don't know anything about that but a year sounds reasonable."

He nods. "It's not like I can't stand her presence. We were together for so long, and I don't despise her or anything. Not even close. I just want to move on, you know? I don't know how to do that when she's everywhere."

"I get how you're feeling."

He chuckles. "I bet you do."

My eyebrows knit together. "What does that mean?"

He shakes his head. "Don't worry about it. How's your mom doing? You haven't said much about her."

"She's good. Worried about me. I haven't seen her since I got back and she's been anxious, wants to make sure I'm okay after the accident. I want to see her, I really do. I'm just worried that when she looks at me, she's gonna see a failure."

"That's ridiculous. Caroline is the sweetest woman that's ever walked this earth. You're her baby. She could never see you as a failure."

"I know she wouldn't. I just can't help feeling like I disappointed her." Even though she doesn't know it, I had a choice. I could've stuck with the military, but instead, I was a coward.

The server brings our food over, mine being an omelet, his being a stack of pancakes.

"That's stupid. You put in seven years of great work. Nothing about that is disappointing."

"Yeah. I'm also worried about her. After Dad passed, she still had us, so she wouldn't feel so alone. Then I left, and Eliana went to college and suddenly she was by herself. She claims that she's happy. Has a bunch of book club friends and loves the people at her work."

"She's always been a pretty positive lady. I mean, she definitely misses you guys, but I'm sure she has a good life going for her."

"Probably. I'm also worried about her financially. When

it became just her, we took a big hit. I picked up a few jobs, worked them through high school and after graduation. When I left for the army, I lied and told my mom that they had started a program to support widowed parents of soldiers."

I take a bite of my omelet. "In truth, it was just a portion of all of my paychecks to keep her and Eliana afloat, along with the trust from my dad's life insurance. She's too proud to take my money. I just don't know how to support her now."

"Look, I know your dad's passing put a lot of weight on your shoulders. You thought that it meant you had to take over his role in the family, but that's a load of shit. You were eleven years old. A child." He shakes his head. "I can still remember inviting you over to play video games and you saying no, that you had to go rake the neighbor's yard or tutor at the library. You took some of the emotional and financial weight of your family on way too young. Your mom is an adult. Have a little faith that she knows how to take care of herself."

I let his words sink in. "I know she can. I just don't want her to have to."

"And that's what makes you such a good son. You're a good man, Sean. Give yourself a little slack."

We let the conversation fizzle into something less serious. "So you know how I've had a new project for the company?"

I nod. "Yeah, the one you've been weirdly cryptic about? Me and the guys have been placing bets on what it is. I guessed a big hotel. Please say I'm right, I don't want to lose a hundred bucks right now."

"You're not correct. I'm very sorry."

"Damn it. Ricky is never letting me live that down."

"If it'll make you feel better, I'm not telling the guys for a while, so you'll have time to scrounge the money up."

I raise an eyebrow. "Okay, I'm not that poor. I have one-hundred dollars."

"Sure. Anyway, the project. I got contacted a few months back about a business opportunity in Oklahoma. Apparently, this guy is trying to get out of the construction business, wants to sell his company. I have a buddy over there who works for him, had him reach out to me and ask if I was interested in buying it."

"Holy shit man, that's great!"

"Well, don't get too excited, it's nowhere near final. I'm still trying to see if I could make having two branches in different states work. There's another company also reaching for it, so that's another thing I have to think about. But if neither of us buy it, they're just gonna liquidate everything, break it up. It just seems like such a waste. I'm going out to see it later next month, meet the crew, talk more logistics. That's one of the reasons why I wanted you to learn the ropes. I want someone I trust watching over things since I'll have to bounce back and forth for a little while trying to figure things out."

I slap him on the shoulder. "Of course! This is amazing, I mean seriously. You're twenty-five and have a great company that's growing. I'm proud of you, E."

"Thanks, buddy. I just hope it all works out. I've been trying not to get my hopes up about it, but it would just be so cool! Can you imagine? I'd be like a real businessman."

"You're already a real businessman."

He looks at me knowingly. "I wear T-shirts and jeans to work every day."

I cringe. "Yeah, you might want to invest in a suit. Or at least a polo or something."

"Unfortunately. Just keep it quiet, will you? I don't want

people freaking out about changes and all that. No reason to get everyone riled up if it doesn't work out."

"It will."

He rises from the booth. "Maybe. Alright, I gotta get home. Maybe my wife will talk to me today!"

I salute him. "Good luck with that."

Summer

I slept like shit. I knocked out after talking with Sean, completely ruining my plan of getting my schedule back on track. It's definitely true what they say about working nights aging you. I look like I'm at least in my late twenties and my bones crack every time I move. It's embarrassing.

I smell something ripe coming from the front of my room and look towards Gouda. "What the hell, bro? You smell very bad."

I walk up to his cage, open it, and scoop him up in my hand. "Do you want a bath today? Would that be so much fun?"

He just stares at me. "Okay. Good talk. Here, you sit in this box while I clean your cage. Then I'll give you a little bubble bath."

I drop him into an old Amazon box that's too tall for him to jump out of. I grab his cage, gagging at the fumes coming from it. "Seriously, your shit does not smell normal. I swear I clean this cage every day at this point and nothing helps. I have to have like four air fresheners running to mask your scent."

This is my life. I am talking to my pet mouse. I shrug, putting on gloves and dumping the old bedding, mixed with rat turds, into a trash bag. Now that I have a fresh canvas, I clean the bars of his cage with animal-safe cleaner and drop new bedding into it. I dump out his water dish, clean it, and fill it back up, placing it into the cage as well. I wash all of his enclosures, along with his wheel, and change the setup so it feels like a new home.

Satisfied, I take the trash out, and grab the box and his mouse shampoo, bringing everything into the bathroom. "Now, I'm shutting the door because I don't trust you, so please don't jump out of the sink because I will freak out and cry."

I start by running the water, checking the temperature, and filling the sink up. I hold him in my hand, pouring a few drops on him so he gets used to the feeling of it. He squirms—and to my delight—doesn't jump out. I grab some of the mouse shampoo and lather him up, making him look like a little marshmallow. "You know, you're usually kinda ugly, but right now you look pretty cute."

Once he's fully clean, I slowly drop him into the water. He freaks out, thrashing, and splashes me completely with water. "Bad Gouda! Not nice! I'm trying to help you."

He stills for a minute before looking up at me and lunging out of the sink. "NO! STOP! DON'T DO THAT!"

I jump onto the toilet as he runs around the bathroom, squeaking. He makes his way towards the door and crawls under it before I can stop him. I stay there for a second, processing what just happened. "Shit."

I throw the bathroom door open, scanning the room for him. I look to see that both my and Eliana's bedroom doors are open, meaning he could literally be anywhere. "Shit. Shit. Shit."

I spent an hour trying to coax him out. I tried everything. I even threw shredded cheese around the room like confetti, but it didn't work. So here I am, on my hands and knees, collecting shredded cheese from my floor. I can't even use a vacuum because I'm scared he would run out and it would eat him. "You are an asshole. A stupid, rodent, asshole!"

"Alright, I get it," Sean says, making me jump.

"Where did you come from?"

"I've been here for the past two minutes. You've just been too busy collecting cheese off the ground to notice."

I ignore him and continue my collection. He kneels beside me, picking the rest up. We throw it away, and he turns to me. "Care to explain what's going on?"

My panicked words burst out of me. "I lost Gouda! I was trying to be a good mouse mom and give him a spa day, but he hated the water and escaped!"

"Are mice even supposed to get baths?"

"I don't know, Sean!" I yell. "But he got one. And his ungrateful ass hated it."

"You didn't google if they liked water first?"

I turn to him, eyes narrowed. "Say one more word, Sean, and I promise I will strangle you."

He puts his hands up in defense. "Alright, alright. Just wait here."

He walks into the pantry, grabbing a box of Cheez-Its. He steps into the living room, shaking the box around, before reaching in and grabbing a few. Laughing silently, he throws them on the ground, and within seconds, Gouda comes running out from behind the TV.

I snatch him up in my hands, squeezing a little. "You are a very bad mouse! Very bad!" I grab a towel and dry him off, walking towards Sean.

"How'd you know what to do?"

He takes Gouda from my hands, walking him back to the

cage in my room. "You do remember why you have this mouse, right? I watched a video on YouTube on ten ways to catch mice. This was method number eight."

I look at him sheepishly. "About that, I never did apologize for releasing a mouse in the house to scare you."

"It was a good attempt," he admits. "Maybe next time don't throw the PetSmart box away at the top of the trash."

I scratch my head. "Huh. So that's how you found out."

"That and the fact that four mouse traps appeared out of nowhere, all of them not loaded with any bait."

"Well, what was I supposed to do? If I loaded them, then he would fall for it and die."

"You could've just not released him into the apartment and that would've worked."

I look at Gouda, sleeping peacefully in his cage. "Yeah, maybe. Why are you still staying here, anyway?"

He scoffs. "Wow. Way to make a guy feel welcome."

"I didn't mean it like that. I just mean I thought you would have booked it out of here the second you had a job lined up."

He shrugs. "I had planned on it. But I can't lie and say that I haven't enjoyed spending some extra time with Eliana. It's nice being so close to family."

"I get that. And having cheaper rent has been kinda nice."

"Sorry I've been putting you out. A part of me might also feel like the second I leave this apartment, it's permanent. My old life is officially over. Maybe I just want to hold on for a little longer."

I look at him thoughtfully, understanding what he means. "Well, you're welcome to stay. You aren't so bad, Sean Jacobs."

"You're not too bad either, Summer Rhodes."

Twenty

Summer

I walk into work feeling pretty light. I was able to cram a nap in after mouse-gate and it has me feeling pretty energized. I clock in and sit at my computer, checking my assignment. God must be on my side today, because it's pretty easy. If Jonah was here, it would be a perfect night.

I get report from the dayshift nurse, check in on all my patients, do a med pass, and chart, all before 9:30 PM. I sit down feeling on top of the world. Nothing can ruin this shift for me.

"Hi, Summer!"

I jolt, turning to my left to see Tammy, my awful manager, sitting next to me. Scratch that.

"Tammy. How are you?" I say through gritted teeth.

She beams. "I am just fantastic! Thank you for asking. Listen, we need to talk."

Shit. Am I seriously getting fired? Did I accidentally forget to change a patient's dressing? What if I subconsciously slipped narcotics into my pockets without knowing?

"Oh no! You're not in trouble, honey." She says, noticing my distress. "Look, I'll be frank with you. You're pretty and young, and at first glance, people really want to like you."

"Thanks?"

"You're welcome. Now when you start talking, that's a different story. But that's not what we need to speak about. I need a favor."

I raise an eyebrow. "You just insulted my personality and now you want a favor from me?"

"Yes! I knew you'd understand. So, as I'm sure you've heard, there's a huge medical conference being hosted at our hospital next month. I need you to speak at it."

"I didn't even know that was happening."

"That's precisely the issue. You put no effort into the culture of our unit. You never pick up shifts. You don't come to holiday parties. You don't interact with anyone but Jonah. When it comes to nursing, we get glowing reviews about you. But your attitude? It's a problem."

I cross my arms over my chest. "I don't see what this has to do with some stupid conference."

She frowns. "Not stupid. Exciting! It matters because you are doing the bare minimum. I need more from you. Management has asked for someone from our unit to represent the hospital by preparing a speech. We also need you to talk about some of the impressive things that we have contributed to medicine in recent years."

"I'm not doing it."

"Oh, you are. Don't forget who controls the schedule, Miss. Rhodes. I can make it so that you work every holiday, every full moon, and every shift without Jonah."

My eyes narrow. "You wouldn't."

She smiles. "I would do it faster than you can count to one."

"You're actually blackmailing me into doing this?"

She tilts her head. "Let's call it motivating instead. I like that much better."

"I am terrified of public speaking. Even if I wanted to do it, which I don't, I think I would screw it up."

"I have full faith in you. Patients love you. When you try, you're really good with people. You're caring and understanding. You're a very bright young lady. I just wish you would stop wasting your potential."

I stare at her, shocked. "Fine."

She smirks. "Wonderful."

She gets up and grabs her bag, walking towards the elevator. "Hey, Tammy?"

She turns around. "Yes, dear?"

"You should be vindictive more often. It really suits you."

She winks and steps away, flipping her hair as she goes.

Sean

After my conversation with Ethan yesterday, I decide to call my mom. We've talked a few times since I've been back, but I've mostly been dodging her calls. I feel guilty about it, but every time I hear her voice, I'm reminded of who I left behind. I bite the bullet anyway and dial her number.

"Hello?"

"Hey, Mom."

I can feel her warmth through the phone. "Baby! Oh, I've missed talking to you so much. Eliana says you have been super busy with a new job!"

"I have been, yeah. You remember Ethan, right? Ethan

Carter?"

"How could I forget! I love that boy so much. He was so good to you after John passed. Had such a pure heart."

"Right. Well, I actually started working with him. He owns that construction business and he offered me a job."

I can hear the smile in her voice. "Honey, that's wonderful! I bet he treats his employees so well. Good for him, he's still so young."

"Yeah. He offered me a management position."

"That's amazing! I always knew you would do something big!"

"It's not that big of a deal. He probably only offered it to me because we're friends."

"Well, I'm proud of you. You have been so resilient through all of this." I can hear her choke up a little. "You have just been through so much. I'm so impressed by the man you've become."

How could I ghost my own mother? All she's ever done is be there for me, and I've been pushing her away. "Mom, I'm so sorry."

"For what, baby?"

"I've been a terrible son to you. I left you to raise Eliana by yourself. I didn't call enough. I didn't visit enough. I have no excuse now and I still haven't changed my behavior. I don't know what's wrong with me."

"Nothing is wrong with you, Sean Jacobs. I put way too much on your shoulders after your father died. I was a wreck. Wouldn't eat, couldn't sleep. I forced you into taking care of your sister. I let you work like a dog when you were way too young. For heaven's sake, I made you think you had to enlist in the military in order to provide for me!"

"Enough mom. I joined the army because it would be best for all of us. You didn't force me into anything. You were grieving."

"And so were you. That is not an excuse for my behavior because I may have lost a husband, but you lost your father. You had to become a man way too early, and I will never forgive myself for that. No wonder you don't want to call me anymore."

I clear my throat. "Me not calling has everything to do with what's wrong with me and nothing to do with you. I felt ashamed of how my life looked, and you were the one person that I didn't want to see me struggling. I wanted to be as strong as you see me. So I thought staying away and letting you think I was okay would be better."

"I'm so sorry I made you feel like you had to hide from me." She sobs. "I just love you so much. You and Eliana are everything to me. You having demons doesn't make you weak, and the way that you are facing them makes me think you're even stronger."

I feel something tingly in my throat.

"Honestly honey, a few months ago you would never open up to me like this. You would be stubborn, try and fix everything on your own, and not let anyone see you as weak. Something has made you change and whatever it is, I'm grateful for it. I feel like my Sean is back."

I cough, letting the lump pass. "He is mom. I'm gonna do better."

"You're doing just fine. I just want you to feel okay again. I'm the one that's going to be better. I promise."

"I believe you."

"Good. Listen, honey, I have to run. Joan's son is getting

married and we're going to dinner to celebrate. But you'll call?"

"Yeah, Mom I will."

"I love you, Seany."

"I love you too."

Twenty-One

Summer

I sit on the couch, excitedly waiting for Sean to get home. Between pottery with Eliana, Tuesday outings with Sean, and work with Jonah, it finally feels like I have things to look forward to in my life. Well, maybe not the work part. But the Jonah part can stay.

I check on Gouda and make sure he's still living after the treat I gave him. The package said organic but when I gave it to him, he choked really weirdly and so I was worried he might die. I even shook the cage violently when I checked on him five minutes ago, but it turns out he was just sleeping. "You are just so cute today."

Sean walks up behind me. "Thank you."

I spin around, noticing how close he is. "I'm talking to Gouda."

"That's the second time you've made that excuse. Either you think you're Snow White or you have a serious thing for me."

"That sentence made me want to puke."

He puts his hand behind his neck, elbow raised. "In like a 'I'm so overcome with lovey-dovey emotions' kinda way?"

"In a 'if that were true, I would have a physical reaction' kinda way."

He smirks. "A physical reaction, you say?"

I blink. "Let's go. We have things to do."

I speed walk to the door, snag my keys, and step out. He follows hastily, grabbing his wallet and shoving it into the front pocket of his jeans. We step into the elevator, both reaching for the L button. Our hands make contact, shocking each other. I jolt back while he hits the button and tuck my hand away.

"So, are you gonna tell me where we're going?"

"No. That literally defeats the purpose of it being a surprise."

He huffs. "Have I ever told you how much I hate surprises?"

We reach the lobby, stepping out when the doors open. "Honestly? That information is completely irrelevant to me."

"Rude."

We step outside and he snatches the keys out of my hand. "I'm driving."

I halt my steps. "Absolutely not. Chuck behaves for one operator and one operator only—me. Eliana tried once, and he broke down within two minutes. We thought it was a fluke, so we made Jonah try. Same thing happened."

He shrugs, placing a hand on my lower back and urging me along. "We'll see."

I try to ignore the burning sensation that is left behind by his touch, even though it was only there for a second. He walks to the passenger side with me, opens the door, and lightly shoves me inside. As if on instinct, he reaches for the seatbelt, buckling me in.

A breath rushes out of me. "Such a gentleman."

He jerks his chin up in a nod, and shuts the door, rounding to the driver's seat. He jumps in, large body suffocating in my normal settings. Knees bent against the wheel, he moves the chair all the way back and adjusts the mirrors, turning to me. He looks me straight in the eye and says, "Let's try it out."

"What?"

He gives me a confused look. "The car? You said it won't work with me."

"Oh. Right."

He puts the key in the ignition and Chuck roars to life. He gives me a knowing smirk. "Maybe I just have the magic touch."

I grab my phone and open the clock app, putting it on stopwatch. I hold it up, starting the time as he puts the car in reverse. He places his large hand at the back of my seat as he reverses, fingertips brushing my shoulder. *Alright, now he's just doing it on purpose.*

I take his phone and he gives me a weird look. "For directions. You don't know where you're going."

He nods. "Four, six, nine, six."

I type in his password and pull up maps, typing in the address. I plug his phone in so the audio links and open up Spotify. His recently listened are all audiobooks.

"Oh no."

He looks at me out of the corner of his eye, pulling out of the parking lot. "What?"

"You're one of them."

He cocks an eyebrow at me. "One of who?"

"Audiobook listeners. You probably think you're better than everyone because you listen to intellectual stories instead of rap music."

"I do think I'm better than everyone, but not for that reason."

I scoff at his arrogance. He smiles. I go to the search bar and find my account, putting on one of my playlists. 'Shape of You' by Ed Sheeran starts blasting from the speakers.

"Oh, you cannot be serious."

"Don't even start with me. Ed Sheeran is an adorable little redheaded leprechaun who makes fantastic music. I will not accept any slander."

"Looks like I won, by the way."

I give him a confused look, and he points at my phone, the timer reading '2:05'. Hm. I guess Chuck likes him.

We spend the rest of the drive in comfortable silence. I serenade him every once and a while with my wonderful singing. He shakes his head, but lets me. I see his eyes light up when we pull into the parking lot of our destination.

"Joe's Golf and Stuff? I used to love this place as a kid!"

I laugh at his childish enthusiasm. "I know. That's why I thought it would be a good place to ease into this."

His brows knit together. "No offense, but I don't really understand how golfing would help with my PTSD."

"You know, I think it already is. That's the first time you've admitted that you have PTSD."

He shrugs.

"Anyway, we're not golfing. Come on, you'll see."

We get out of the car and head in through the front. The inside is loud, with kids and teenagers laughing and playing in the arcade. I walk to the front desk. "Hi!"

The teenager with short black hair and a septum ring looks me up and down. "Hi."

I ignore her lack of enthusiasm. "We need two cards, both

for laser tag. Can we do three games on each of them, please?"

She stares at me. "K."

She types it into the computer and loads the cards. "Thirty dollars."

I reach into my bag for my wallet when Sean steps right behind me. I can feel his breath coming down on the top of my head and the heat radiating off of his body. Before I can hand her my card, he reaches around me, thrusting his card into her hand.

"You don't have to do that. It was my idea."

He turns his head so that his face is all but two inches away from mine. "Don't be ridiculous." He says, grabbing his card back from her without looking away.

"Damn girl. Go off." I turn back to the girl with an eyebrow raised and she shrugs.

We walk towards the laser tag area and wait for the current round to end. When it does, a worker comes out and explains the rules, then opens the door to the intermission area. I look at Sean as he stares at the gear, knowing exactly what he's thinking.

I thought that if I could bring him to an environment that he's already comfortable in, and has positive memories of, then he would feel more relaxed. It was a good way to go through the motions of the kind of stuff that led to his accident, even if it's on a much lesser scale.

He picks up a vest with the guns hanging off it. He doesn't put it on, just holds it, and feels its weight. He looks like he's almost about to put it back when he's interrupted.

"You're big!"

I look to see a little girl with pigtails staring up at him, giggling. She's drowning in her vest, and her little hands probably can't even hold the guns. His hard expression morphs into a much softer one as he kneels down to her level. "How about now?"

She giggles. "You're still really big."

He plays dumb. "But how? I'm at your level now!"

She giggles again. "Is that your girlfriend?" She asks, pointing to me.

He hesitates, and I step in, bending my knees. "I'm not his girlfriend. Boys are smelly."

"Boys are smelly!" She agrees, "I have a brother named Noah. He's right there."

She points to a little boy gearing up on the opposite team. He sees her staring and rolls his eyes, turning back to his friends.

Sean frowns. "It looks like we're on the same team. I'm Sean and that's Summer. What's your name?"

"Lily."

I smile. "That's a beautiful name."

She looks down shyly. "You aren't on my team yet, though."

Sean pouts. "Why not?"

She laughs. "Because you don't have your vest on!"

He takes a deep breath before throwing his vest on, trying to click the buckle. His chest ends up being too broad, so he lets the straps hang. I put mine on right as the doors open, and kids rush into the arena.

Sean gets on his feet but stays bent over, reaching his hand out for her. "Ready?"

She gives him a toothy smile, placing her small hand in his. "Ready."

He turns back at me and I give him a nod that he returns before they run in.

I spend the first round following her mean brother around, hiding behind walls and shooting him every time he reloads. He gets angry and sits in a corner pouting, claiming his vest is broken. I count it as a victory.

I see Sean a few times with Lily, her running with him following after her. They work as a team, him shooting people, and her pointing them out. I can see how experienced he is with the act, even if it's just with a laser gun.

His position is effortless, eyes calculating, fingers nimble. I can see him relax more with every shot, getting comfortable in the motions again.

The round ends and we say goodbye to Lily, heading back to the intermission area for round two. This time, I go to the blue side to get a vest.

"Done being my teammate, sunshine?"

"Yeah, I decided it would be too easy for you without any real competition."

"Hey!" Some random kid says from beside me.

"Sorry," I respond.

Sean laughs at my antics, putting a new vest on. "Don't be offended when you lose. This was my job for seven years."

"You were a pro laser tag player? No way! Can I get your autograph?"

He rolls his eyes. "Funny."

"I know. Now stop talking to me, I need to get in the zone."

We wait a few more minutes for enough people to join, then head in. Luckily for me, while he was distracted last round, I memorized the arena. I know all the best hiding spots, and where there are bonus targets to shoot.

I head for a wall in the far corner and duck behind it, looking through the small window. I see Sean walking towards me lazily, oozing with confidence.

"I know you're back there, sunshine."

I try to mask my voice into one of a male child. "Sir, please back away. You're scaring me."

"Oh, you haven't seen scary." He says, maneuvering his gun around the wall and shooting me in a matter of seconds.

"Hey! No fair. You're targeting me."

"Damn right, I am."

I pout, before booking it out of there. I run for a few minutes, trying not to barrel down kids in my wake. I eventually find another one of my spots and kneel down, looking through a small peephole. I don't see him anywhere, so he must've gotten lost in the madness.

"Looking for me?"

I jolt at the sound of his voice and look up to see him towering over me with wild eyes. His face is lit up red from a target nearby, and his jawline is accentuated from the shadows. Without breaking eye contact, I lift my gun up, shooting his vest.

He slaps a hand over his chest, faking an injury. "You wound me."

I duck out from under him and head to my next base, shooting at some kids on the way. I get settled, looking around at every angle this time. He rounds the corner quickly, and I raise my gun. He pins my hands to the wall behind me, making me drop my gun in the process. He steps closer, dropping his head so our faces are closer.

"When are you going to learn that anywhere you run to, I will always find you?" I gulp, trying to think of a response. He licks his lips, awaiting my answer. I reach for my gun, but he stops me. "Never thought I'd see the day where Summer

Rhodes was at a loss for words."

I open my mouth to respond but he leans closer, dropping his mouth to my ear. "As much as I'm enjoying this, I'd prefer your sweet voice any day."

The lights flip on, and our vests stop glowing, signaling the round is over. He winks, then throws an arm around me playfully and drags us out to the leaderboard.

They dramatically add the points up.

"OH MY GOD! I WON! I BEAT YOU!"

He smiles at my gloating, watching me jump up and down, making an L with my hand. We both know that he let me win, based on the fact that he set a new record for the place last round, but he lets me have my moment.

"How about we do this last one together?" He asks.

I look up at him. "Okay. We do make a pretty good team."

We gear up for the last time, running in. We decide that we'll run everywhere together, him shooting people, me shooting targets. Then, if he gets shot, I'll take over until he is revived.

The plan works perfectly, and we take down all the eight-year-old boys that are playing. One of them even cries, yelling that it's his birthday, so we can't target his team. We burst out laughing, which only makes him cry harder.

We finish strong and check the leaderboard. He was the overall lead scorer and our team won by a landslide. I snap a picture of it, and then follow him out to the car.

He does the same thing as before, opening my door and buckling me in. This time, he knows the way back, and makes me listen to one of his boring audiobooks. Not that I'd ever admit it, but it isn't actually that bad. I look over at him, seeing a calm smile on his face. I'd call week one a success.

Twenty-Two

Summer

We walk into the apartment, both of us in pleasant moods. I peek into Eliana's room but she must not be home. I'll text her later.

When I walk back out, I don't see Sean, so he must be in the bathroom. I walk past the door, stopping when I hear him grunt in pain. I stand by the door, resting my ear on it. He makes another noise and I knock.

"Are you okay?"

He stays silent for a moment. I can hear him letting a long breath out, and he turns the water on to mask it. "I'm fine. Please, just go away."

After the day we had, I thought we got past his need to hide secrets. He's spent too long trying to keep everything to himself and I'm tired of it. Before I can overthink it, I open the door.

He's standing by the sink, staring at the mirror with his shirt off, front angled towards me. There's sweat beading on his forehead, face red.

"What the hell?"

He whips his head up at me, and that's when I see it. I walk closer to get a better look.

"Sean. This is bad."

"Don't you think I know that? I look disgusting."

"It's not you, but it has been way too long. This should be healed by now."

I stare at his scar. It looks like the stitches had ripped at some point, causing it to not heal correctly. All the skin around it is beat red, clearly irritated. The scar itself is crusty, with yellowish liquid oozing from it.

I close my eyes, pinching the skin between my eyebrows. "Have you not been going for checkups? The doctors should have noticed something like this."

He looks at me sheepishly. "No."

I sigh, walking back to my room. I grab some supplies and come back, ordering him to sit on the counter.

"What? Why?"

"Please don't argue with me right now. I'm not very happy and you pissing me off isn't going to make it better. Take your pants off."

He looks at me, shocked.

"I'm going to flush it and when I do, there's gonna be fluid everywhere. I don't really want to ruin your sweats, so take them off. Leave your boxers on."

He looks like he's going to say something, but sees my facial expression and decides against it. He bends down, grunting a little. The sweats come off and I look away for a minute, trying to stay professional.

His quads are huge. They look like they could strangle me.

His legs are covered in little scars, and he has a larger one running down the side of his thigh. I let out a cough and walk beside him, pointing to the counter. He hops on and gets settled so that his back is against the wall, while I step to one side of his leg, dropping my supplies.

"I'm going to clean this up and put a new dressing on it. Then we're getting back in the car and you're going to the hospital so they can reassess and get you on some antibiotics. It's clearly infected."

He starts to argue, but I shoot him a glare, and he stays quiet instead. I wash my hands and throw on some gloves. I grab a few flushes and open them. "This might hurt."

He bites his bottom lip as I soak the scar with saline, getting some of the gunk out. He recoils when I pat it with a clean gauze. "Sorry."

I try to clean it at another angle, but with the way he's sitting, it doesn't get fully drenched. I look up at him. His eyes are closed, brows furrowed. Without thinking, I walk around and step between his legs to get better control.

His eyes shoot open, taking in my position. He snatches a towel from the rack and throws it over his boxers. I ignore the motion and spray the wound again, distracting him.

"Why do you even have all this stuff?" He says through gritted teeth.

"Nurses take shit like this from the hospital all the time. Why would I pay for a first aid kit when I have an abundance of supplies at my job?"

"I like seeing you in action." I roll my eyes and flick his skin a few inches away from the wound, making him wince. "Too close."

"You're fine."

"You know, you aren't being very sympathetic."

I give him a pointed look. "You're right. I don't feel much sympathy for you right now."

He looks away, dodging my glare. I keep flushing it, trying to make the saline run clear so we don't have to spend too much time at the hospital when we get there.

"I'm going to put this dressing on and tape it so it stays, then put your clothes back on and meet me by the door."

I grab a few of the dressings, holding them up for sizing. I pick one and open it, shoving his chest back a little so I can place it without wrinkles. I tape it down and trash my gloves, washing my hands again. I grab my stuff and walk out, shutting the door behind me.

I return my supplies to their spot and walk to Gouda, sighing. "Why are men so stupid?"

He looks up at me and blinks, then sprints to his wheel and starts going crazy on it. "K. Good talk."

I walk to the front door and put on my shoes, grabbing my keys. He walks out of the bathroom and I leave the apartment, him following me like a kid in trouble.

He tries to open my car door for me but I slam it shut and stand there until he rounds to the passenger's side, getting in on my own. We drive to the hospital in silence, no music or audiobooks in sight.

I park in the employee garage so I don't have to pay, because there's no way I'm wasting money on him right now. I get out and walk towards the door, not waiting to see if he follows. I scan my badge and walk in, urging him to go inside. We walk to the emergency department and I step to the desk to check in.

"Summer! Hi sweetie! Are you okay? What's bringing you

in?"

"I'm fine. Just doing some charity. He's the patient."

I point to him, and he steps up, giving her his information. After he gets checked in, I point to a chair, and he sits, looking like he's in timeout.

"Is that your boyfriend? He is very cute." The older nurse says, wiggling her eyebrows.

"Absolutely not."

"Oh. Well," she drops her tone of voice. "I moved you guys to the top of the list so you don't have to wait."

"Thanks, I owe you."

She winks. "Nonsense."

The ED nurses tend to like me because I don't ask much of them. Whenever they call to give report, I always say it's unnecessary, that we are both busy and I am perfectly capable of reading the patient's chart. They seem to appreciate that.

I plop down into the chair next to him, rubbing my temples.

"I'm sorry."

I look at his face. "I know."

A nurse calls his name, and we follow her back. She's floated to my unit before, so we chat a little and she lets me stay in the room even though I'm not his family.

He sits on the bed, and I sit in a chair while she asks him admission questions. I sit on my phone for most of them, scrolling through Instagram.

"When was the last time you were sexually active?" She asks, staring at the computer to ignore his expression. That piques my interest and my gaze flies towards him, his eyes bulging a little.

"A while."

I smirk before morphing my face and voice into looking

like an overprotective mother. "She needs an accurate answer, Sean."

He turns towards the nurse, throwing on a charming smile. "Listen, Abby, is it?" She nods. "It's been a little while and I don't have anything, that's all you need to know, right?"

She clears her throat awkwardly, typing his response into the chart. "Yes, I'm content with that answer."

"Wonderful." He throws me a cocky look and I stick my tongue out at him. He smiles slightly and I resume my stern expression, remembering I'm mad at him. They continue with the questions, and I lose interest again, turning back to my phone.

"Okay. That's everything I need from you. Now it looks like your attending that was on the case, Dr. Brown was it?" He confirms. "Right. He's not here tonight but his junior resident is, and he's going to swing by."

"Sounds good. Thank you, Abby."

She blushes and waves to me before walking out. We wait for a little while, Sean looking stressed. He messes with the hair at the back of his neck, legs fidgeting.

"It doesn't look super bad. I don't think you need to worry."

He nods, still not saying anything. A knock at the door pulls our attention. "Come in."

The resident comes in, recognizing me immediately. "Summer! How are you? I've missed your unit so much. Always had the best nurses," he says, winking.

"I'm good! How are you? Still liking it?"

"Something like that."

Sean clears his throat, getting the doctor's attention. I look to see him shooting daggers at the guy, who is completely unaware.

He slaps Sean on the arm. "Oh hey there buddy! I didn't even see you there!"

Sean's jaw clenches as he stares at the spot the doctor touched. "Weird, since I am the patient."

"Right! I'm Dr. Alder, I was one of the residents on your case a little while back. So what brings you in? I see that you never scheduled a follow-up appointment."

"His incision is infected."

Dr. Alder turns towards me. "Alright, well, let's take a look."

He throws on some gloves and sits in the rolling chair, scooting up to the bed. "Take your shirt off for me, boss."

Sean rolls his eyes but listens, grabbing the shirt with one hand and whipping it off. Dr. Alder puts on his gloves and stares at the gauze taped to Sean's abdomen. "This dressing is perfect. You always were the best at them"

Sean looks at me as if asking, "Who the hell is this guy?" I shrug, and silently answer, "Just listen to him, will you?"

Dr. Alder takes the dressing off and nods, inspecting the wound. "It's definitely infected. How long has it looked like this?"

"A few weeks."

He sighs. "You're lucky it didn't progress much. It looks pretty gnarly, but it's surface level. If it gets like this again, you need to come in immediately, or you could get sepsis."

"I will be monitoring him closely this time around. Very closely. No need to worry, doc."

"Good. Alright. I'm gonna prescribe some antibiotics. Like I said, Summer did a great job of cleaning it and I trust she will continue to." He folds my dressing back over it, resealing the tape. "I'm going to send you home with some cream for when it's healed a little more, along with extra supplies to take care of it. All instructions will be in the discharge paperwork. I'll send some mild painkillers for the first few days. I'm shocked the pain didn't bring you in. You didn't leave with many pills the first time."

"I was in the army, I can handle a little pain."

He blinks. "Okay. Well. Other than that, you're good to go."

"Thanks, doc." We say in unison and he heads to the door.

He turns back, looking at me. "Well Summer, if you ever wanted to go out sometime…"

Sean shuts him up. "Keep walking."

"I'm gone."

He leaves, and Sean turns towards me, grabbing his shirt. "What the hell is his problem? What happened to professionalism nowadays?"

"Sean, I don't know if you've noticed, but you've made me a little angry in the past hour. Maybe let's just stay quiet, okay?"

He lets out a breath. "Yeah, okay."

The nurse comes in and goes over discharge. I say goodbye to everyone and drag him to the car, making him carry the supplies.

We get in, leaving the garage to go to the pharmacy before it closes. I make him go inside, refusing to do the drive-through. He gets his prescription, and I start driving back to the apartment.

"You hungry?"

Sean

"You seriously did not just ask me that." She looks over at me with narrowed eyes.

I scratch my head. "I mean I did."

"Am I hungry? Yes. Do I want to spend any more time with

you today? No. Not really."

"Why are you so mad?"

She scoffs. "Why am I mad? I don't know, why do you think I'm mad?"

"Last time I checked, you still hate me. So I'm not really sure why you're so interested in my health."

She shakes her head. "Unbelievable. I thought we were done with that shit."

"You don't get it."

"I don't get it? ME? That works in a hospital? I don't get it?" Her hands tighten on the steering wheel. "YOU don't get it. Do you know how many people I see come onto my unit and never leave because they don't take care of themselves properly? People that could've had a simple recovery but didn't come back when they saw the signs, so they leave in body bags instead?"

"I wasn't thinking."

"No. You weren't. Do you know how Caroline, Eliana, and Ethan would have felt—how I would have felt—if something happened to you? Maybe if you looked past your own idiotic self, you would've seen that."

"I'm sorry. It won't happen again."

She clicks her tongue. "Damn right, it won't. I'm doing your dressing changes from now on. I will spoon-feed you those drugs if that's what it takes. I am now your mother, Sean Jacobs."

"Don't love that."

"Well, me neither." She rubs a hand down her face. "Eliana is gonna freak."

I sit up. "You can't tell her."

"What?"

"You can't. She and mom are already worried enough about me. She has too much going on. I can't involve her in this."

She pushes her hair back with her hand, clearly uncomfortable. "You want me to lie to my best friend?"

"Please. It's for her. Not for me."

She stays silent, thinking it over. "You owe me. A lot."

"I know."

"I just don't understand why you wouldn't just go back to the doctor."

I tuck a stray hair behind her ear. She looks pretty even when she's mad at me. "Grab dinner with me and I'll tell you."

Twenty-Three

Summer

We grab a booth at the 24-hour diner I remember going to as a teenager. My parents disapproved, saying that diners are for crime and hoodlums. I went anyway, loving the chaotic ambiance of the place.

"I haven't been here in forever."

He puts a straw in his water, then hands me one. "I came with Ethan the other day. There are not many places in the actual city that I went to as a kid, but this is one of them."

We sit there awkwardly, me waiting for him to open up to me like he promised. I wasn't trying to push him, but it's in my blood. I tell my friends everything. I just wish he would let other people in.

He stares at the menu, pretending to read it over. We both know that he gets the same thing every time, he's just that person. But I let him, giving him time to start talking.

The waitress comes by and takes our order, her eyes lingering on Sean for a little too long. He doesn't notice.

He waits until she walks away, then begins. "I'm scared of hospitals."

I nod, figuring that was the reason. "I assumed as much. Is it because of the accident? You have bad memories from your recovery?"

"No, I've always hated them." He runs a hand over his upper lip. "Did Eliana ever talk about our father passing away?"

I shake my head.

"Not surprised. It became almost a taboo in our house, all of us finding it easier to pretend it didn't happen. He was a great man," he smiles. "The best dad I could ask for. He was a hard worker, always picked up extra shifts. We weren't super poor, but he wanted to give my mom and us anything we ever wanted.

"He didn't want money to hold us back. He was so good with time management, freakishly so. He could always manage working and our lives. Never missed my sporting events or Eliana's gymnastic meets. He made time every month to take my mom out, never wanting her to feel like he prioritized us over her."

The waitress brings our food and we start eating. "I remember this one time, I had accidentally let our neighbor's cat out of the house. I was there to have tea with her because she was an older lady who got lonely at times. Awful woman, super mean. But my dad knew she enjoyed speaking with kids since she never had any and roped me and Eliana into going over every so often. I freaked out, ran home crying. My dad spent the whole night searching for that stupid cat."

I grin. "Did he find it?"

He laughs. "Turned out the cat was house trained, had a door to leave whenever it wanted. It came back a few minutes after I let it out."

I giggle. "You didn't check?"

"No!" He says playfully. "I wasn't going to admit to her that I lost her cat. I was scared she would skin me!"

His smile dims a little. "Anyway, he was just a good dad. He was a provider. Never wanted anyone to worry or fuss over him."

"Can I ask how it happened?"

He takes a bite of his omelet, chewing slowly. "He was sick. Cancer."

I bite my bottom lip. "I'm so sorry."

"The worst part is he didn't tell anyone. He knew for a full year before it got really bad. I should've noticed."

"You couldn't have."

"I could have. There were signs. He couldn't do things the same as before, he got winded easily. He was sleeping more, always sneaking off somewhere." He licks his lips. "Turned out he was going to the doctors all the time. Chose to do chemo through a pill so that he could keep it a secret for longer.

"I was so mad at him. I remember he had collapsed one day. I was the only person home. I remember laying there, pounding on his chest, screaming for him to wake up."

Tears well up in my eyes, threatening to fall.

"I ran to grab his phone, called an ambulance. They stayed on the line with me. I just sat there yelling into it, praying for them to come faster. I didn't know if he was breathing or not." His eyes darken and drop to his plate. "I rode with him to the hospital, where my mom met us. Eliana was only six. We didn't want her to see him. I stayed with him there but refused to talk to him. I couldn't believe that he could keep such a big secret from me, from my mom."

He chokes up a little. "I wasted so much time. He got discharged, but I stayed angry for weeks. At him. At the world. At everything." He takes a long sip of water, throat clearing. "He spent the next year in and out of the hospital. We kept it from Eli for as long as we could, but eventually I told her. My mom was mad, but my dad understood. He didn't want her to be mad like I was.

"He died in the hospital. I was in the room with him, telling him about some stupid drama on my football team. He listened, but I could see his chest rising and falling harder. I tried to call a nurse in but he stopped me, a tear falling from his eye."

He covers a hand over his mouth, blinking rapidly. I feel myself crying, but wipe the tears away, trying not to upset him.

"He told me that he loved me and that I needed to take care of the family. The monitors started going off, nurses ran into the room. I was ushered out, but could hear the code blue alarm going off throughout the unit.

"I collapsed to the ground, a nurse holding me. They announced the code over the loudspeaker in the hospital, and more people came to help. That's how my mom found out. She was downstairs getting me something to eat. I remember seeing her running down the hall, shoving into his room."

I don't stop the tears from falling now, and he reaches over, clearing them from my face. "I'd never heard anyone scream like that. Eventually, she came out of the room, and I knew he was gone."

"I had no idea." I shake my head. "I am such an idiot. I yelled at you, called you selfish."

"Stop. What I did was selfish. I should've been more inclined to go, if anything, but every time I do, I just think of that day. I felt so guilty. Because I was hungry, I stole his last moments away from my mom."

"You didn't steal anything. You had every right to be there."

"Maybe. The weeks after were the worst. Eliana didn't understand, slept on the couch by the door, waiting for him to come home. She couldn't process it. Eventually, when she did, I had to be there for her. My mom was checked out. Never left her room, barely ate or showered.

"I took care of both of them like he asked me to. We ate food that people brought for us for weeks. I'll never look at a casserole the same again. Things got easier over time, my mom came back slowly. Eliana had counseling and learned to grieve."

"And what about you? Who took care of you, Sean?"

"I did."

I shove away my plate, no longer having an appetite.

Twenty-Four

Summer

"Now, you're probably wondering why I called this meeting."

I sit across from Jonah at the lunch place he made me meet him at, claiming he has something to confess.

I crack my neck. "Yeah, everything about this is scaring me."

"Honestly, it affects you, so you have every right to be scared."

"That didn't help."

He points at me. "Wasn't supposed to. Here's the thing, I am now a virgin."

"You are the furthest thing from a virgin."

"Let me rephrase," he says, frowning. "I am a born-again virgin. Celibate. No more sexy time for Jonah."

"Okay."

His head jerks. "Okay?!" He exclaims, clearly taken aback. "That means we can no longer sleep together…"

"Jonah, we haven't done anything in a while. Plus, there

were never any romantic strings between us."

"I know, but I expected you to be a little upset. Our chemistry is a major part of this friendship."

I take a bite of my Caesar salad. "Not really. Most of our friendship is talking shit."

"I really wanted you to take this harder," he whines.

"Do you want to start again?"

"Yes. Hey Summer, I have something to admit." He sighs, gaze softening. "I can't sleep with you anymore."

"WHAT?!" I yell, grabbing the attention of most of the restaurant. "You asshole! You just slept with me and now you've lost all interest? Unbelievable."

A small table of girls having brunch cheers. "You tell him, girl. Don't let him get away with this!"

He grabs a menu and uses it to hide his face from them. "Okay, I'm done playing now."

I lean in with a panicked expression. "Same. What do we do?"

He puts on a fake smile. "Just kidding! Love you, baby."

I laugh loudly. "Oh, honey! How you jest."

Everyone turns back to their conversations, ignoring us completely. "Let's never do that again."

I nod in agreement. "Never. We aren't built to be actors. So, are you going to explain where this sudden vow of abstinence came from?"

"Celibacy."

"Celibacy is more long-term."

He blinks. "Of course you would know that. Whatever. You get what I mean. I've come to the realization recently that I'm a bit of a manwhore."

"Oh! Well, who would've thought?" I say sarcastically.

"Funny. I was out on a date the other day and-"

I tilt my head in confusion. "Date? Jonah Hart doesn't date."

"Your lack of faith in me is offensive. I was trying something new. Anyway, I really liked this girl, and we ended up getting to the conversation."

"What conversation?"

He waves his hand towards me. "You know. The conversation."

" . . . "

He sighs. "The sex conversation. Body count range. That conversation. I forget how inexperienced you are at dating."

"No need to point it out. Continue."

"She asked for a range and I said I didn't know. She then looked at me shocked and asked, 'Over twenty?' and I laughed. I thought she was joking."

I cover my mouth with my hand. "Jonah I think you forget that over twenty sounds like a lot for most people."

"Like who?"

"Me? Mine is barely over ten and I think that's a lot."

"This is just making my choice more obvious. Anyway, she got upset and asked why I was laughing at her, and I explained that my body count was well over twenty. She basically called me a slut and left."

"In what words?"

"She said and I quote, 'That's a lot of experience. I don't think I'm comfortable being with someone who expresses their body so freely.'"

"Oh."

"Yeah. Oh. So to prove her, and myself, wrong, I will not be partaking in sex for the time being."

"Because you want to get her back?"

His face morphs in disgust. "Hell no. Her timeline included babies within the next two years. Clearly, she's crazy."

"Well, as riveting as this conversation has been, it's my turn to rant now."

He interlocks his hands, elbows resting on the table. "I'm ready."

"You know our perky manager, Tammy?"

He shivers. "Unfortunately."

"She blackmailed me the other day. Like full-on threatened."

"Gasp. With what? What dirt have you been hiding from me, Summer?"

"None. She said that if I didn't speak at that conference next month, she would never schedule us together again."

He stabs the rest of his burger with a fork. "That bitch."

"I know! So now I have to do all this research about the hospital and talk about why I love my job."

"But you hate your job."

"Exactly!" I groan. "As we've established, acting is not for me. How the hell am I supposed to go up there in front of a billion smart doctor people and tell them how great it is?"

"Maybe you could just quit before it? And I'll come with you."

"I am pretty poor, so I'm not sure that's for me."

He sighs. "Well, I'm out of ideas. You'll be fine. You are a smart girl who is charming sometimes, you'll do great."

"Actually, if I do bad, maybe they'll fire me anyway!"

"And I can quit!"

I stand up, grabbing my keys. "Sure. I gotta go. I'm gonna be late for pottery."

"Say hi to Pam for me!"

* * *

I meet Eliana at the shop since Jonah insisted we have lunch today. She's already there when I pull in, and she hops in my car after I park.

"I'm so excited! Ceramic Saturday is my new favorite day of the week!"

I pull the sun blocker down and flip the mirror open. I apply some lip balm and flatten my hair a little so the wave isn't as intense. "Is that what we're calling it now?"

She holds her hand out, and I pass her the tube. She applies a thin layer and drops it into my center console. "Yes! Don't you think that's so cute?"

"It's definitely something!"

She swats at my arm. "Don't be a hater, Summer."

"You seem pretty chipper today. What's going on with you?"

She folds her hands in her lap. "Well, you remember that one pilot I talked about a few months back? The hot mean one?"

"Yeah, didn't he ban you from his flights?"

"Yes! But I just found out that he's flying to Bora Bora and that's my dream spot!" Eliana has always loved to travel for whatever reason. For me its an absolute nightmare.

I traveled often as a kid, mostly just so my parents could flaunt their wealth some more. My parents never wanted to deal with me on the trips. They normally hired a nanny to come along and had them babysit me the entire time. Claimed that vacations were for relaxing, and that they couldn't do that with me yapping in their ears. Not that it mattered, anyway. My dad would spend most of it locked away working, and my mom would storm off to a spa somewhere.

Sometimes it was fun. If we went somewhere near a beach, the nanny would take me, let me play in the water. I have some of my fondest memories there. Usually, it was a big city. They didn't deem it safe enough for me to join, so they left me in the hotel room.

When I got older, they stopped bringing me along, which I was fine with. As a preteen, I would invite Eliana over, something I wasn't normally allowed to do. As a high-schooler, I threw ragers. I was proud of my position as the constant host.

Eliana never got to travel. Her family couldn't afford it, and it was nerve-wracking for her mom to travel alone with two kids. Becoming a flight attendant was her way of seeing the world.

I pull my hair back into a ponytail, unsatisfied with how it poofed back up. "Why don't you just wait until another pilot goes?"

"I would, but there's a waitlist for flight attendants to go to cool areas like that. I'm at the bottom, but a friend of mine isn't, and she got assigned to it." She wiggles in her seat, doing a little dance. "Her son ended up getting sick and she can't go!"

I give her a concerned look. "I don't think you should be celebrating that."

"He's fine."

"Sure. But how are you gonna get on the flight? Won't they just give the spot to the next person in line?"

She nods. "Normally, yes. But since the flight is so soon, they can't because of policy. So she offered it to me!"

"That's nice and all, but you're still banned from his flights."

Her smile turns mischievous. "Yes. But that manager still

owes me for not telling her husband that she made out with a pilot in the employee bathroom."

My jaw drops. "WHAT?"

She scratches her head. "Oh, I never told you about that? My bad. Well anyway, she's gonna write me on the flight board under 'Eli' so he doesn't notice until we're in the air. I'll just have to dodge him until then."

"Well, I'm excited for you! How long will you get to stay?"

"Two nights. Normally they would fly right back, but there's some celebration happening for the villas, so not enough people are leaving."

"Oh my gosh. You should bring your sexiest bathing suit and sleep with the pilot!"

She blinks. "What makes you say that?"

I cock a brow. "He's hot?"

She clicks her tongue. "That could be fake news. I still haven't met him, it could just be the uniform. Anyway, we should go inside. Pam is probably waiting for us."

"Or rigging our wheels so we can't participate."

"Or that."

We get out of the car and walk into the shop, elbows interlocked. We're greeted by the same lady as last time, Shelly. "Hi, girls! Ready to shape some clay?"

"You know it!" Eliana cheers.

"Wonderful, let me check you in. Remind me of your names."

"Summer and Eliana."

She looks at the computer, confusion shaping her face. She navigates around for a while before snapping her fingers. "Oh! It looks like you have been moved up to the intermediate class!"

We turn to each other with wide eyes. "Oh? Do you know why?"

She shakes her head. "I don't. But you did say that you guys had a raw talent. Maybe Pam noticed it too!"

I run my tongue along the inside of my bottom lip. "Who teaches the intermediate class?"

"Brenda! She's very good."

I let out a laugh of disbelief. That bitch took us out of her class. "I'm sure she's amazing, but here's the thing, Shelly."

She looks up from the computer.

"Pam had such a way of teaching. She really touched me and Eliana here," I say, Eliana nodding vigorously. "So, is there any way we could be moved back to the beginner's class? I would just love to continue working on my fundamentals with such a…patient woman."

She places a hand over her heart. "I am just so glad that you've connected to the art through one of our instructors. Let me check to see if she has any openings." She clicks a few keys. "You're in luck! She has two open spots for her class right now!"

Eliana beams. "Wonderful! See you after!"

When we walk in, she's in the kiln room, distracted. We sit down in the front row, right in front of her wheel, and get comfortable.

She walks out and almost drops the pot in her hand. "You?!"

I clap happily. "Us! We saw that you had us moved out of your class because of our progression but we just couldn't leave! So it looks like we'll be together again!"

She slams the pot down onto the table and clenches her jaw. "Wonderful."

"Isn't it?!"

Me and Eliana chat while more people file into the class. I see the kid who judged me last time and throw him a dirty look. His mom ushers him to the spot furthest from us. I grab my phone out of my pocket and check my email while I wait. I skim over one from Tammy titled "Stop procrastinating your speech preparation!" I send it to trash.

"Alright, class! Welcome back for session two. Reminder, you have two more classes after this one that come with the bundle. For today's class. and the next one, we will be continuing to make new pieces. On the last day, we will glaze everything and then the studio will call you when it's all ready to be picked up!"

People around us sit up enthusiastically. "Excuse me, Mrs. Pam, I have a question."

Her smile drops as she looks at my raised hand. "Yes, Summer?"

"Oh, you know my name! I love that. It's like we're real friends!"

Eliana snickers beside me while Pam looks unimpressed. "Your question?"

"Oh, yes. Will we actually get to pick what we make this time, or are you going to choose for us again?"

"Not that it matters for you since you picked your own design after my specific instructions not to last time," she grits out. "But today I will be picking again. The last session is the artist's choice."

I pout. "What are we making?"

"Maybe, if you let me get through my introduction, you would find out! May I continue, or do you have anything to add?"

"All you, Madam Pam."

She gives me a side-eye. "Today we will be making plates! When you glaze them later, we will use food-safe glaze so that they will actually be kitchen-safe. You may stay at the wheels, but we won't actually be spinning them today. Everything about this project is controlled by you."

"Can I turn mine into a jewelry holder?"

She huffs. "No, Summer, you cannot. Like I said last time, this is a new skill and so we will all do the same thing so that everyone is on the same page. Will you be able to handle that?"

"Yes, Lady Pam."

She continues, ignoring my remark completely. I look over to see Eliana struggling not to laugh at my attempts to make Pam break. She sees me looking and urges me to stop with her eyes. I flutter mine back at her innocently.

Pam passes out the clay, water, and sponges. She then sits at her wheel, moving the pedal away and having us do the same. "Okay! Let's get started. Go ahead and flatten the clay to the wheelbase. Don't worry about it sticking, we will use a wire at the end to detach it."

I start to flatten it by pressing my palms into the clay. Eliana tries to do the same, but her elbow slips and she ends up smearing the clay down the wheel. She looks at me, panicked, and I try to not let the laughing start again. I look away, finding control of it, and turn back to her.

Pam sees her mistake but says nothing. She gets up, and walks to the back, returning with two aprons. "I wanted to see if you girls could handle yourselves this time around, but I have a feeling that you won't be able to."

The little kid laughs again and I turn around, sticking my lower jaw out in warning. He shuts up immediately, and his mother gives me a glare. I smile sweetly and turn back around, putting on the apron.

We continue to flatten the clay, trying to get it all at one even level. Pam instructs us to pour a little water on the top and smear it around, helping it to even out. I do as she says, but end up spilling too much water and it runs all over the wheel. I scramble to try and contain it but end up hitting the pedal that I moved, making the wheel spin out of control. My clay stays put this time, but the water does not, and it sprays onto me and Eliana once again.

Pam takes a deep breath and looks at me. "At least we were wearing aprons?" I say, and she nods curtly, continuing on with the class.

Once the top is all smooth, we grab the sponges and get any remaining cracks out of the clay. Neither I nor Eliana make any mistakes this time, so we must be improving already.

"Now, for these plates, we will be doing a flattened bottom and adding walls. Some of you may have these types of plates at home, others may have the kind that has a circular base and almost curves up. Both can be done with clay, but the kind we are making today is easier for beginners."

She brings us each a strip of clay that she cut up for us and shows us how to slip and score around the base of our plates and the strip so that we can attach them. While scoring, I end up stabbing the base, but I recover before she can notice. I attach the edges correctly and see Eliana struggling a little, but she does as well.

We then add a little coil of clay along the inside and smooth it all together so that it blends nicely. "Nice work girls, I'm impressed."

Pam walks away to help some of the others. "Did you see that?" I whisper.

"Do you think that means we're her favorites?" Eliana asks.

"Oh, definitely."

We continue to smooth the plates while everyone else finishes, and Pam goes to the back again to get her supplies.

"Now, just like last time, we are going to use the tools to make designs on the plates. Not to worry, if you do well glazing, they will still be food-safe. Just keep in mind that the more ridges there are, the more thorough you will have to be."

She watches me closely, but has to walk away to help someone else. I grab some extra clay and make designs on my plate that I think she'll love.

When time is almost up, she comes around to collect our plates so that she can set them out to dry. Eliana has attempted roses this time.

"Wow, Eliana! That is definitely some abstract art."

We all stare at the ball sacks on her plate. She sighs. "I don't know why this keeps happening."

Pam walks to me and clicks her tongue. "You made a jewelry dish."

"No, I made a plate that has dimension."

"You made a jewelry dish."

"It is a plate that can be used for pasta. The noodles wrap around the little hills."

"You made a jewelry dish."

I grin. "I made a jewelry dish."

"Do you enjoy disobeying me, Summer?"

"Of course not! I just think we have artistic differences."

"We definitely do. Artistic and otherwise."

She grabs the plate and sets it with the others, silently dismissing us. We walk towards the exit, waving to Shelly when she stops us.

"Girls! I know that you really enjoy Pam's class, but I wanted you to know that she won't be teaching you for the rest of your course."

My mouth drops open. "What? Why not?"

"It seems she has planned an impromptu visit to her son, who lives in Europe. She will be staying with him during the days that your next classes are scheduled, so she won't be here to teach you."

"What a shame! I just don't think we can learn without her instructing us." Eliana says.

"Well, could we continue our course when she gets back?"

Shelly thinks for a moment. "Well, I guess I could put your other two sessions onto her books for when she returns."

I beam. "Wonderful! Just do me a favor, put our names down as something else, so it'll be like a surprise."

Shelly claps with delight. "Oh, I just love that idea! You got it, girls. Enjoy the rest of your day."

We leave, feeling victorious again.

Twenty-Five

Sean

"Are you sure this is the right place?"

Summer and I stand outside of an old church, her recheck-ing the address. "Yep, this is it. Week two of your desensitiza-tion starts now!"

She skips towards the front door, me lingering behind. After last week, I was expecting something fun again. This looks like she's enlisting me into a cult. I grab her arm before she can walk inside. "Summer, what are we doing here?"

She drags me inside. "It's a therapy group for individuals struggling with their mental health."

I jerk away. "Hell no! Who knows what kind of people are in there?"

She scoffs. "If I had to guess, probably people like you, Mr. Judges-a-lot."

"Whatever." I grumble.

A lady at the welcoming table notices us. "Come in, folks! No need to be scared. We are here to help."

I grab onto the bottom of her shirt, rubbing the material between my fingers. "I don't like this, Summer."

"It's too late now!" She whispers out of the corner of her mouth. "She already saw us!"

"We're sitting closest to the door." I rush out.

The front desk lady waves us forward. "Okay! Go ahead and grab a name tag!"

I turn away, whispering into Summer's ear. "Don't write your real name. I'm still not convinced this is a real group."

She nods.

"Welcome Kurtis and Jenny! Where does that name originate?"

Summer blinks. "France?"

"Huh. I never would've guessed that. Now, are you both participating today?"

She shakes her head. "No, he's the one that struggles." I elbow her in the stomach and she yelps.

"I'm sorry to hear that. Well, we only allow spouses to be present for support, so you will have to wait out here with me."

Summer quickly wraps an arm around my waist, leaning her head into my chest. "Perfect! We're married."

I cough, and she pinches my ass in response. "Yep!" I throw an arm over her shoulders, yanking on a strand her of hair. "This is my wife."

The lady's eyes widen. "Oh! My apologies. You both just seem so young, but I shouldn't assume."

Summer attempts to smile, but it ends up looking like she's in pain. "Newlyweds! You know what they say, when you know, you know."

"And I knew!" I add. They both turn to me, giving me a

concerned look.

"Well, that's so sweet." She coos. "Let me see the ring!"

Summer yanks her hand away, putting it in the back pocket of my jeans. "We actually don't believe in rings. Chaining our love to a simple strip of metal felt shallow."

The lady looks down at her own ring, frowning. I turn into Summer's neck, whispering to her. "Look what you did."

"You got us into this, Jacobs."

I scoff. "Actually, I had nothing to do with any of this."

The lady pulls our attention back, ushering us to go in and join the other people. The room has a circle of metal pullout chairs in it, a man who I assume is the group leader sitting in front of them all. "Welcome in. Please grab a seat."

We wait while other people file in, all looking abnormal. I silently fume, counting down the minutes until this is over. I fidget with the strings of my hoodie, untying and retying them again.

"Okay everyone, it looks pretty full, so we can start." The instructor looks to be in his late sixties. He's wearing a blue polo with tight ripped jeans and has a pencil behind his ear. *This simply cannot be real.* "We will start this meeting like normal, and go around the room explaining why we're here today."

It starts with an older man who looks like he could be here for a similar reason as me. "I'm Clint. I am here because my wife left me for my brother forty years ago." *Or not.*

"Welcome Clint." Everyone choruses back to him. Summer and I look at each other, her stifling a laugh.

"My name is Joana, and I have an addiction to stealing small items from the dollar section at Target." I drop my head, rubbing my temples.

"Welcome Joana."

The process continues on, each statement getting more and more outrageous than the last. When it gets to me, I do my best to put on a serious face. "My name is S- Kurtis and I have PTSD from getting shot in the army a few months ago." A chair squeaks and someone whispers "Oh."

"And this is my wife, Jenny. She's a sex addict."

Summer lets out a honk, coughing on the water she had just taken a sip of. She bites her lip, looking at me with a threat in her eyes. She throws a hand onto my thigh, saying, "Yes, it's true. I just can't get enough of this guy."

There's silence for a few moments. "Welcome Kurtis and Jenny."

The rest of the people take their turns airing out their secrets while I try not to fall asleep. Summer listens to them intently, clearly fascinated by their exaggerated problems.

"Now that we've all been introduced, I'll take a turn." The instructor starts, "my name is Joel, and I was a cocaine addict for twenty years."

"Finally." Heads suddenly turn towards me and Summer removes her hand from my thigh. *Oops.* Guess I said that out loud.

He ignores my comment, continuing. "We are here today to get some clarity on the issues we are facing. To start, I would like you to all write down a word to describe a feeling you have at this phase in your life."

He passes out notecards and pencils, and we write down a word without our names on it, as he instructed. He then has us crumple the paper up, and throw it into the middle of the circle. He gets up and lays in the middle of our papers, making a snow angel with them. I look down at him in horror.

He stands back up, dusting off his pants. "Now that they're all mixed, I want everyone to grab one and unfold it. Then we are going to take turns reading them."

I reach down and grab two, giving one to Summer. I unfold my paper and let out an uncontrolled chuckle. 'Horny.' I guess she stuck to her role.

We read out the words, most of them being pretty basic. Bored, happy, sad, etc. When we get to Summer's, people shoot her a look but say nothing. Mine ends up being read by the last person.

"Aching."

I can feel her eyes on the side of my face, but I don't look over at her. Instead, I focus my eyes on Joel, him explaining the importance of having a schedule in everyday life. It's all a load of shit.

"Alright. Now, I would like you all to turn the card over and write the reason you can't move on from your current problem. It can be a simple answer, or it can be long. Whatever you feel, write it down."

We do as he says, some of us writing more than others. Summer takes a total of two seconds to finish her card. I'm not sure she even wrote anything. I doodle in the corner of the card while I wait.

"Now, drop your card on the ground." He demonstrates with one of his own. "And stand up," we do. "And stomp all over it."

No one moves. Joel then begins to jump up and down on his card, grabbing it and throwing it, then jumping on it again. He stops for a moment, looking at us expectantly. We tap our feet over the cards, slightly fearing him.

"More! More! Smash the card. Demolish it! Let all of

those emotions out!" I clench my jaw, slowly twisting my head towards Summer. She cringes and begins jumping on the paper.

People follow her lead, one of them even letting out an angry scream. I contemplate my entire life and stomp a little harder.

"Wonderful!" He yells, motioning for us to sit back down. He collects the crushed-up papers and trashes them, then sits down to join us. "Wow. That was a lot of energy shifting. Did you guys feel it?"

I grunt.

"Okay. Well, it looks like we're getting close to the end here, so let's wrap it up with a final conversation. I never wanted to be a cocaine addict, I just thought it would make me seem more mysterious. It did not."

I cock an eyebrow.

"It's not important. The point is, our problems don't spiral out of hand on their own. We continuously overthink them, distort our own thoughts, and make delusions that are untrue. We tell ourselves that we are failures, that our unhappiness is because of our own poor decision-making. We say that we put ourselves into this situation so we must deal with it alone.

"The truth is, that's bullshit. We're all human. And getting help is the only way to get through our problems. Anything else is just a distraction. Now, as your homework, I encourage you to try and confess something about yourself to someone else. Thanks for showing up, everyone. Refreshments are at the back table."

Summer and I launch from our chairs, booking it out of the church. I rip my nametag off and shove it in my pocket. She does the same and snickers. "So, got anything to confess?"

I open her door for her. "I do, actually."

She looks up at me.

"I hate you."

She punches my arm and climbs in.

Summer

I let him play another audiobook in the car because I feel a little guilty. In my defense, the group looked really promising online! It had good reviews from people who seemed truly mentally unstable. How was I supposed to know their problems were a little less than relatable?

I go to skip an ad on his phone when a text pops up, making me stop in my tracks.

"Hey Sean :)"

HUH? I click on it without thinking, pulling up a text chain with some girl named Macy. I'm about to put the phone down when another text comes through.

"I've been thinking about you. We should talk next time I'm in the city."

What. The. Actual. *Fuck.*

Twenty-Six

Sean

Summer gets out of the car a little quicker than usual. After being weirdly quiet for the whole drive home, she storms towards the apartment complex, leaving me confused. I grab my phone from the cup holder and jog after her, calling out her name. She keeps walking.

We get near the elevator and she jumps in, rapidly pressing the 'close door' button. I sprint towards it and shove my arm in just in time, making the doors open. I step in, clicking our floor, and cornering her into the back wall.

"What the hell was that? If anything, I should be mad at you right now."

She avoids my stare. "I have no idea what you're talking about. No one is mad."

I cross my arms over my chest and step closer to her, invading her space completely. "Clearly. Now, are you gonna tell me what's up?"

She stays quiet and I feel a vibration in my pocket. I keep an eye on her, but reach in, pulling my phone out. I click on the text and can't help but laugh. It only makes her expression darken further.

My laughing becomes uncontrollable, to the point where I'm gasping for air. "You can't be serious!"

She huffs and frowns harder, turning completely away from me. "Still don't know what you're on about."

I step closer so that we're almost touching and drop my mouth to her ear. "So it has nothing to do with these texts?" I say, holding my phone up.

"No. God, what is taking this elevator so long?!"

"She's the wife of one of my old buddies from the army. He ended up passing away. and I organized his stuff to be returned. She still checks up on me every once in a while."

Her expression softens a little, but she stays turned away.

"Nothing ever happened."

"You never slept with her?"

My eyes widen. "Are you asking?"

She shrugs.

"No, sunshine. I haven't slept with her, nor do I plan on it. Any more questions?"

"Nope!" The elevator doors open and she prances out, leaving me laughing in her wake.

Summer

"UGH!" I shove my laptop down slumping against my headboard. I've already taken three breaks in the past twenty minutes and my speech is going absolutely nowhere. I look over at Gouda, who is happily munching on a Cheez-It. "Do you want to write my speech for me?"

He completely ignores me and keeps chewing. I never

thought I would struggle with something research-related this much. I was always a good student, had all A's, didn't really have to try ever. Learning came easily to me, and so did research—until now, that is.

Either I'm out of practice, or the hospital seriously has done nothing of interest in the past year. Praying he might know more than me, I call Jonah for backup. "I need your help."

"What's up, my lovely?"

I let out a long groan. "I can't do this stupid speech. I'm supposed to talk about the success of the hospital. The problem is, I haven't seen any."

He walks with the phone to the bathroom, propping me up and dropping his pants.

"Ew, Jonah! What the hell?"

He shrugs his shoulders and moves the phone until he's out of the frame. "Sorry, that was kinda instinct." He says and finishes peeing, coming back into the frame. "Don't act so disgusted. You used to love this smoking body."

I turn my nose up in disgust. "Key word being used to. Why is showing yourself peeing an instinct? Is that a thing now?"

"I hope not. I meant cameras following me. I've been told that I photograph flawlessly."

I shuffle lower into my bed and curl up under the covers. "You're distracting me. Go get your laptop and help me research."

"What? Why?" He whines, throwing himself face down onto his bed.

"It's pretty much your fault that I'm in this situation in the first place. Now you have to pay for it."

We spend the next hour researching the hospital. We find a few new surgeries that have been making the hospital a lot of money and learn that robotic surgeries have become the standard in a lot of specialties at our branch. Jonah ends up getting tired and hangs up, leaving me to my own mind. I keep working for a little while longer and write the first half of my speech.

I'm about to call it a night too when I hear voices outside of my door, one of them being a woman's voice that I don't recognize. I gasp. Did he bring that Macy chick into my house? I leap up from my bed, sprinting to the door.

"Summer, you're here! Oh, you look so beautiful. Come here, honey."

My jaw drops when I see who it is. "Caroline?"

* * *

We sit down at the table and start eating the dinner Sean made us. Caroline explains that she had been waiting for an invitation from him for too long, and decided she would just drive into town herself. Seeing her again healed a part of me.

Even though my mom was never very—well—motherly, I still found myself missing her from time to time. Or maybe not her actual self, but the version of her that I wanted to believe was real. No matter how much I hate her, she's still my mother, and I've never been able to let go of that. My father never showed any interest in me. Not having him as a part of my life hasn't been a struggle at all. Caroline filled the role of both parents for me, but replacing my mom with her always brought up some guilt.

"So, Summer, tell me about work. You are such a compassionate girl." Sean snickers and she swats at him. "Don't you start with me! She is very nice. You just don't give her a reason to be. You can't blame her for that."

"Yeah. You can't blame me for that." I mock, contemplating my answer. Although work is usually the last place I want to be, I can't imagine myself doing anything else. It's like a toxic relationship. The more I hate it, the more I attach myself to it. I'm too far in to think about another career. "It's fine. I don't love my unit, but I make it work."

She takes a sip of her wine. "That's quite alright, work isn't everything. I never really loved working in the office." She works as a secretary for a small law firm. "I felt like everyone looked down on me, and the stress started consuming my life. After a while, I realized how much else I had to be grateful for. People work way worse jobs for a way lower wage. I'm lucky to have a job at all."

I nod, finding some truth in her answer. Nursing isn't the worst gig out there, and there are parts of it I do love. Maybe I just need to stop focusing on the negative so much. "We should watch a movie tonight like we used to."

Caroline beams. "I love that idea! You guys used to watch that one movie on repeat."

Sean jumps in. "Teen Beach Movie. The only thing we could ever agree on."

Eliana looks up at the ceiling, reminiscing. "Ross Lynch. The man that you are."

Caroline shakes her head. "The only reason you all agreed is because you girls had a crush on the blonde guy, and Sean had a crush on the brunette girl."

Sean rubs a hand along his jaw. "I was so convinced that I could pull Maia Mitchell that I sat through a two hour long movie listening to your guys' awful singing."

"It wasn't that bad!" I say, picking at my food. "I would have thought the dancing would be worse for you. We would cover the screen for a second and you'd be yelling about how fat we were."

Caroline gasps. "Sean! You did not!"

"Not my best moment. We should watch it tonight."

We all agree and shovel the rest of our food down, throwing our dishes into the sink. I get changed into some comfy clothes and grab some snacks, sitting down on the couch.

Sean crosses the room to me. "You know we just ate, right?"

"You're already fat shaming and the movie hasn't even started yet."

The girls file in behind him and grab a seat next to me. He sits on the floor in front of my feet and I pull my legs to my knees to give him more room. Eliana grabs the remote and finds the movie, turning it on with an excited squeal.

Brady and Mack both pop up on the screen and all three of us cheer, remembering why they were our childhood crushes. "I need to follow him on Instagram."

Caroline chimes in. "Oh, I already do! He's like a rockstar now or something."

Sean turns his head towards his mom. "You follow Ross Lynch on Instagram?"

She shrugs. "What, because I'm a mother I can't have eyes? He's a handsome young man."

He blinks and takes a peek at me, seeing me curled into a ball. He turns back to the screen without a word, but reaches behind him and grabs my legs, hooking them over his shoulders so that I can stretch out.

Eliana is too focused on the male abs on the screen to notice, but Caroline does, and grabs her phone to snap a photo discreetly. Turns out the flash was on and we all end up getting blinded.

"Oops! I was trying to open up that Messages app." She turns to me and winks, and I raise a brow in return.

We continue watching the movie, snacking at about halfway through. I'm trying to focus on the screen, but Sean keeps ahold of my ankles and is rubbing them with his thumbs. Why is every swipe sending electricity up my body? I've made out with guys and felt less.

Caroline yawns and we look over at her, as she's basically falling asleep sitting up. "Maybe we should just finish the movie tomorrow," Eliana suggests.

"Okay, sure. You kids go to bed and I'll sleep here on the couch."

Sean lets go of my ankles and stands up, stretching his arms above his head. "Absolutely not. You aren't sleeping on the couch, Mom."

"Agreed," Eliana says. "Mom can take my room, and I'll stay with Summer." She links her arm with mine and we stand up, heading to my room.

Caroline holds her hand up, stopping us. "No way, Eliana. You have flights over the next week and will be coming back during the day. I don't want you waking Summer up."

"Shit, I forgot about that. Okay, I'll take the couch and Sean will sleep in my room with Mom."

Sean vetoes that plan immediately. "Absolutely not. It's your house, Eli. I don't want to make you sleep on the couch."

"I don't mind! Plus, we all pay the same in rent and you've been sleeping on the couch for months, so I'd prefer if you got a bed for once."

"But I work early. I don't want to wake Mom up."

Caroline cuts in. "Well, Sean and Summer have opposite

schedules, do they not? She goes to bed after he gets home and he falls asleep after she leaves. So no one would wake anyone up, right?"

Eliana hesitates. "Right."

"So then it's settled! Sean and Summer will sleep in her room, Eliana will take the couch, and I will sleep in Eliana's room!"

Twenty-Seven

Sean

We stand in her doorway, staring at each other. After Mom makes her mind up about something, there's really no changing it, so here we are. In her room. Both of us. *With one bed.*

"I'll just sleep on the floor."

She smacks her lips. "K!"

She goes into her closet and grabs an old blanket, throwing it on the floor. Then she walks over to her bed and chucks down a decorative pillow. I think she's joking, but she just hops into bed, getting comfortable.

Alrighty, then. I step onto my makeshift bed and reach behind my head, pulling my shirt off. I fold it and place it on the floor in my section. When I look back up, I see Summer, eyes bulging, mouth hanging open. "What are you doing?"

"… getting ready for bed?"

She tucks a hair behind her ear. "I mean, why is your shirt now on the floor?"

"Because I don't sleep with a shirt on? Aren't you supposed to be telling me to make myself at home?"

"I'd actually prefer it if you didn't. You don't see me stripping down."

"Unfortunately," I mumble.

She moves her head closer to me. "What was that? You mumbled."

"Nothing." I sit down on the floor and pull the blanket over me, the carpet scratching up my back. I try not to move so it's less itchy and lay my head back on the pillow. It's quite literally the hardest pillow I've ever felt in my life. "Goodnight, sunshine."

"Night." She reaches over to her bedside table and shuts the lamp off, retracting back under the covers.

I lay there, listening for her slowed breathing. I'm about to drift to sleep when she flips the light back on. My eyes shoot open, squinting from the sudden brightness. "Yes?"

"Just get up here."

"What?" I ask, sitting up. I rub a hand on my back and see that the carpet has made imprints on my skin.

She huffs. "It's making me feel guilty."

"What, the fact that you gave me the most uncomfortable pillow in the world? Or that your carpet is practically sandpaper?"

She rolls her eyes. "Let's not be dramatic. I was feeling more guilty about the fact that when everyone falls asleep, I let Gouda out of his cage so that he can run around my room. Sometimes he poops on the carpet and seeing how your back sticks to it kinda grosses me out."

I go perfectly still. "Are you admitting to me that I probably have rat shit on my back right now?"

"No! He's a mouse. But I clean it up really well, it's just the principle of it. Like what if the poop molecules soaked in before I could get all of them?"

I leap to my feet, jumping on the pillow so that I don't have to stand on her disgusting carpet. "That's it. I'm sleeping on the floor in the living room."

She jabs me with her toe. "Stop. It's fine. Just sleep with me."

"Alright, we don't really have that kind of relationship, so please stop begging."

"Shut up," she says, kicking me this time. "You know what I mean. My bed is king size, you can stay on your side and I'll stay on mine. We're both adults. We can sleep in a bed together without it being weird."

"Why are you even sleeping? It's nighttime."

"I messed up my schedule again and only napped today, so I'm tired. Are you gonna get in or not?"

"As long as you're sure.." She pulls the covers back and gestured for me to hop in. I slide in next to her, almost moaning at the feeling of her soft sheets mixed with the warmth her body left behind. She scoots to the far end of the bed and throws the covers over both of us, turning away from me. I reach over and flip off the light, letting myself drift away into the darkness.

* * *

Summer

I wake up to my blanket being wrapped around me perfectly, warming my cold body. I nuzzle further into it and feel something hard against my back. Shit. Did I fall asleep eating again? Last time I did this, a fork almost impaled me in my sleep. I reach back to get it when my blanket moves on its own.

I open my eyes and turn, seeing black fluff next to my face. "What the hell?" The fork pushes further into me, and that's when I remember.

I fling myself out of the bed and land on the floor with a thud. Sean's head pops up, and he groans when the sun hits him in the eyes. "What's wrong with you?"

"THAT WAS NOT A FORK!"

He flinches, squinting at me. "What are you yelling about?"

"You were touching me! Like your body was fully wrapped around mine!"

He shrugs. "I don't know if you've noticed, but your room is freezing cold. My body probably just drifted towards yours for warmth."

"But your legs were basically tangled with mine!"

He runs a hand through his hair. "Yeah, that is usually what is included with cuddling? Have you never been held before?"

I shake my head.

"Come here."

A laugh bubbles out of me. "No, I'm good, thanks."

He opens his arms a little. "Stop making it weird. Friends cuddle each other all the time."

"Who even are you right now?" Is Sean a clingy man? Never in my life would I have guessed that. "And since when are we friends?"

"I think we're friends."

"So you cuddle with Ethan?"

"Well no. But I know you do with Eliana, I've seen it. And I'm her brother, which basically makes us the same. Now come back, I'm freezing."

I think against it, but stand up to join him anyway. It is freezing, and he's basically a human furnace. And that was the best sleep I've ever gotten. I slip in and turn away from him again, and he shifts closer. He wraps his arms around me and pulls me in, throwing a leg over mine.

Nope. Too weird. I'm about to shift away when he nuzzles his head into my neck, drifting back to sleep quickly. Not wanting to move him, I close my eyes and do the same.

I wake up about an hour later to pounding on my door. When it opens, I fling myself out of bed again, not wanting anyone to get the wrong idea.

Caroline marches in. "Sean! You made this poor girl sleep on the floor? What is wrong with you?"

I jump in, wanting her to stop talking so loud. "It was my choice! It's called floor therapy. It's supposed to make your breasts bigger."

She looks down at her own. "Huh. Maybe I should try that sometime." Seeing that her son still hasn't woken up, she stomps toward him and whacks him on the leg. "Sean! Get up! You're going to be late for work!"

"Mom!" He yanks his leg away, rubbing it. "It's supposed to rain pretty hard later, so Ethan just gave everyone the day off since we've been working extra lately."

"Oh! Well, now that you're up, let's have breakfast together."

He scratches his head. "Sure."

She pats his arm. "Oh, honey, I wasn't talking to you. Eliana, Summer, and I need a little girl time."

His mouth makes an 'o' shape. "Wasn't the whole point of you coming here to see me?"

"No need to be jealous, Seany." She walks over to me and

helps me up off of the floor. "I'll make up some time for you."

He flops back into my bed, knocking out once again. We walk into Eliana's room and get ready together. We decide to dress cute so that we feel a little more dignified, and it almost feels like I'm in high school again, getting ready for prom.

We walk to the place since it's close and get a table outside. The weather is perfect, breezy but not cold. Autumn in the city is like nothing else. The restaurant is adorable. It's on the corner of the block, and is decorated for the season, with little centerpieces that look homemade.

I look around at the loud buzz of the city. People speed walking to their destinations, businessmen angrily yelling on the phone, taxis honking, and friends hugging. I think it's what makes me feel at home here. My house was always so quiet, it made me uneasy. But here? There's never a quiet moment.

My attention is pulled back to the table, and I loop my purse around the back of my chair. We look over the menu and place our orders, getting mimosas to drink.

"So, Caroline, how long are you planning on staying?"

"I was thinking just a few days, if that's alright with you two, of course."

Eliana taps the table excitedly. "You should stay until Thursday! Summer has a big speech coming up at the hospital. You have to go!"

"Oh, I don't know, honey. That seems like an awfully long time."

"It's fine! Then you can spend extra time with Sean."

"I mean, I would love to stay a little longer, if you are both sure. It's so nice to be with you girls. I've missed our little hangs."

I grab onto her hand from across the table. "Same. And we're sure. I feel like we haven't done this in forever."

Eliana takes her other hand. "We need to do it more. We don't live far enough away from each other to be away this often."

"It's my fault." She squeezes our hands. "It was hard not having Sean around, and I missed you both so much. I felt like I lost all of my babies so quickly, and I just got used to being alone."

"Caroline! I had no idea you felt that way. It's not your fault. We've been busy and neglecting everything that isn't right in front of us. We need to get better at it."

"Agreed," Eliana says, grabbing her mimosa that had just arrived. She takes a big sip. "I've been so busy with work and writing. I feel like I just need a break."

"We should all go somewhere this winter. Get away from the cold, go to the beach or something."

"We should." Caroline gives our hands one last squeeze and lets go to take a sip of her drink. "On another note, I want to hear about your love lives. Any new men in the rotation?"

"No!" Eliana blurts, making us give her a weird look.

"It's okay, honey." Caroline rubs her arm. "You are very young, no need to settle down just yet. What about you, Summer? Still going out with that nice boy?"

"If you mean Jonah, we were never going out."

Eliana chimes in. "He's a virgin now."

"Oh. Um. That's nice?" She says with a concerned smile. "So no one else, then?"

I shake my head. "No. You know how I am."

She sighs. "Yes. Look, honey, I know you had a rough go of it in high school, but you're a bright girl. You deserve to be loved."

Caroline didn't know the full extent of everything that happened while I was in school, but she had an idea. She would see me come to her house drunk and say nothing. Instead of lecturing, she would take care of me, knowing I couldn't go home. She knew I spent a lot of time with boys. And when it happened, she never judged me for the shape I was in after.

I chug my whole glass. "Sure. What about you, Caroline?"

Eliana's eyes snap to mine, mouth down-turned. Caroline doesn't find my question shocking. "No, I've experienced love. John was a great husband. No one else would be able to compete. Plus, I'm happy with my life. I have great friends, two fantastic kids, and a bonus one." She says, looking at me. "What else could I possibly need?"

Eliana looks visibly uncomfortable at the mention of her father, but doesn't say anything. Our food comes and we dive in, conversation becoming minimal. We talk some more when we're done and order another round of drinks. Caroline picks up the check, even though me and Eliana protest, and we take a small walk before heading back to the apartment.

When we get back, Sean is finally awake, and busy lounging on the couch. I go on a run—that ends very quickly—and take a melatonin in an attempt to tire myself out. I let myself have a long, hot shower, and get into bed so that I can get my sleep schedule back to normal. But for some reason, I can't get comfortable.

Twenty-Eight

Summer

Sean and I don't see each other much for the rest of the week. Even though we're sharing a room, he's been working every day and spending any extra time with his mom. I accidentally scheduled myself for three shifts in a row, so I spent most of my time sleeping and working.

It's Tuesday again, and I'm a little unsure about my plan for this session. Honestly, I don't think they've been doing anything, based on the fact that Sean hasn't mentioned the panic attacks stopping. Maybe pushing a bit harder will end up helping him.

He gets home a little earlier than usual and I wait for him to shower and change. He leaves his shirt off so that I can change his dressing again, like I've been doing since we went back to the doctor.

"It looks so much better. Honestly, I don't think we'll need to cover it again after this one."

He nods. "Good, the gauze makes it so itchy."

He puts his shirt on, and we leave the apartment, grabbing a snack before we go. I drive this time, but he still insists on opening my door and buckling me in like I'm a toddler.

"Did I tell you my mom found the antibiotics?" He asks.

I face-palm. "Well, that couldn't have gone well. You didn't hide them?"

"They were in the bottom of my suitcase. How was I supposed to know that she would snoop?"

"Have you met your mother?"

"True. Anyway, she basically cornered me and threatened me into telling her what was going on. She freaked out and got mad at me for not saying anything."

I turn onto the street that houses the building we're going to. "Huh. I didn't even notice she was upset with you."

"She got over it fast." He looks up and sees where we are, sitting up quickly. "What the hell are we doing here? You just said that I was all better!"

I park in the garage of the hospital, unbuckling my seatbelt. "You are. We're not here for anything medical. We're going to volunteer for a few hours. I want you to see the positive parts of medicine."

"I can't do it. The only reason I was fine last time was because we stayed in the ED. I don't think I can walk around the normal rooms."

I rub his arm. "You can do it. I'll be there with you, we'll take it slow, and if we absolutely need to leave, we will."

"I don't like this."

"I know." I bite my lip. "But sometimes we have to get out of the comfort zone."

He plays with his hands, deciding whether or not he's up for it. "Okay."

I smile proudly. "Okay."

We check in and I can tell he's nervous. We get our volunteer vests and go to the gift shop to pick up flower orders. Our job is to deliver them to rooms, so I show him around my work as we do.

We walk up to the door of the first room and he grabs my arm, preventing me from knocking. "I don't think I can go in there. All I'll see is him."

I knock with my other hand. "Well, good thing it's her!"

The patient tells us to come in and we do. "Hi! My name is Summer, this is Sean. We brought some flowers for you."

It's a sweet older lady that seems to have a broken arm. "Oh, how lovely! I'm Poppy. Come in, come in. Have a seat. Chat with me for a minute here."

We sit on the bench next to her bed and she offers us some chocolate that she smuggled in. We refuse it. "So, how has your stay been here?"

"Oh, not too bad," she says, sniffing the flowers. "The staff is very kind, I'm just ready to go. There's talk of them sending me to a nursing home, but I've been living by myself for ten years just fine. I have dogs at home, I can't leave them."

I take hold of her hand. "Let me tell you a secret. If you truly can stay at home on your own, then show them that. Take walks in the hallway, brush your teeth, take a shower, and prove to them that you can take care of yourself. If you find yourself struggling, there are a lot of different kinds of nursing centers. You could try a more independent or assisted living facility, which a lot of them allow animals."

"Really? I could take my pups?"

"Of course. Then you would still have your independence, but there would be resources there if you needed a little extra help."

I can see her start to tear up. "Thank you, honey. Everyone is so busy that they don't really have time to explain things to me, I appreciate you doing so. I was so worried."

I squeeze her hand, then let go. "You're welcome. Now we have some more deliveries, but you get better, okay? Enjoy the flowers."

She beams. "Thank you, both of you. Have a good day."

Sean waves to her as we leave, stepping into the hallway. "I understand now."

"Understand what?"

"Why you're a nurse. For a while, I couldn't see it. You just didn't seem happy. But the way you were just now, it was amazing. I mean, you could see the worry just ease off of her. You're a natural."

"Thanks. It means a lot." I look up at him thoughtfully. An alarm goes off in one of the rooms we walk by and I barely notice, being so used to them. I feel him grab onto my shoulder, and I remember.

His face morphs into one of worry, and I can almost feel his heart beating. I pull him aside to a little alcove and cradle his face with my hands. "You're okay. See?" I move my wrist down to his neck so that he can feel my pulse. "You're here with me. Got it? Don't go back there."

He nods, melting into my touch. The alarm stops, and he stays still, breathing starting to slow. "See? It's okay. Everything is fine."

He pulls back and we continue on. "Sorry."

"Don't be. If anything, you know now that you can get through it. You don't have to let the memories take control of you."

He doesn't answer and we head to labor and delivery for the next drop-off. It ends up being a really sweet couple and they encourage Sean to hold their baby. He does, and I swear my hormones shoot through the roof. What is it with men and babies?

We continue doing deliveries and I can see his tension ease a little with every unit we go to. Him being able to see that not all parts of the hospital are encased with death really seemed to help, and I was glad one of my ideas finally did something.

We get the last bouquet and I check the card, seeing what unit it belongs to. "You meet me in the car, I'll finish this one up."

"It's okay, I'm actually starting to have a little fun. Plus, we have to return our vests." He grabs the card and sees the location, shutting up.

Oncology.

"Seriously, Sean. Don't push yourself. You've made a lot of people happy today."

He shakes his head. "I should come with you. I need to."

I start walking in the direction of the room hesitantly. He follows. "I know, but it still could be hard. A lot of these rooms look the same, but even just stepping on that floor, you can feel the weight of it."

"I want to do it."

We get to the double doors. "Okay." I push them open.

He walks next to me, taking in his surroundings. I can tell the stress is coming back, but he keeps it under control, masking it well. We make it to the room and I hesitate to knock. He reaches around me and does it instead.

"Yes?"

We step into the room, and I look at the patient. It's a young girl, probably similar to our age, room decorated so it no longer looks like a hospital. "Can I help you guys?" She asks.

Sean speaks up. "We're here to give these flowers to you."

She gives us a sweet smile. "Actually, could you give them to someone else? I'm leaving next week. I finally beat it. Seven years of fighting and I actually beat it."

I walk up to her, wrapping her in a tight hug. "I am so proud of you. You are an absolute warrior, you know that?"

She squeezes me back. "I prayed every night for another shot, and God gave me one. Now I get to pray for someone else to have the same chance."

Sean walks up next to me. "We'll be right there with you. Congratulations, seriously. Ring the bell for yourself, and for the people who couldn't."

She stares at him as if she can see right through him. "I will."

We say goodbye and I stop by the nurses' station as we leave, giving them the flowers for a patient who needs them.

"You're making this hard for me." He says when we get back inside the car.

I cock a brow. "I'm making what hard for you?"

"Just giving me things to think about."

"You think about me?" I joke.

He turns to me, a serious expression on his face. "Yeah, sunshine. I think about you. A lot more than I should."

I dip my head, and try to ignore the butterflies dancing in my stomach.

Twenty-Nine

Summer

When we get back, we all eat dinner, and then I banish myself to my room to finish my speech. Once it seems long enough, I practice saying it, but stutter over every line. "This is not good, Gouda. I procrastinated too far this time."

Sean comes in to go to sleep since Caroline will still be in the city for two more days. I stay sitting up, typing away on my keyboard. He plops down beside me, yawning.

"Right, sorry. I'll turn off the light, but I need to stay on the computer a little longer. Is it gonna bother you?" I ask, reaching over to shut it off.

"No, no. I'll stay up with you."

"You can't. You have work tomorrow," I say, rubbing my eyes. He grabs the comforter and throws it over our legs, then pats the space around mine, tucking me in. "Plus, you look tired."

"Wow, thanks."

I whack him. "You know what I mean."

190

"I do. I can stay awake for a little while longer. Finishing up your speech?"

I sigh. "Trying to. It's in two days and I don't have any of it memorized. I just don't understand. I'm perfectly outgoing most of the time and never get anxious speaking to people. But the second it's on a stage and they're all staring at me, I want to crawl out of my skin."

"Maybe you're scared of being judged?" He reaches over and grabs the laptop, ignoring my protest. "Let me see."

He scans through it for a minute with narrowed eyes. "You hate it."

He shakes his head. "I don't hate it, it's good. It's funny but educational, has good transitions."

"Then why do you look like it's the worst thing you've ever seen?"

"I'm just trying to get through your atrocious grammar." He starts at the beginning and adds adjustments to the speech.

I blink. "I'm going to be saying it, so the grammar doesn't matter…" *Idiot.*

"You still have to know how to form an actual sentence. Seriously, have you never taken English?"

I lean my head back against the headboard. "Will you stop complaining and just fix it, please?"

He takes the next twenty minutes to show me all the mistakes I made and fixes them. Then he makes me flashcards so that I can get comfortable memorizing it. At around midnight I tap out and decide to nap, while he sleeps for the night.

I turn the light off and get comfortable, moving as far away from him as possible. He just scoots closer and drags me back into his chest, then he flips around. He grabs my arms and wraps them around his large frame, sighing happily when I don't let go. We don't move for the rest of the night.

* * *

Sean

I'm getting out of my car after a boring day in the office when I feel a hand grab me. Suddenly, I'm being yanked into the passenger seat of Summer's car, and she throws us into reverse. "What the hell are you doing? I didn't even lock my car."

She bites her lip. "Oh. Well, it's fine. We live in a safe-ish neighborhood." She grabs her phone and turns on Spotify, humming along to her playlist. "I needed to fit in an extra session this week and I didn't think you would agree to going."

"Tell me where it is and I'll let you know."

She looks at me out of the corner of her eye. "Nice try, no."

I lean my chair back and shut my eyes. "Why did we have to do this today? We literally did something yesterday."

"Just take a little rest and we'll be right there."

I open my eyes and see that the car has stopped. *How long have I been out for?* I turn to my left and see Summer playing games on her phone. I sit up and see where we are.

"What the fuck?"

She widens her eyes. "Don't freak out."

"Don't fr-" I take a deep breath. "Don't freak out? You had no right!"

She pulls at her hair. "Just hear me out."

"No! I'm not hearing you out. I've let you push me, but you went too far! I mean seriously, Summer."

I recognize the place instantly. It's the cemetery my dad is buried in. I've been here once, when they were putting him in the ground, and never came back. I couldn't bring myself to, and she knows that.

"I want to leave."

"No."

I snap my head to look at her. "Are you kidding me? I want to leave. Either drive, or get out, and I will."

"No!" She slams her hand onto the steering wheel. "You never processed his death. And you can lie to yourself all you want, but it's true. You took care of everyone else after, so you wouldn't have to. You left for the military so you wouldn't have to. And now you can't move on because of it."

"That's bullshit!" I throw my hands up. "If I'm having an issue, it probably has to do with the fact that I got fucking shot!"

"Maybe. That's part of it. But I think you got over that. You didn't go back to the hospital because your dad died there. You cut your mom off because she reminds you of when he died. And you have panic attacks because you're terrified of dying and making anyone feel the way you did after he passed. Tell me I'm wrong."

I turn away from her, tired of hearing it.

"I'm not saying this to hurt you." She grabs my shoulder, making me look at her. "I'm saying this because I care. Everyone in your life lets you cruise, but I won't. You deserve to be happy, Sean. And I don't think you can be until you fully accept his passing."

I feel something wet roll down my cheek. She reaches over and swipes it away, then grabs hold of my hand. Electricity shoots through my body like it does every time I touch her. She doesn't look at me with sympathy like everyone else.

When I came back, our bickering was the only thing that made me feel alive.

Everyone tiptoed around me, made me feel fragile. But she never did. She called me out on my shit, she pushed me into getting my life together, and she was there for me at the times I couldn't.

I interlock my fingers with hers, and she gives my hand a reassuring squeeze. "You can do this Sean, you know that. You just have to be willing to."

I step out of the car and shut the door behind me. She tries to follow, but I shake my head and she turns back, knowing I need to do this alone. I walk to where I remember them burying him, the memories flashing in my mind.

I spot his gravestone and slow my pace, working myself up to it. I kneel down in front of him, giving the stone a small rub. "Hey, Dad."

I drop my gaze, staring at the grass. Dead flowers lay beside his grave, shriveling up. "I'm sorry it took me this long to see you. I just got busy, I guess.

"Actually," I scoff. "That's a lie. I've been hiding from you. You really fucked me up, dad. No matter how hard I try to stop being mad at you, I can't. I understand why you lied. I would've done the same. But I can't forgive you for that."

I drop to the ground, sitting back with my legs in front of me. "I could have made better use of that year. I would have asked you about your teenage years, the times you got caught sneaking out or drinking. I would have had you tell me the story of how you proposed to Mom. I would have wanted to know you.

"I don't remember your voice. I first noticed when I was fourteen, it was my first day of high school. I tried to think about what advice you could give me, I was so nervous. But I couldn't. Because I couldn't remember how you used to sound."

I feel a tear roll down my cheek, and I brush it away. "Then I forgot how you looked. I would spend hours staring at pictures of you so that I could keep you in my head. But then it would fade again.

"I spent years hating you for leaving me. I was hurt that you left Mom and Eliana, but I hated you for leaving me. You were my person. I loved you in a different way than everyone else. If I had a problem, you were who I wanted to go to. I could rely on you every single day. And then you were gone."

Another tear falls. "You left me alone. And if I grieved you, then I knew that at some point I would get over the way you looked when you knew it was over. So I stayed mad instead.

"And I'm sorry." I run my hands through the grass, pulling at it. "I'm sorry for hating you because loving you was harder. I'm sorry for blaming Mom for the way she left me after you died. And I'm sorry for making you watch."

I stayed silent for a little while, just soaking in his presence. And then I talk. I tell him about my new job and the possible extension. I tell him about Summer and her attempts at helping me. I tell him about our living situation and her stupid rat. I tell him about Eliana and how proud he would be of her. And I assure him that I'm gonna do better.

"I love you, dad." I kiss my hand and place it on the stone, rising from the ground. "I'll be back. I promise."

"Sean?" I whip my head around and see my mother, standing with a bouquet of flowers. "What are you doing here?"

"I'm seeing Dad."

She places the new flowers next to him and grabs the old

ones. She wraps her arms around me, pulling me in for a tight hug. I let go in her arms, letting the years of pent-up tears fall. "Let it out, baby."

"I never cried." I sob, dropping my head to her shoulder. "My dad died, and I never cried about it once."

"It's my fault. I never gave you the chance to."

She pulls away, but keeps her hands on my face, cradling me.

"I failed as a mother." I go to argue, but she stops me. "Don't start. It's true. After your father died, I fell into such a bad depression. I didn't know how to live without him, let alone raise two kids. So I didn't do anything. I slept and I ate, and that was it. You raised Eliana during the months that I couldn't, when really, I should've been taking care of both of you. He was your dad. And I never let you have the chance to grieve him. And I hate myself every day for that."

"I don't want you to hate yourself. I wanted to take care of you guys, I had help."

She scoffs. "Like that fake grant you made up?"

My jaw drops. "How'd you know about that?"

"Honey, I'm not naive. I know that the army does not sponsor every family in need, or the government would have no funds left. I knew that you would have found a way to help us no matter what, so if you wanted to do it secretly, I let you."

I nod. "It's what he would've wanted."

"No. He would've wanted you to watch out for us, sure. But he never would have wanted to see what his death did to you. The way you shut down, stopped talking to us. I thought that we had lost you."

She turns towards the car, where Summer is pretending not to watch. "But then suddenly, my boy was back. You were smiling again, opening up, letting other people help you. She's good for you."

"I know."

She turns back to me. "Don't let the way my relationship ended affect the start of yours. If I could do it all over again, I would. Because I got to be loved. And that's a feeling that everyone should have at some point in their life."

I let her words soak in. Maybe I've been worried about the wrong things this whole time.

Thirty

❧❦❧

Summer

I walk into the hospital feeling like a total imposter. I'm wearing a pantsuit that still has the tags on it, tucked way inside. The second this day is over, it's going right back to Nordstrom.

My hair is in a slick back bun because Eliana said it made me look more professional. I'm wearing some classy gold jewelry—fake, of course, and black high heels that are already ripping apart the back of my feet. I have my flashcards in my pocket so that I can look them over while I wait, but decided against using them during the speech.

I check into the conference and head into the hospital's auditorium. I go backstage and stand there, staring at the chaos in front of me. "First time?"

I look to my right and see a petite girl with dark curly hair and tan skin. "And last, hopefully."

She laughs. "It's not so bad. When are you speaking?"

"No clue. I'm trying to figure out where I'm supposed to be,

198

actually."

She wraps an arm around my elbow. "The conference coordinator is this way, she should have all the information. I'll take you."

We find her and she tells me that my speech is at the end of the introduction ceremony. Like an ending punch. *Yay!*

I get settled in my reserved seat near the front and wait for people to start arriving. The girl who I met, named Kaydee, ends up sitting next to me and we talk while waiting for people to file in.

"So what's your presentation about?"

I fiddle with the tag that's jabbing me in the hip. "I'm actually not presenting, just giving a speech on behalf of the hospital."

"Oh!" She turns in her seat. "I didn't know you worked here. Are you in management?"

"No, I'm a nurse."

"Same! What department?"

"Just Med-Surg."

She cringes. "Yikes. Well, some people love it, right?"

I shake my head. "I wouldn't know. Where do you work?"

"Not far from here. I work at another hospital in the city. Oncology."

"Do you like it?"

Enough people have arrived by now, and they dim the lights. The president of the hospital comes onto the stage and welcomes everyone. Kaydee leans in. "I love it." She whispers.

The president gives a presentation that contains the itinerary for the conference and welcomes the next speaker. We listen to the boring speeches for about an hour, and just when I'm certain that I'll fall asleep, the coordinator taps me on the shoulder and takes me backstage.

"Okay. The president will introduce you and you'll walk out. We've cued your presentation with the photos, and there's a clicker on the podium that controls it. Good luck!"

And then she's gone. I can feel my heart rate jump, my palms turning sweaty. I can barely hear what he's saying, and then suddenly he's staring at me, waving me onto the stage.

I step out from behind the curtain, the lights blinding me. I recover quickly and walk towards the podium, my sweaty feet slipping around in my shoes. I look out and see all the people staring back at me, a room full of professionals with country club memberships and stacked 401Ks.

I think about my options. I could run away crying, but that probably wouldn't look too great on me. I could scream and yell "FIRE!" but when there isn't one, they might think I'm schizophrenic. Oh! Maybe I could pretend to pass out!

"So with that being said, take it away, Summer!"

I see the president walk off and look back to the crowd, all of them expecting me to start talking. I feel my throat start to close, my mouth turning painfully dry. I'm about two seconds away from going with option one when I see *him*.

Sean is sitting close to the exit, arms crossed, legs spread out in front of him. He has a relaxed expression on his face, and when he sees me staring, he gives me a reassuring grin. "Grammar." He mouths.

And just like that, a small smile forms on my lips. I clear my throat and start speaking, looking back at him every few seconds. I get through most of the speech, only slipping up a few times, when it gets to the part about my experience.

"I've only been a nurse for about a year and the truth is, it's not easy. No one told me it was, but I tend to have a bit of an ego." That earns me some chuckles. "As I'm sure a lot of us in this room do. I struggled a lot in the beginning, always felt dumb, and like someone was looking over my shoulder.

"When I made a mistake, I expected to walk into the nurses' station and hear everyone making fun of me, but no one did. And so that's probably my favorite part about working at this hospital. Even if I don't get along with everyone on my unit, when it comes to patient care, we're all on the same team."

I see some nods in the crowd. "I never have to ask my techs to grab a set of vitals, they already have it done. I never need to remind another nurse that I have a medication to waste, they followed me in the minute I asked. And every time I forget to clock in, my manager fixes it the second I send an email. Simply having people around me that drop everything to ensure that patients are getting everything they need makes my job a lot easier, and my days a lot shorter."

I run a hand over my hair. "So that being said, I hope everyone here enjoys being in this lovely hospital, and learns something from one of our wonderful presenters. Thank you."

I practically run off of the stage, slouching when I step behind the curtain. I take a deep breath. I lied. The part about my coworkers being helpful was true, but me saying that I love this hospital? It's not true. I still feel like I'm not where I'm supposed to be, and that fact makes me feel heavier as I leave the auditorium.

I feel a pair of arms wrap around me. "You were amazing!" Eliana shrieks, jumping up and down.

Caroline follows, squeezing me tight. "You looked so mature up there, so smart. I am so proud of you, honey."

I make eye contact with Sean and catch him already staring

at me. He gives me a knowing smirk and I bite my lip, trying not to return it. His gaze settles behind me and hardens.

Caroline lets me go and large arms wrap around me from behind. "Bitch!" An older physician glares at Jonah as she walks by. I feel him shrug. "You did so good! Way better than I could have."

He lets me go and stands beside me. "I know I did." He goes to ruffle my hair and I smack his hand away. This slick back took me thirty minutes and I will not be letting anyone near it.

Caroline grabs both of them, along with Ethan, who apparently tagged along, and takes them to a poster about Arthritis. Sean waits until they are far enough away and lurches forward, scooping me up in his arms.

"Sean!" I shriek as he spins me around. "Put me down!"

My giggles fill the hallway, and he slowly lowers me to the ground, keeping his arms on my waist. "You were amazing. Seriously. I might want to be a nurse now."

"Please do not. I've seen the way you talk to patients."

He rolls his eyes. "Don't be jealous of my charm. We should celebrate. Dinner before my mom leaves? My treat."

"Italian. I have to stay for a little longer, but I could meet you guys there?"

"Sure. I'll send the address."

He walks towards the rest of them, and they leave, heading back to wait at the apartment. I even see Jonah walk with him, and try not to gasp at the sight. Once they're gone, I head back into the auditorium to wait for the first presentation. Kaydee finds me and we suffer through it together, groaning when we see how many are left. This is going to be the longest day of my life.

* * *

Sean

Mom, Eli, Ethan, Jonah (unfortunately), and I all ended up at the apartment after Summer's speech. She didn't end up going on stage until about 11:30 AM so we got back, ate random snacks from the fridge, and sat around until around 6 PM when Summer said she could probably sneak out.

We load into two cars and head to the restaurant, me and Ethan in one, Eliana, Mom, and Jonah in the other. I see Summer's car and park next to her, then get out and open her door.

"That was the worst day of my life." She looks up at me, grabbing the hand I offer. She limps onto her feet, wincing at the contact with the ground. "These are the stupidest shoes ever. Why are we still torturing women with these? It's honestly medieval."

I grab onto her waist so she can lean into me, taking some of the pressure off. We walk into the restaurant with everyone following after us while Jonah tells the story of how he totaled his car last week.

"How many?"

"Six," I tell the host, and he leads us to the table I reserved and hands us menus. Summer sits next to me, with Eliana on her other side. Mom sits across from Eli, with Jonah in the middle and Ethan across from me. Jonah is still yapping—loudly at that—and Ethan laughs, giving me an amused look. I kick him.

"What the hell?!" He whisper-shouts.

"We don't laugh at his jokes."

Summer elbows me and turns back to Jonah, who is

completely unaware. We order a round of drinks and toast to Summer when they come.

"Thank you guys for coming, I really appreciate it."

Eliana pulls her into a side hug. "Of course we came. Jonah even tried to smuggle Gouda in, but Sean said no."

Jonah frowns. "I just wanted you to have a support base. But instead of your child, he brought this random guy," he points to Ethan.

Ethan shrugs. "I'm always down for a day off. Sorry, your rat couldn't come."

"Mouse." Summer corrects. "But thanks for showing up, I guess. It's good to see you."

"Yeah, you too." I kick him again.

Our food comes, and we eat, mostly being entertained by Jonah's stories. I try to block him out, but it's impossible because of his extreme volume. Eliana and Summer cackle at his ridiculousness while my mom just beams, shaking her head. Ethan seems genuinely interested, which I'll have to talk to him about since he's supposed to be my friend. Overall, it was a surprisingly fun group.

We leave the restaurant slightly buzzed and full, piling into the cars. Mom goes on her own, heading straight home and Eliana takes her car and drops everyone else back at home so that Summer can get home quicker since her feet hurt. I ride along, ready to call it a night too.

We pull into the complex, and Summer stumbles out of the car, complaining about her feet again. Tired of hearing it, I scoop her up bridal style and walk with her into the building.

"SEAN! Put me down. If I rip this suit, then I won't be able to return it."

I shush her mouth with my finger. "I'll pay for it."

She bites my finger, and I yelp, giving her a glare. Satisfied, she leans her head onto my shoulder, too tired to fight it any longer. I carry her to the door and fumble with my keys, opening it to see that the lights are open. "What the hell?!"

I stare at the couch, where two older people sit, a man and a woman. Summer pokes her head up to see what caused my reaction, then leaps out of my arms, somehow landing on her feet.

She stands there, mouth wide open. "Dad?"

Thirty-One

Summer

I stand in the living room staring at the people in front of me.
I haven't seen my parents since I left for college. I graduated
from high school in May, five years ago. They didn't come,
but still threw a huge graduation party so that they could brag
to their friends. I wasn't allowed to invite any.

The summer had consisted of them avoiding me completely.
They went on random "business" trips back to back until it
was time for me to leave. They didn't say goodbye, just stayed
in their bedroom until Eliana and I packed up my room and
left.

But here they are. Mom looks the same, probably the Botox.
Her long blonde hair mirrors mine, but hers is pin-straight
at all times. She says that textured hair is just another word
for unruly. Her frame is petite. We never could share clothes
because I was at least two sizes bigger than her. Her eyes are
the same too. Soft, pleading, nothing like the rest of her.

Dad, however, looks like he has aged twenty years. His

brown hair has turned mostly gray, and his wrinkles have tripled in quantity. He's wearing a suit, like always. I can't remember the last time I saw him out of one. When I was a kid, they used to get ready before I got up and get unready after I had gone to bed. He looks like he's gained some weight and now has a slight beer belly. Huh. Guess business isn't booming.

"I'm just gonna wait over there." Sean backs out and B-lines for my room, shutting the door quietly once he's inside.

After that day, I truly thought that I would never see them again. I stayed on campus over breaks and went to Eliana's on holidays. I was fully prepared to walk myself down the aisle one day. I was ready to tell my children that they didn't have any grandparents on my side. And when they passed, I thought I would read about it in the papers.

I had made peace with the fact that they were done with me, and me with them. I worked through school, got scholarships, and paid my loans off. I never wanted to rely on them again, financially, or otherwise.

I put my hands behind my back and fiddle with my fingers. "What are you doing here?"

Why does their presence unsettle me so much? I was certain that when I saw them again, I would tell them to shove it. But here I am, cowering like a kid again.

My father stands, and my mother follows, like always. She could never be her own person and had to go along with everything he said, even if I could tell she disagreed. "We came to visit you. Maybe you could act a little less ungrateful about it."

My mother grabs his elbow. "Exactly. We drove all the way over here and you haven't even offered us something to drink."

"Maybe because you weren't invited."

His face forms into disgust. "How could we have raised a daughter so impolite and rude? We came here thinking you had gained some class after your stunt back home."

My jaw clenches. "Don't know where you got that idea."

Mom puts a hand on her hip. "Our friends sent us a post of the itinerary for the conference you spoke at today. Do you know how embarrassing it was? Having to pretend like we knew our daughter was speaking at a major conference?"

I say nothing.

"And that we weren't invited." My dad continues. "So we showed up. Watching you up there, I thought, 'Maybe she is my daughter after all'. I was ready to offer you that spot in my company. You looked so professional up there. I wouldn't even require marriage right away."

"I'm not interested."

"Oh, not to worry." He cuts in. "The offer no longer stands. I can see that you haven't matured one bit. Who is that guy you ran in with, Summer?"

I grit my teeth at the mention of Sean on his lips. "None of your business."

"Is he your boyfriend?" Mom buts in.

"No."

Dad sighs. "Just as I thought. You run in here with some random guy, laughing like a delinquent? Grab your shit, Monica. Our daughter is the same slut as before."

"What the fuck did you just say?"

Sean

I can't listen to another word of it. I sat here, ear glued to the door, trying to not barge out and stop them from disrespecting her. But after that? No way in hell.

I burst through the door, stepping right up to his face. At my height, I'm towering over him, but he doesn't seem to mind. He lifts his jaw in defiance, puffing his chest out.

"He didn't mean it." The woman, who I've gathered is her mom, says.

"Oh, I fucking meant it. She's a slut." He glances over at Summer. "At least in high school, you picked guys with a future. Maybe you have changed after all."

"I'm gonna give you five seconds," my tone turns deadly, "to get the fuck out of our apartment, out of respect for her. She is single handedly the brightest, most resilient woman I have ever met. So, if I get to five and you're still here, I'm taking it as a sign."

He backs down slowly, grabbing onto his wife's wrist. He pulls her away as she's grabbing her coat, and yanks her towards the door. She whips her head back, looking at Summer one last time before they're gone.

She crumbles and I catch her. We lower to the ground, her falling into my arms, sobbing. "I don't know why I let them get to me."

I put my mouth to her hair, kissing it softly. "It's nothing to do with you. They've tried to instill power over you since you were young. It's normal that it would stick."

"They're right." She sobs. I grab a reach for a tissue from the coffee table, handing it to her. She blows into it and I take it back, giving her a fresh one. "About all of it. They're right."

I grab her face, forcing her to look at me. "Don't you dare say that shit ever again. You're nothing like what they say you are."

"I am." She curls into me, dropping her head to my chest. "Or I was, at least."

I sigh into her hair. "You don't have to tell me."

"I want to."

I rub her back, before picking her up and settling her on the couch. I put a blanket over her and stand up, walking to the kitchen. I grab the kettle, fill it with water, and throw it on the stove to let it heat up. I don't even know if she drinks tea, but it seemed soothing. I look through the cabinet, but all I find is hot chocolate. Will she still drink it if I used water? Should I just restart? But I don't want to make her wait.

Screw it. I throw the powder into a mug and fill it up with hot water. I bring it over to her and sit down. She takes a sip.

"Did you use water in this?"

Shit. "Yeah?"

She takes another sip. "How'd you know I don't like it with milk?"

"I know you." *Smooth.*

I sit there watching her take sips, clearly avoiding talking. It feels like this is becoming a common theme with us. I mean seriously, how did we get here? Just a few months ago, we couldn't be in the same room without attempting to annoy the other person. And now, we have these deep conversations constantly.

"I had a rough few years in high school. I don't know how much Eliana told you…"

"Not much. Just that your parents had some high expectations that you felt like you couldn't match."

She nods. "Exactly. Except their expectations weren't just high. They were impossible. I remember when I started playing chess, they put me into a competition fit for adults.

I was nine. I didn't even like chess, thought it was stupid and boring. But to them, it was a dignified and classy sport. Something a professional should know how to do.

"Not that I was supposed to be a real professional." She puts her mug on the coffee table and settles further into the couch, wrapping herself in the blanket like a burrito. She tries to stretch her legs, but I'm in the way, so I place them over my lap. "I was paraded around just for appearances. So that they could show everyone the business was still in the family, but it would be a man, my husband, running it."

"That makes no sense."

"To them it did. I was going to play-dates with their friends' sons since I was in diapers. They wanted to see who would look best with me, who would be a good representative of the company. The older I got, the more I hated it. The guys were jerks, all they cared about was money and collecting the perfect wife, AKA doll."

She leans back, snuggling into the pillow. "When I met Eliana, I finally realized what having true friends was like. They wanted to separate us immediately, didn't see her as a 'fit friend' for someone like me. That was the first time I rebelled. Told them that if they separated us, I wouldn't attend another dinner. That I would sabotage every business operation they had. I was thirteen."

I run a hand down my face. "Jesus."

"They said that if I behaved perfectly, that I could keep her as a friend. But it didn't matter. I saw the power that I could have over them for once. There was no chance that I was giving it back. So, I pretended to behave for a little while. And then I just got tired of pretending.

"Instead of golfing or boating with their friends' sons, I

started sleeping with them. The guys were fine with it, because why wouldn't they be? But it made them uninterested in me as a wife. They saw me as flighty, unreliable, a slut. And so did their families. My parents lost every chance at an arrangement that they could get. They were furious."

I rub her feet, urging her to continue. I had an idea of what had happened when she was younger. She never tried to make it a secret. She wasn't ashamed of her past because of how she had grown from it. But when you add her parents into the mix, that's where her regret roots from.

"They found out why and threatened to disown me. They planned to never let me see Eliana again, to send me to boarding school, anything they could think of, really. They said the only way that I could redeem myself was by lying low for the rest of high school. Stop partying, stop sleeping around, just focus on grades and college. I was supposed to go for business, an Ivy, just like my dad.

"I did what they asked for a while. I was scared of losing Eliana and never liked the life I was living, just felt like I had to keep some sort of reputation for myself, even if it was a bad one. But then I met Noah."

My grip on her feet tightens a little and she kicks me, giving me a knowing look. "Sorry."

"Sure. Anyway, he was the son of my dad's competitor. Was supposed to take over his dad's company like I was sort of supposed to take over mine. I didn't know who he was when I met him. We were at some charity banquet, and he invited me to dance. I was going to say no, I had lost all interest in guys at this point. But he was different. More charming than any guy my age, had so much confidence, such a good energy around him. I couldn't refuse.

"When my dad saw us together, he flipped out. I had never seen him that mad. He told me I could never see Noah again, but that just made me want to see him more. Our paths started crossing often, I went to parties again just to see him. I was obsessed. More about how my parents disapproved than anything, but I liked him at least."

"We started dating." She yawns, clearly trying to stop the sleep from coming over her. "I was hesitant to have sex with him. I didn't want him to be like one of the guys from my past. But he was insistent, knew of my reputation, and thought that my refusal meant that I didn't like him or wasn't attracted to him. Eventually, I got tired of fighting and we slept together.

"He had me leave right away and claimed that his dad was supposed to come back soon but that he'd call me. I went home, and when I got there, I found my dad in a fit of rage. Turns out that Noah had recorded us, and sent it to my dad to mess with him."

My eyes widen. "Are you fucking kidding me?! Where is this guy?"

"Doesn't matter. He wasn't planning on actually doing anything with it. I was hurt by the situation, but mostly because I didn't think of it first. I wouldn't have done what he did, but realizing that he had found a way to use me to make my father mad, it just about killed me. My parents stopped talking to me after that.

"I was done with that life, anyway. I kept my head down until graduation, secured a spot at the same university as Eliana, and left as soon as I could. Today was the first time I saw them since."

"I'm so sorry, sunshine. You didn't deserve them for parents."

"Maybe. But the loss wasn't big. I had never loved them as much as a kid should love their parents, nor did they love me like that. If anything, I mourned the fact that I never got a family, not that I had lost mine."

I pick her up, taking her to her room. I couldn't hear her talk about them anymore, and I could see how tired she had become. I tuck her in and lean down to kiss her forehead.

"You didn't lose your family. We're right here."

I turn to leave, but she grabs my wrist, stopping me. "Stay."

So I do.

Thirty-Two

Summer

"We have a problem."

Jonah and I are in our normal spot at the nurses' station, snuggled up with our blankets. Ever since I agreed to speak at that conference, Tammy has been extra nice with the schedule.

"Great. It's always something." Jonah grumbles, leaning his head back against the top of his rolling chair.

I pout, noticing his grouchy attitude. "Is the abstinence not going as well as you predicted?"

"Not quite," he sighs. "I seriously had no idea how much of a role sex had in my life. I feel like I'm annoyed all the time."

"Maybe try a hobby."

He shoots me a glare. Jonah and I used to bond over the fact that we had no real interest in relationships. We both were very pro-casual people. But recently, neither of us has been acting that way.

"I think I like Sean." I bury my face in my hands. "Like a lot."

I peek at him through the gaps in my fingers and see him

staring at me with a bored expression.

"That's it?"

I throw my hands into the air. "What do you mean 'that's it?' this is bad!"

"Why would this be bad? There are worse people to like. Sean is a great guy, who has a family that loves and accepts you, and you've liked him for a while."

"Excuse me?" I pull my knees to my chest, resting my face on them. "This is a new revelation."

He throws me an obvious look. "You have liked Sean since the minute he got to your apartment, probably even before that."

"You are ridiculous," I say, nose wrinkling. "I had absolutely no interest in him until we started spending more time together."

"Maybe consciously. But no one else in your life has had such an impact on what you do. When Eliana and I tell you to do something, you take it into consideration. When he does, you trust his word more. Plus, he's the hottest guy you've ever seen."

"I trust your word." I won't argue with the other part because I'm not a liar. "I just didn't realize how much depth he had to him. And he's a genuine guy. Like a true gentleman, says things that make my insides turn warm. And he's clingy. Which I didn't even know I wanted, but I'm realizing that it makes me like him more."

He smirks. "Yeah, you want his hands all over your body."

I blink. "Stop. This is serious. He doesn't like me back."

"Alright." He grabs my hands. "Enough with that. That man looks at you like he wants to have your babies and rip your clothes off all at once. He also looks at me like he wants to burn me alive, just because I have a past with you. So what do you think that means?"

"He's homophobic?"

He drops my hands and shakes his head. "Seriously. That man likes you back. So stop wasting time."

"I have to sit with this for a while." I stand up and stretch my legs, and grab a wipe to clean off my computer. I wipe down my phone and water bottle for good measure, too. "It wouldn't matter if he did. I wouldn't risk losing Eliana."

"Summer." He says in a bored tone. "I am slowly losing patience here. Eliana is your best friend and his sister."

"That's the problem." He glares at me for cutting him off. "Sorry."

"She would never pick between you. And it wouldn't be a big deal, anyway. Sean is probably planning on moving out soon, so the only time you would see him should something go wrong is holidays, which are usually awkward either way."

"I guess." I print out my report sheet and start highlighting. Is Jonah right? Could Sean actually feel the same way? But I don't want to lose him if it's not mutual.

"So that's it? We're not gonna talk about your parents randomly showing up at your apartment for the first time in five years?"

"I'd rather not." I grumble.

"Look." He snatches the highlighter out of my hand, capping it. "I've let you get away with being dark and mysterious for too long. I'm worried that one of these days everything's just gonna explode out of you and instead of a nurse, you'll be a patient. On the psych floor."

I reach to take the marker back, but he shoves it in his back pocket. "One, absolutely not. I've met some of those nurses, and I'm scared. And two, there's nothing bubbling up. I'm fine. Great even! My asshole parents showed up and told me I was the same slut they remember. Big whoop."

"I'd say." He cocks a brow. "Talk to me. You have to be a little bothered by this."

"Not really. I gave up on them a long time ago."

"Sure, but it still has to hurt."

I rub my forehead. "I don't know. It opened up old wounds, to be sure, but I feel like it should have hurt more? They're my parents. No matter what I do, they're still my blood. But I'd be fine to never see them again."

"Even your mom?"

"Especially her."

He bites the inside of his cheek. "I thought he was worse?"

"He is." I nod. "But she let him control my life. Nothing I did was good enough. I remember one time, I had gotten a perfect score on my spelling test. I was seven. My teachers knew that I was the smartest in the class at everything but spelling.

"I studied non-stop until the next test. When I saw the score, I was ecstatic. I thought that he would finally be happy for me. I practically skipped into his office when I got home. I didn't know he was in a meeting."

I chuckle softly. "He was so mad. I can still see the look on his face. Wild eyes, sweat sheened across his forehead, flushed skin. He looked at me like I was a stranger. At that moment, I realized that he hated me. That he would never look at me as a child, only his biggest disappointment."

"You were a child."

"You don't understand." I snap. "I am not some broken girl with daddy issues. I don't sit at home and pout about my nonexistent childhood. I have a life. I have friends, and a job, and millions of things to be grateful for. I hate my father. But not enough to ruin my adulthood, too."

Jonah pats my head soothingly. "I'm sorry. I didn't mean to pry."

"It's fine. But to answer your question, yes. I hate my mother too, because when I walked out of that room with tears welding in my eyes, you wanna know what she said? 'Your father is working. Stop bothering us and go to your room'. Didn't look at me when she said it. I am an inconvenience to both of them."

He plasters on a goofy smile. "You aren't to me."

"I know I'm not. I'm a treat. And neither of them will ever understand that. I'm okay with it. So yes, they showed up at my apartment. And I don't plan to invite them back."

"Okay."

I nod. "Okay."

One of his patients hits the call light, and he groans, then gets up. I sit back down and put my head on the desk, resting it over my folded arms. I just want this week to end.

Stupid parents. Stupid work. Stupid Sean. Everyone and everything is stupid. My wallowing is interrupted by a tap on my shoulder. I look up to see Mia, another nurse on my unit. "Hi, Summer."

I sit up more. *Seriously, can I catch a break today?* "Uh, hi Mia."

She welcomes herself to my area and sits in the spot Jonah was just occupying. She places her hands in her lap, then looks back at me. "I went to the conference, listened to you speak. You did good up there. I was surprised."

"You came over here to give me a backhanded compliment?"

Her eyes narrow. "No. I came over here to be nice, but you tend to make that pretty impossible. Ask me why I was surprised."

I lean back with caution. "Honestly, I don't know if my ego can take another hit right now."

"That's fine," she mirrors my position, putting her short brown hair into a small ponytail. "I'll tell you, anyway. The truth is, we all were expecting you to freeze. Mess it up completely."

My jaw drops. "Wow. Thanks for having some faith in me."

"Look, believe it or not, I actually don't dislike you, unlike most people on this unit." She leans against the desk, cocking an eyebrow. "Humor me. Why would management give you the speech when most people here are open about their distaste towards your attitude?"

I slouch, already bored with this conversation. "Tammy said they wanted me to do it because I'm pretty and young and people like that."

"You seriously believed her? Since when did hospitals pick representatives based on how attractive they are?"

"Honestly, I didn't care enough to think about it."

"That's your problem." She snaps, pointing at me. "You don't care. About anything. The patients love you, and your actual etiquette as a nurse is fantastic. But you don't try to get along with anyone but Jonah. You don't respect the older nurses. You don't go to any holiday parties or get-togethers. You don't try."

"I don't get paid to try. And my respect is earned."

"Unfortunately, that's not how this profession works." I think this is the longest conversation I've ever had with Mia. I mean seriously, she usually sits at the station quietly and reads in her free time. Since when was she keeping a record of me? "Management asked the staff who should do the speech. No one wanted to do it, so they volunteered you because they like you the least."

My jaw drops again. "What the hell? I get that I might not be that involved, but since when did everyone hate me?"

"We don't hate you, I don't at least. The problem is, we can tell that your heart isn't in it. You don't like working here, and it rubs off on everyone else. It's no secret, so why are you still here?"

The truth is, I thought everyone in nursing was burnt out. Even though I've been barely working here for a year, I want to cry every time I realize that this could be where I might stay forever.

"Because where else would I go? I haven't been working here long enough to give it a fair shot. I come in everyday, praying that nursing will become the career that I imagined in my head. And every day I leave disappointed."

She grabs my hand. "I worked in the ICU before coming here, did you know that?"

"No, I didn't."

"You didn't because you've never talked to me before." She gives me a small smile. "I started there as a new grad. I worked so hard to avoid Med-Surg because I didn't want to be like all of my classmates who got stuck in units like this. I was there for about a year and hated every minute of it. I wanted to talk to my patients, to see them get better. But I saw more people discharged to the morgue than anywhere else.

"I knew that I had to get out. So I applied to transfer units. The only spot they had open was this position, and I took it as a filler. I thought that I would just come until they had something more attractive open up. But I never left. Because this unit was everything that I was missing."

"That's great, but I don't really understand why you're telling me this."

She drops my hand, playfully rolling her eyes. "I'm telling this because you need to find a place that looks like everything you dreamed of. Every field of nursing is different. Just because you don't like this one, doesn't mean you hate the profession as a whole. Go find your dream unit, Summer."

She gives me one last smile of encouragement, then walks away.

Jonah slips beside me, looking confused. "Were you just talking to Marly?"

"Her name's Mia. And she's actually pretty cool."

Thirty-Three

Summer

"Can one of you give me a ride before you go?"

Eliana and I are in the middle of getting ready for pottery class when Sean barges in, saying that he needs us to drop him off somewhere. I glance at him, trying to control the butterflies that appear in my stomach when he smiles at me. "We're riding together so you can just take Eliana's car."

He throws a bag over his shoulder. "Actually, I'm going to the airport, so I'll need dropped off."

Eliana whips her head around. "The airport? Why?"

"There's a business trip in Oklahoma that Ethan needs to attend." He steals her charger, shoving it into his bag as well. "Apparently, he wants me to go with him."

My face morphs into confusion. "You guys work in construction. What business would there be in Oklahoma?"

"Um," he lets out a cough. "I'm not sure actually, Ethan just dropped this on me last night. So, ride? On the way to pottery?"

"Ugh." Eliana starts rushing around her room, throwing clothes everywhere. "Sean, it's not really on the way! But fine. Now get out."

He holds prayer hands up at her and walks out, shutting the door behind him. We look at each other. "That was weird, right?"

I nod. "Totally weird."

We make him sit in the back seat and sing at the top of our lungs to torture him a little for the detour. We kick him out at the front door, and he tells us to send Pam his love after we make him promise to be safe. Once he's out of the car, we book it out of there, knowing Pam won't appreciate us being late.

I throw the car into the parking spot and we jump out, sprinting into the studio. Shelly is at the front desk, like always, and beams when she sees us. "Girls! So good to see you. Come in quick, the class just started."

"Yes, ma'am!" We yell, running towards our normal room. We push through the door and every set of eyes turns to us. Our classmates are different than usual, but Shelly set our new sessions up so that they are all on week three like us.

Pam doesn't notice at first, because she's helping a student near the back of the class. She looks up to flip a hair out of her face and that's when she sees us. Her eyes flutter shut, and she places a hand across her forehead, looking like she got an instant migraine.

I grin and walk towards her, throwing my arms around her small frame. "Aw, you missed me!"

She jerks at the contact and tries to wiggle out, but Eliana comes around behind her and closes us all into a group hug. "We couldn't continue in our pottery journey without you, so we had Shelly reschedule us as a surprise!"

She huffs. "I should've known Autumn and Elena were you two."

We let her go, and she heads straight to the back, returning with two aprons. We accept them graciously, and take the only open seats that are conveniently front and center.

"Sorry class for the interruption," her eyes cut towards us. "I will continue with what I was saying earlier. I've already passed out clay, so I will grab you girls some when I'm done. Now I know I'm a new face for some of you…"

"Don't be silly Pam! We're old friends!"

She ignores my outburst and continues with her introduction. "Like I said, SOME of you have not met me before. My name is Pam, and I primarily teach the beginner classes here. You've learned two basic pottery techniques up until this point, so we like to give you creative freedom for the last project. Then, next week, we will glaze the pieces so that they have some color.

"With that being said, I will leave all creative decisions up to you. I'll pass out tools should you need them, and you may go! I'll be around in case you need anything."

I take a moment to decide on what to make, but then it comes to me, and I get started. Eliana turns to me with a frown. "What are you making? I have no idea what to do."

"Just a gift for someone. Maybe you could make a decoration for your room? What about a little plane to represent your work?"

Her face lights up. "Yes! That's so cute. You're so smart, S."

We get to work on our projects. She attempts to make some fancy plane that she always ogles, its name being some arrangement of letters and numbers that I can't remember. It ends up looking like a potato with wings, so she decides to make a paper airplane instead.

My project is going exactly how I envisioned it. Even though I have a feeling I'll never admit to Sean that I like him, I want to give him something to remind him of our outings, something he'll have to remember me by when he eventually moves out. With there only being one more of our sessions planned, and him getting a promotion at work a little while back, I have a feeling he'll leave soon.

With no more excuses to spend time with him, Eliana will be the only connection between us. Even if we've started a friendship of sorts, I don't think he'll put any effort into it once he finds his own place. It was for convenience.

So I decide to make him a toolbox. It's small, and decorative, not meant to have any function. On the outside, I keep it simple, so he can put it up in his house someday if he wants. But on the bottom, I put our names and the date that he first opened up to me. Without me witnessing his panic attack, I don't think I ever would've seen the kind of person he truly is, and I want him to know that.

When the shape is done, I make little tools to go inside. A wrench, for the time we played laser tag. A hammer, for the time we went to that awful therapy group. A screwdriver, for the time we volunteered at the hospital. A drill, for the time we visited his father's grave. And a nail, for the last day I have planned.

The tools end up being about the size of my palm each, so I have just enough space to write the dates of all of our outings on them. I take time on all of the pieces, making sure they are detailed and neat. When I'm done, they don't look professional by any means, but they look like I tried while making them.

Eliana clears her throat from beside me, pulling me out of my concentration. "This looks beautiful, Summer."

I look down, suddenly self-conscious about the project. What if he hates it? Or thinks it's weird that I put this much thought into it?

"Look at me." She turns her body so that she's facing me fully, and waits for me to mirror her position. "It's for him, isn't it?"

I let out an awkward laugh. "Who?"

She gives me an obvious look. "Sean." My eyes go wide. "Don't give me that look. Even if I hadn't noticed anything, you literally made a toolbox, and he works construction. It doesn't take a genius to figure out."

"What do you mean by, 'even if I hadn't noticed anything'?"

She sighs. "Summer, I love you, but you can be very unaware of your surroundings. Did you seriously think I wouldn't notice the two of you sneaking off every Tuesday at the exact same time? Or the fact that he continued to sleep in your room even after Mom left? Or just the googly eyes you guys make at each other? I'm an adult. I know when two people are together."

"What?!" I scoff. "That's ridiculous. We aren't together. We just have a friendship that has planned hangouts."

She rolls her eyes. "You're really trying to tell me you haven't slept together?"

"No! We haven't!"

Her eyebrows knit together. "Oh. Well, it doesn't change the fact that I can see you like each other, maybe even more than like."

I bite my lip, starting to feel the embarrassment. "It's one-sided, at least I think. Are you mad? I swear I wasn't trying to hide it from you. I just realized it recently and didn't want to make anything weird. I won't pursue it, I promise."

"I don't want you to promise that." She grabs my clay-covered hands and places them within her own. "You're my best friend. Why would I ever want to take something away from you that could make you happy? It's the same with him. He's my brother, and I want him to be with someone who deserves him. And you do. If anything, he doesn't deserve you."

I feel a small tear run down my face. Why am I crying? "Even with your blessing, I don't think I can do it."

She squeezes my hands. "You have to."

"Why?"

"Because I've always wanted a sister."

At that moment, Pam appears out of nowhere, making us break apart. She peeks over our heads and makes a small noise of approval.

"Well. I won't lie and say I'm not surprised. This really is fantastic work, both of you. Eliana, your airplane has no inappropriate look to it, and Summer, your piece has a lot of meaning behind it, I can tell. And we got through the day with no accidents. It's truly a miracle."

I grin. "Exactly! Maybe we can even abandon the aprons next time!"

Her smile drops. "I wouldn't go that far."

She takes our pieces and our aprons, silently dismissing us. We wash our hands and leave the room, prepared to chat with Shelly before we leave.

"Girls! Was Pam surprised?"

I put an elbow on her desk, leaning my head against it. "She was ecstatic. We had a real breakthrough today."

"Oh! Well, that's just fantastic! The only problem is Pam has a doctor's appointment next week during your lesson."

Eliana snickers from beside me. "Oh, you know what? Why don't you just throw us into one of her classes?"

"Hm." She starts typing away on her computer, looking for some availability. "Shoot. I have some bad news. Pam doesn't have any more beginner's classes for a while."

No. We haven't gone this long with Pam for her to duck out on us on the last day. I'm about to ask for a spot in whatever her next class is when an idea pops into my head. "What about private lessons?"

She tsks. "We could set you up with one, but it couldn't be next Saturday. I could do it a few weeks after, but there would be an up-charge since it's private."

"Pam's time is priceless to us."

She places a hand over her heart. "That is just about the sweetest thing I've ever heard. I'll add the two-hundred to your tab."

Eliana elbows me in the side. "Oh! How…great. Just like last time, put us under different names. Maybe ones that are a little less obvious."

She winks. "Will do! See you then."

"Was that really worth two-hundred dollars?" Eliana says out of the corner of her mouth as we leave.

"To see the look on Pam's face? Absolutely."

Thirty-Four

Sean

Ethan and I get to the hotel and drop our bags off, deciding to head down to the bar. We'll be here until Monday, but don't have to do any work until tomorrow. The company that's selling wanted us and the other potential buyer to come to a party they're hosting, almost like a last hurrah. Then, while we're here, we can decide if we're interested, and they can see who's a better fit.

We sit down on the wooden stools and wave over the bartender. "Scotch, for both of us, please."

She nods and leaves to grab it. Ethan spins towards me, resting an elbow on the counter. "We gotta have self-control this time, man. It didn't go so well on our last outing."

I cringe. "This time is different. You aren't getting freshly divorced. Or you might be? I actually don't know."

"Nothing has changed. I wanted to keep this trip under the radar, so I'm pretty certain she thinks I'm cheating on her."

I slap a hand against my forehead. "Jesus."

230

He scratches the side of his head. "Yeah, not ideal. Let's talk about tomorrow. I think this could be really good for us, so try to be extra charming."

"I'm always charming."

He blinks. "If that's you being charming, then I need you to multiply it by like a hundred. If all goes well, we could end up putting an offer in before we leave. I've been working through everything with a lawyer and he says it's all set."

I slap a palm on his shoulder. "I'm so excited for you, man! So what will that mean for you? Are you going to hire a manager out here, or jump back and forth?"

"In the beginning, I'll probably split my time just so I know both places are running the way I like." Our drinks arrive and he grabs one, throwing it back in one gulp. "I'll have you run everything back home in between, unless you would be interested in taking over out here?"

I grab my drink, taking a sip. "I hadn't thought about it."

"You don't have to give me an answer right away, I know you just got back and probably want some stability. Just think it over. You could even come for a trial, to see if it's something you would consider."

"Maybe."

We decide to call it a night, knowing one drink should be a cut-off when we're together. We head up to our rooms, going our separate ways, and I step into the bathroom to get ready for bed. I go through my normal routine, feeling uncomfortable about the silence that looms. Normally, I would be able to hear Summer's music through the wall, but not here. Because she's not here.

I lay on the uncomfortable hotel bed, staring at the ceiling. I think about what Ethan mentioned. Could I really leave?

Even though it's probably time for me to find my own place, I just got reunited with Eliana, and Mom isn't too far away. Moving states could make them feel like I'm abandoning them all over again.

I eventually drift to sleep, with all of the questions replaying in my mind on repeat.

* * *

I wake up to the sun shooting through my eyes, making me groan on instinct. I throw an arm over my face, twisting away from the light. Grumbling, I try to hide back under the covers and trick my body into believing I never woke up, but it doesn't work. Overall, probably the worst sleep I've ever gotten. And I know why.

I'd gotten used to being with her. I found myself trying to make our schedules overlap, even if it was just for a few hours so that I could sleep with her in my arms. The feeling of having someone beside me when I woke up, the warmth that radiated from her body to mine, was unbeatable.

I don't think I can go without it again. I miss her. I've been away from Summer for a day, not even, and I miss her. I miss the smell of her hair, how the soft strands would tickle my chest. I miss the cute dance she does when she likes the food I make. I miss the huge T-shirts she wears, the ones that make it look like she's not wearing any pants. And I miss the sound of her laugh after I make a joke just to hear it.

I'm fucked. Completely and totally fucked. Somewhere along the way, I caught feelings for Summer Rhodes.

Summer

I honestly feel like a preteen that's crushing on a celebrity. Even though Sean has an actual presence in my life, he's always felt so far away. Before he left, it was because he had no interest in getting to know me. He also felt untouchable. He was my best friend's older brother, completely off-limits. Then he went away, and the distance made him seem almost fake.

And then he came back. Like a force of nature, Sean Jacobs has thrown the balance of my life off track entirely. He's been gone a day, and I miss him. Me. The girl who's never felt anything real for a man in the history of ever. I miss the smell of his aftershave, the one that's woodsy and smells unexplainably like a man. I miss the feeling of his stubble against my cheek when I wake up to him wrapped around me. I even miss the stupid smirk he makes when he's being an arrogant jerk.

I thought the best way to go about it would be to ignore it, and let the feelings fizzle away once there's distance between us. But now that I've experienced the distance, I can confidently say that my feelings are only getting stronger. Maybe Jonah is right. Maybe I have liked him for longer than I realized.

I'm pulled away from my thoughts by a knock at the door. I groan, knowing Eliana probably forgot her key again. I get up from the cocoon I've made for myself in bed and trudge over to answer it.

"You really need to be more responsible-" my voice trails off when my eyes collide with a pair of cold blue ones.

"Summer. You look…comfortable."

I ignore her comment. "What are you doing here, Mom?"

"I'm leaving your father," she rushes out. She eyes me

expectantly, waiting for me to open the door further. "Are you going to let me in or what?"

I stand shell-shocked and she huffs, squeezing her way in. I follow in after her and start looking for an offering. "Would you like some orange soda?"

Her nose turns up in disgust. "No, thank you."

We stand there awkwardly staring at each other. I gesture for her to sit and she does, then I settle in across from her.

"I'm sure you have some questions."

"Not really." I shrug. "Actually, maybe one. What took so long?"

She rolls her eyes. "Try not to judge. I know I was a terrible mother. I think about it all the time."

"I don't."

She crosses her legs, straightening the wrinkles out of her skirt over and over again, almost like a tic. "You don't what?"

"Think about it." I lean further into the stool, staring straight into her eyes. "Ever since you guys dismissed me, I haven't thought about you. That's what you would want, isn't it? To still have control over me, even when you have no presence in my life?"

She scoffs. "I never wanted you to be unhappy, even if it seemed like it at the time. The truth is, my parents had arranged my marriage to your father when I was young. His influence has hovered over me for my entire life. I thought that by turning you into the perfect daughter in his eyes, I could ensure that you wouldn't have to do the same thing that I did."

"Bullshit," I spit. I tried to stay civil, but for her to come in here and try to make an excuse for her controlling behavior? I shouldn't have expected anything else. "You thought that every decision I made was the wrong one. And a lot of them were, but only because your lack of warmth drove me to them. I never had a mom. I had a mother. Instead of teaching me how to live happily, you taught me how to be the perfect wife to some trust-fund kid so that I had to live the same horrible life that you do. You took your anger out on me."

Her face forms into regret. "That wasn't what I was trying to do! I swear. I agreed to let you know the sons of your father's friends, just because it would keep him busy. I thought that if I could make you into someone he saw fit to take over the business, you could make your own life for yourself. Everything I did was because I wanted you to never live like me."

"I don't live like you. And I am the only one that played a role in that." I stand up and back away, feeling the tension radiating off her. "No matter what your reasoning is, you knew that after I started acting out, he wouldn't give the company to me, no matter who I married. So what's your excuse for that? You saw that I was making a life for myself, one that you didn't agree with, so you shut me out."

Her facade breaks, a tear slipping from her eye. "I thought it would be easier. I knew that you hated me, and if I sided with you over your father, I knew how he would react. I thought that if I just let you hate me, you wouldn't have to live with him while he blamed you for my disobedience."

"Stop lying. You stayed with him years after I moved out. It had nothing to do with him. You just hated me."

"I didn't!" She sobs. "I don't. Summer, please."

She jumps up, walking to me. She grabs my face in her hands, cradling my cheeks. "You are the only good thing that came out of my marriage, and I'm sorry it took me so long to see it. You have to understand, I was raised to be his wife. Everything I have in life is connected to him. Without your father, I am nothing. I was scared. Of what he would do when I left. Of how alone I would become. I was scared."

A tear rolls down my face. "So what changed?"

"You did. No matter what anyone says, you have become an incredibly strong and successful woman. You were raised with shitty parents, you went through hell and back in school, you had every odd against you. And here you are. You have a life, you have people that love you. So I thought, 'if my daughter could become someone as strong as she is, then I can do this one thing.'"

"How are you gonna do it?"

"It's already done. I left him this morning, packed my things, and drove off."

I nod. "You can't stay with me."

"I know." She backs away, moving towards the door. She grabs her coat and keys, then turns back to me. "Maybe you could call sometime? When you're ready?"

I don't bother agreeing, and she leaves.

Thirty-Five

Sean

Ethan and I get to the party at around 5 PM. We spent the entire day on the job site, meeting the crew, and checking out the environment. I can practically feel the happiness radiating off of him, and if we get the chance to buy, I know he's going to take it. We didn't get to meet the CEO. He was spending the day setting up the venue.

His hard work paid off to be sure. It's an open-spaced ballroom, but they used rustic construction gear as decoration. An old bulldozer with flowers sprouting out of it, a crane holding dangling glasses of champagne. For a construction send-off, this definitely is not what I had in mind.

"Satisfied?"

I turn to my left to see an older man dressed in a suit. He gives me a bright smile, extending his hand out. "Jamie Woods, you're with Carter Construction, yes?"

I shake his hand. "I am. Sean Jacobs, it's nice to meet you, Mr. Woods. The place looks amazing."

"My wife's doing. I just did the heavy lifting."

Ethan shows up beside me at that moment, reaching his hand out as well. "Mr. Woods, it's such a pleasure. I'm Ethan Carter, we've spoken over the phone."

He clasps his hands over Ethan's. "Jamie, please. You are so much younger than I was expecting!"

"Oh," Ethan's face morphs into worry. "I hope that doesn't affect your decision at all."

Jamie smirks. "It does, but in your favor. I was eighteen when I started my company. Had nothing, built it from the ground up. I understand what it's like to be young and ambitious. It worked out for me. I'm sure it will for you too."

"Thank you, sir," Ethan says, beaming. "If I could be half as successful as you, I would consider myself lucky."

"My boy," Jamie chuckles, "you are already more successful than me. Just try and hang onto it if you can."

"Mr. Woods," I cut in and he grunts. "Jamie. Can I ask why you're selling?"

Ethan elbows me in the rib, and I hiss. He gives me an obvious look, eyes popping out of their sockets.

"It's quite alright. I'm selling because I'm too old to be in the game anymore. The guys I have managing alongside me are at the same stage in their lives, and no one on my crew wants the responsibility. When I was young, I planned on passing the legacy down to my children. Then my wife and I had two beautiful daughters that scream when dirt gets anywhere near them."

He lets out a loud laugh, and we follow. "Anyway, it made more sense to pass it on to someone who could help it grow, who had a passion for the work. And I think that's you, Ethan."

I see his eyes go wide, jaw-dropping. He sputters for a

moment, readjusting his suit jacket. "Jamie, are you sure? What about the other company?"

"They're too corporate for me." He puts a hand on Ethan's shoulder, giving him a hard pat. "You have heart. I can tell you'll run it right, plus my crew likes you a lot better than the other guy. And they think Sean here is scary, which I like."

Ethan barks out a laugh. "Sean? They think Sean is scary?"

"I'm very intimidating." I pout.

"Yeah, like a puppy."

I shoot him a glare and Jamie laughs again at our antics. "You boys. I should make my rounds, but if you contact your lawyer now, we could announce this by the end of the night."

He leaves to greet some other guests and Ethan snatches his phone out of his pocket, running to make the call. I take the time to circle the room, eyeing the pictures of how the company grew throughout the years.

"I'd remember if I saw a face like that around here before."

I look over to see a girl around my age, with short brown hair and olive skin. Pretty, but has nothing on Summer.

"I'm with Ethan Carter. He's the guy that's taking over the company if all goes well."

She smirks. "Good. I wanted to make sure that my father's legacy was being placed in good hands." She peaks down at the glass of scotch I'm holding. "I can see now that it is."

I peek down at my feet, feeling awkward. Why does it feel like I'm doing something wrong by talking to her? Even just looking at her, all I can see are the reasons why Summer is better. While this girl looks like a flirt, Summer is more bubbly, like her sarcasm can make you feel good inside. This girl's hair has tight curls, but Summer's is long and wavy. It reminds me of sunshine at the beach.

"Did I lose you?"

I blink. "Sorry, what were you saying?"

"I was just asking you for a dance."

I cringe, trying to find a way to reject her politely.

"You have a girlfriend?"

Summer's face flashes into my mind. "Something like that."

She shrugs, heading off to find her next victim. *Something like that? What am I saying?* I can't remember when the lines blurred, but Summer has started to occupy every thought across my mind.

I can't go there. I know I can't. I would never want to jeopardize her friendship with Eliana, or her place in my family. I'm not good enough for her. I can't force her to deal with the baggage that comes with me. But most of all, I can't let her get hurt because of me. I need some distance.

Summer

I turn my car off, letting out a long sigh. For the majority of the time I've worked on this floor, I knew that I wasn't happy, but I didn't think I had any other option. Now, with Mia putting ideas in my head about seeing what else is out there, it feels like every shift is even harder.

I trudge up to the unit and almost walk out when I don't see Jonah's name on the board. *Great. Just what I needed.*

I sit down while I have a few minutes before report to stalk my patients a little. I open the first patient's chart and try not to cry. Ninety-five years old, full code, Q4 dressing change, A&Ox1, incontinent, NG tube, combative sundowner, no sitter available. *Kill me now.*

"Summer! I haven't gotten to see you since your speech! You did amazing, by the way, really made us proud."

I cringe at her peppy and loud voice. Honestly, I don't have the energy to be nice to Tammy today. I spin around in my seat so that I can see her. "Can I ask you something?"

"Of course."

"Did you only ask me to give a speech because no one else wanted to do it, so they volunteered me?"

Her eyes widen, jaw going slack. "It really wasn't like that! I mean, yes, no one had much interest, but I wouldn't have had you do it if I didn't think you could."

"I don't like this job."

She nods slowly. "I had a feeling, but it's important, so you have to push through, anyway."

"I don't feel important."

She grabs onto my shoulders, bringing me to my feet. "But you are! We need someone in your position, and the patients love you! You are a valued member of this team."

The words fall out of my mouth before I can stop them. "I don't think I want to be on this team anymore."

She lets go of me, placing her hands at her sides. "You don't mean that."

"I do." My posture straightens a little. "I mean it. I don't fit well into the staff here, I don't like the acuity, and the patient population isn't what I expected. I can't do it anymore."

Her voice drops an octave. "What are you saying?"

"I quit."

She stands there, mouth wide open. "But…you- you can't just quit! That's neglect."

"I'll finish this shift and the rest of my schedule. But after that, I'm done. I need to see what else is out there. My letter of resignation will be on your desk in the morning."

I walk away, leaving her sputtering behind me. I take report from the dayshift nurse, who hugs me, and says she's proud. If I'm being honest, I don't even remember her name.

I meet all of my patients and do a med pass, then excuse myself to call Jonah. He picks up on the first ring. "Heyyy."

"I think I just quit my job."

The line goes silent, and then I hear a loud cackle. "Finally! I hated that place, it was about time."

"You can't leave too!"

He groans. "I'll wait it out a little longer, but I couldn't leave you there alone. Now there's nothing holding me back."

"You're ridiculous."

"You love it."

Thirty-Six

Summer

I've spent all day tossing and turning in my bed. Not that I'd ever admit it to anyone, but knowing Sean is coming back tonight has me more excited than I've been in a long time. I'm going to do it. I'm going to tell him how I feel, and if he doesn't feel the same, then at least I'll stop being tortured with the uncertainty.

Eliana worked today and her flight gets back at around the same time Sean's does so they're riding back to the apartment together. No longer being able to wait, I pad over to the couch and stare at the door, urging it to open.

After about 30 minutes, I feel myself giving in to the sleepiness. I grab a blanket and settle further into the couch, nodding off, when I hear keys jingling. I jerk up, leaping from my spot and onto my feet.

Eliana stumbles in first, mumbling, and heads straight into her room. Sean comes in after her, dressed in gray sweats and a black hoodie. Is it possible he got even more attractive in a weekend?

We make eye contact, and his eyes avert mine. Weird. "Hey!"

I walk to where he's standing, but he doesn't look at me, just continues to drop his bag and place his jacket on the hook. "Hi."

My heart drops. Did something happen while he was gone? He hasn't acted this cold towards me since before we became friends. Not even then. Maybe I shouldn't tell him. I could just wait-

No. I'm doing this. I can't chicken out now.

"So." I place my hands behind my back, fiddling with the waistband of my sleep shorts. "I have something to tell you. I think I have feelings-"

"Actually." He cuts me off, grabbing his bag. He steps away from me and drops it on the couch, then turns towards the bathroom. "I'm kinda tired. So."

He eyes me, then looks towards my bedroom door. "Oh! Right. Sorry."

I cross my arms over my chest and go into my room, leaving the door open so he can follow. When he doesn't, I turn back to see him making a bed for himself on the couch. I shut my door, flipping on the lock.

* * *

I had the worst sleep of my life. I woke up multiple times, hoping that if I opened the door, I would see him sleeping on the ground outside of it like a sad puppy. Was it the most realistic thought? Maybe not.

I walk out of my room to see him and Eliana in the kitchen, getting ready to eat breakfast. He slides her a plate, sees me,

and slides me one too without a word. At least he doesn't want me to starve.

Why does he have to look so good even when he's being an asshole? His hair is messy, making it look softer than normal. He isn't wearing a shirt, so I can see every outline of his body, scar included. Now that it's healed, it makes him look rougher, sexier. His pants hang low on his hips, the waistband of his underwear popping out.

Maybe he really was just tired, and his attitude wasn't about me at all. "So Sean, tell us about your trip!"

Eliana points her fork at him. "Yes! We still have no idea what business you could have in Oklahoma."

He shrugs. "Not much to tell."

So it wasn't a fluke. What has got him in such a mood? "Okay, well, I see that you aren't working today, but I need us to leave at around the same time as usual."

His eyes flick to mine. "That won't be necessary. I won't be needing your assistance anymore."

My chest hallows, and I begin to panic. What could I have done to make him act this way? I spent the whole time he was gone counting down the seconds until he was back. It felt like a part of me was ripped away. And now he can't have the decency to tell me what's wrong?

"Too bad. We have to go."

"Why?"

I blurt out the first thing that comes to mind. "If we don't, I'll lose my deposit. Of a thousand dollars."

Great. Now he's turned me into a liar.

The water he had just sipped gets caught in his throat, and he starts violently coughing. I run around the counter and wrap my arms around him, jerking him into the Heimlich maneuver.

He spurts out a laugh. "What the hell are you doing?"

"Saving your life! Obviously."

He grabs my hands and returns them to my sides, shaking his head. "What could possibly cost a grand, and why are you spending it on me?"

"I can't tell you, and it'll only cost that much if we don't show up."

He pinches the skin between his brows. "Fine. Be ready at five."

He then walks out of my reach and into the bathroom.

Sean

I splash some water on my face, hoping that if I'm lucky, I'll drown. I grab a towel and pat my face dry, peeking up at myself in the mirror.

I don't know if I can do this. I feel myself getting too close to her, too involved in her life. I won't allow myself to hurt her. I couldn't. But no matter how hard I try to push her away, the second I look into the warm pools of brown in her eyes, I feel my heart lurching towards her.

I decide to go out for the day, that way I can avoid her presence until tonight. I wander around the city, walk through parks, check out the library. I don't even like reading, but maybe I'll get some new audiobook inspiration. I try a new lunch spot and go to text her about it, before remembering I can't.

Eventually, the day gets away from me, and I trudge back to the apartment, mentally preparing myself to stay strong. I walk in the door and all thoughts vanish from my brain.

She sits on the couch, waiting for me. She doesn't notice that

I'm here, and continues to mess with something on her phone. She's wearing a short yellow dress, with a cream cardigan over top. Her hair is a beautiful mess, and her long legs are cleanly shaven. Shit.

"Let's go."

She jolts at my words and peers up at me. When she sees my expression, she gets up and walks straight out the door. As she passes, I smell her sweet perfume mixed with the shampoo she uses. I rub a hand down my face.

"Shit."

She turns back, confusion drawn on her face. "What'd you say?"

"Nothing," I mumble, snatching the keys from her hand.

The drive is long and antagonizing. She plugged the address into my Maps, and I don't even bother to hook Spotify up. We sit there in silence. Me brooding, her passive-aggressively sighing.

We arrive, and I park the car, reaching over to unbuckle her seatbelt. "Why are we at a dentist's office? Are you trying to say something?"

She rolls her eyes and opens her door. "Just follow me."

We walk next door, and I read the sign. I'm about to turn around when she stops me, grabbing my elbow with her soft hand. "Just hear me out."

"No. I don't need therapy."

She throws her hands over her hair, slowly dragging it back. She takes a long, scary breath and turns her eyes towards me in a deadly glare. "No. I am tired of your shit, Sean."

"W-"

She reaches up and places her hand over my mouth, silencing me. "No! It's not fair. For the longest time, I let you get away with being an idiot. You screwed with your physical, and mental health, without anyone else in mind. You flirt with me. You compliment me. You act like you care about me. You make me fucking feel things."

"I didn-"

She tightens her hold on my face. "Stop! You did. You fucking did and you know it. You are an asshole, Sean Jacobs. You made me feel things and then you come back and act like nothing changed between us. You dismissed me yesterday, and you dismissed me this morning and I'm done with it. I'm done with these games, I won't do it.

"And whether you like it or not," she removes her hand from my mouth, "you need therapy. A lot of it. You still have panic attacks, even though you try to hide it from me. You've made progress in processing everything that's happened, but you need help. And I am nowhere near a professional. So even though you acted like a stupid dickwad-"

"Seriously?"

She stomps her foot. "Seriously. I still want to help you. So you are going to go inside, and you are going to make an appointment with Dr. Wilson, and you are not going to say one word about it. Go."

I stay still and she kicks my shin, arms motioning towards the door. "Go!"

I understand why she's upset, I do. No matter how much I tried to control it, my feelings got in the way. I made her believe that there was potential for something to happen between us. Why can't she understand all the reasons it can't?

We're too different. She tries to put out this persona, and I wasted so much time believing it. She makes herself seem incapable of loving. She wants people to believe that she's cold and fearless, when in reality she's the opposite. She feels and yearns like everyone else. She is warm and contagiously bubbly. I would just bring her down.

Five years ago, maybe. But every extra day I spent fighting for my country was another layer of tissue added to my heart, scarred and tough. I can't be what she secretly hopes for. And she knows it.

"Jeez. Okay." I stumble towards the door, completely stunned about everything she had just admitted. I make an appointment like she asked, and walk back out to find her sitting on a bench with an annoyed expression. She sees me leave and gets up, walking towards the car. I follow, and she waits at her door for me to unlock it.

But what if I'm wrong?

"No." I turn in the opposite direction, walking away from the car completely. I trek through the parking lot, having no idea where I'm going, just that I'm not getting back into that car.

I hear her tiny stomps behind me and hear her screeching at me. "Sean! Get back here now. You have the keys, and I want to go home."

I keep walking, ignoring her protests. I hear her steps pick up into a run and she snatches my arm, twirling me to face her.

"You said something."

She crosses her arms over her chest, letting out a cute huff. "I said a lot of things. Thanks so much for noticing!"

"You said something about feelings."

She looks down towards the ground and I step into her, grabbing her chin and forcing her to look at me. "Tell me what you meant."

"What? So you can say nothing? Again?"

"Tell me." I plead.

She says nothing, eyes pouring into mine. "Fine. I have feelings. And I don't know how they got there or what to do with them, but they're here."

I smirk. "You like me."

"You are an asshole."

It turns into a wide smile. "I know." I look down at her lips, and she licks them on instinct. I tip her head up and tilt mine so that our mouths are an inch apart. "Tell me what to do and I'll do it."

She looks away and I hold her face, forcing her to meet my eyes. "We can't."

She's scared. I can see it all over her face. My family is all she has, it would be selfish of me to risk taking that away from her. She knows what would happen if things went wrong. She's dealt with enough loss in her life. But in this moment, I don't care.

I don't care what it means for the future. I don't care that I may not be ready. All I can think about is her. My heart is in my hands, my reason forced to the very back of my brain. I can deal with the consequences later. Right now, I need her. "Tell me, sunshine."

"Kiss me."

Thirty-Seven

Summer

He complies instantly, slamming his warm lips onto mine. One hand grips my hip, pulling me in so that I'm flush against him. His other cups my face gently, rubbing my cheek with his thumb. I let out a small moan at the sensation and he growls, inching me backward until I make contact with the cold exterior of someone's car.

He pins me to the door and pulls back. "What are you doing to me?" He asks hoarsely, before diving back into my lips.

My body is on fire from his touch, and I reach my hands into his hair, tangling it and tugging.

He groans and cups my hip harder until I can feel him against me. His tongue forces its way through my lips, demanding entrance. He's dominant and selfish, controlling and skilled. He nips my bottom lip and I yelp, then he runs his tongue over the now sensitive skin.

Our tongues intertwine in perfect harmony, like a dance that should never end. He attacks my mouth feverishly, taking his time, as if he wants to memorize every corner of it.

"Excuse me?!"

His body straightens and I duck out from under him, checking at whose voice interrupted us. I hear the car behind me unlock and a lady stands near the trunk, giving us a horrified look.

"This is my car."

My face turns beat red, and Sean stares at her before letting out a low chuckle. I smack his chest, but it only makes him laugh harder, triggering a giggle out of me. The lady stomps her foot and snatches her phone out of her purse, threatening to call the police and report us for public indecency.

Sean ignores her and grabs my waist, then throws me over his shoulder.

"Why does this keep happening?!" I screech, and he picks up his speed, jogging back towards our car.

He unlocks it with one hand and opens my door, lowering me to the ground, and helps me in. He leans over to buckle me in and stops at my face, giving me a peck on the lips. He shuts it and rounds the car, getting in next.

I stare straight ahead, a blush forming across my cheeks. He laughs again and starts driving, reaching over to place his hand over my own.

The tension within the car is high during the drive back, and I can feel him growing more and more frustrated at every red light we hit. My stomach is exploding with butterflies, and I'm unable to wipe the grin off my face. No one has ever kissed me like that, made me feel as important as he does.

When we finally get back to the apartment, he throws the car into park and jumps out. He gets to my side and yanks the door open, grabbing my hand, and drags me out. He interlocks our fingers and pulls me towards the entrance, threatening to throw me over his shoulder again.

We get into the elevator and he slams the 'close door' button, but someone rounds the corner and hops in before it goes into effect. The man seems completely unaware of the glare Sean throws at him, and the ride up to our floor is long and painful.

When we get into the apartment, he shoves me against the door, claiming my lips again. I can feel his grin against my mouth and I match it with one of my own. He picks me up and wraps my legs around his waist, carrying me into our bedroom. He stumbles over a shoe and sends us both flying into the bed. We lay on our backs, laughing.

He turns his head towards me. "Summer, what are we doing?"

I move my hand to his waistband, slipping it inside. "I can think of a few things."

He stiffens under my touch, enchanted by the feeling, before he snaps out of it and lets out a groan. He grabs my hand and pulls it back out, interlocking our fingers. "We shouldn't, not yet."

I snap up into a sitting position, turning away from him slightly. "Oh, okay."

"Hey." He sits up too, and grabs my jaw, forcing me to look at him. "I didn't mean it like that. I want to. You don't even know how much."

I sniffle. "You don't have to say that. It's fine." He grabs my hand, placing it over the front of his sweats. My eyes widen. "Oh."

"Yeah. Oh." He chuckles darkly. "I just don't think we should. Not like this. Not in secret."

He wraps his arms around me and pulls me down so that I'm lying on my side. He grabs the blankets from underneath us and pulls them up, then yanks me back to his chest. I flip around so that we're facing each other, him tracing the side of my face with a finger.

I run a hand down his arm, moving to his back and letting my nails trail down it. He shivers at my touch, leaning into it.

"What's your tattoo?" I've always been curious, and have seen him shirtless countless times, but have somehow never been able to look at it clearly.

Giving me a lazy smile, he lies on his stomach, stripping his shirt so that I can see it, and turns his head towards me. I try not to gawk at the sight. His arms bent over his head, muscles popping out.

Inked across his tan skin is the back of an eagle, wings spread, head down. On the head, there's a small date etched in Roman numerals, one I quickly recognize as the day his dad passed.

I run my hands down it, trying to memorize the picture with every touch. "A bald eagle? For America?"

He shakes his head. "The day of my dad's funeral, they were putting him in the ground and I couldn't watch. I didn't want my last sight of him to be of him leaving, so I looked up instead. I wanted him to see my face, to look down at me at that moment. Then I saw an eagle, flying between the breaks in the trees."

He moves back onto his side, propping himself up on an elbow. "I don't believe in reincarnation, but I thought it could maybe be him. Or a sign from him or something. I got it tatted before I left, wanting to always have a piece of him with me. I also just liked the idea that I was fighting for a country that had the eagle as a symbol. Made me feel close to him."

I cup his face with my hand. "You are a lot more than you let on to be, Sean Jacobs."

He scoffs. "Alert the media."

I roll my eyes. "Do you have any more?" He yields no reaction. "Tattoos."

He lets out a snicker, turning his head towards the ceiling.

"No!" I smack his arm. "You have to show me now. You can't give an evil laugh and then just turn away."

He catches my arm, drawing my hand in for a kiss. I snatch it back, then swing my leg over his hips, hoisting myself over him. I hold his arms against the mattress, pinning him so he can't move. "Show me!"

He laughs. "No."

I move one hand down, attempting to tickle him in the stomach. His body goes still, and he makes a blank face. "Did you just try to tickle me?"

"Uh-"

In a flash, I'm flipped onto my back. I look up to see him hovering over me, then he attacks. My body jolts at the sensation, him sending ticklish waves through me.

"Stop!" I say between giggles, getting breathless. "Please! I surrender!"

He reluctantly complies, and his face sobers when he notices our position. His hands framing my face, hips hovering an inch away from mine. I look up at him and he groans, returning back to his spot from before.

"You really want to see it?"

I nod eagerly. He pulls at his pants so that they're barely covering him. There, written low on the right side of his pelvis, reads *"Why not?"*

My jaw drops. "When did you get that?"

He smirks. "That's a story for another time. I'm tired, come here." He pushes me so that I'm facing away from him and pulls my waist back so that we are touching everywhere. He nuzzles his face into my neck, leaving a trail of open-mouthed kisses.

"What are we?" I ask softly.

He sighs. "I don't know. But I can't stay away from you, even if I should."

"Why should you?"

I wait for an answer, but turn my head slightly to see him fast asleep. I smile at his tired face, calm and relaxed. I shut my eyes and let sleep come over me as well.

* * *

I wake up with a smile still lingering. I yawn and reach behind me. When I don't feel contact with him, I turn and find that his spot on the bed is cold. I look around the room to see that his shirt that he had on is no longer on my floor.

I sit up and swing my legs over the side of the bed, sliding my feet into my slippers. Grinning, I run a hand through my hair, wanting to look somewhat presentable. I pad towards the door and crack it open, expecting to find him in the kitchen.

I walk out and see the kitchen lights off, him not in sight. I check the time, but he normally wouldn't leave for work for another hour. I look in the bathroom next and see no sign of him. I open his drawer to see it completely empty. Panicked, I throw the shower curtain open and see that his soap is gone.

I run out to the living room to find his bags gone as well. I can feel tears pricking my eyes, fighting to break through.

I go to Eliana's room next, hoping to find his stuff in there. Her bed is made neatly, no sign of her, or Sean, anywhere.

I sprint back to my room and do a scan, seeing nothing of his. It's like he was never here.

A tear falls from my eye, and I rip my phone off the charger, checking his contact. No call, no text, nothing.

I walk back to the kitchen, hoping that I missed something that he left. A sign that he didn't pack up and leave after yesterday.

A piece of paper on the counter catches my eye, and I grab it, checking to see if it's from him.

My heart drops when I see that it is.

Thirty-Eight

"I'm sorry." -Sean

Thirty-Nine

Summer

3 weeks later.

"Get your ass up."

I hiss at the bright light shining into my eyes, courtesy of Jonah yanking my curtains open. I throw an arm over my face and let out a long groan.

"Now!" He grabs a pillow from under my head and smacks me in the face with it. He then hands it to Eliana, who does the same.

"Ouch! Get out please. I'm in mourning."

Eliana pries my eyes open with her fingers. "You aren't in mourning. Don't be dramatic."

"Exactly." Jonah sits at the side of my bed, laying a hand on my shin. "Look babe, we know you're hurt, but you can't let some guy that you weren't even dating mess with you this much."

Eliana leaps onto the bed, plopping halfway on top of me.

"Even if he's my idiot brother."

I twist my head so that I can see her. "I'm sorry. This is exactly why I didn't want to go there. I knew it would screw everything up."

"It didn't screw anything up with me. I'm not mad. I just want you back to your chipper self."

Jonah clicks his tongue. "Well, as chipper as you normally are! Look, you called out of all your shifts this week, so no one even got to say goodbye. You are no longer employed, and all you do is lay in this bed and watch sad movies. It's not good for you, and it's not good for Gouda. No mouse should be surrounded by this much darkness."

I sigh. "Metaphorical or literal?"

"Both. Now get up, we're going out." He snatches the blanket I wrapped myself in off, and grabs my hands, pulling me into a sitting position.

I rub my eyes. "I don't know if you've noticed, but I'm not really in the mood to hit the clubs."

Eliana hops up, then pulls me into a standing position. "Not to worry! Jonah isn't going to clubs right now because he can't leave by himself, and his abstinence is going too well for him to quit. It's also eleven in the morning. We're going to get snacks and come home and shit talk."

"I'm not hungry."

"Um, no." Jonah shoots me an annoyed look, then goes into my closet to start picking me out something to wear. "We're not playing that game. The Summer I know and love is always hungry."

"Are you calling me fat right now?" I put a hand on my hip and so does Eliana.

He looks back at us over his shoulder. "Oh, come on, Eliana, you're supposed to be on my side here. No, I'm not calling you fat, and no you can't guilt me into letting you bed rot some more. You need to get your shit together."

He throws an outfit on my bed and they leave the room so that I can change. I stare at the yellow shirt, the same shade as the one I wore the last time I saw him. I didn't realize how prominent his presence was until he was truly gone.

Even when he went on that trip, some of his things were still left around the apartment. I would look at them, or sniff his shampoo when I missed him. Creepy, I know, but it was comforting. I considered buying a bottle but decided that would be going too far.

He called Eliana the day after he left. It was quick. All he said was that he was moving to Oklahoma. Apparently, the trip was about expanding the construction business, and he was planning on leaving the whole time.

That's the most confusing part about all of it. If he knew he wasn't staying, why did he start something with me right before? Why would he tell me that he had feelings for me, and then just leave? I truly thought that he was a good guy, someone dependable and honest, but maybe I was wrong about him.

I think the worst part is the fact that I've never liked someone, not really, until him. When I was young, I was so focused on pissing off my parents that I hadn't paid attention to guys that were likable in general. Then I went to college and was too focused on myself and my career to pay them any attention. I opened myself up to him, and he did the same to me. That's why it feels like I'm being stabbed in the gut every time I hear his name.

I wake up thinking I feel his breath on me, and look over

to an empty bed. I refuse to look at the couch, knowing how many times he'd slept there. Every time I wash my hands in the bathroom, I see him sitting at that counter, and think about how I took care of him there time and time again. He's everywhere. He marked everything in my life, everything that's supposed to be mine, and left nothing of his.

I want to hate him. And the fact that I don't makes me want to even more.

I pick out a different shirt, but get dressed like I was ordered to. I shuffle into the living room and ignore their cheers. Jonah tackles me into a hug and Eliana jumps in, crushing my ribs. "Can't. Breathe."

"Oh!" She jumps back. "Sorry!"

Jonah steps away, but keeps an arm around my shoulders. "I'm a proud father. You're gonna be just fine."

Eliana cringes. "Sorry, but you calling yourself her father is too weird, considering the history here."

"Trust me," he snickers, "she didn't mind calling me daddy."

I elbow him and Eliana gags. "Didn't need to know that."

We pile into Jonah's Bronco, me in the front because sadness equals princess treatment. We drive to a store outside of the city, them claiming that we need a new environment that isn't tainted by any memories. I don't argue.

We sing along to my playlist, and I skip every Ed Sheeran song. *Great, now my favorite artist is also ruined.*

I get lost in my thoughts, replaying everything that happened in my head, like I've spent the last three weeks doing. It's pathetic, but I can't shake it. I can't shake him out of my head. I hear his voice, I feel his presence. I say I'm in mourning because I am. I'm mourning the idea that I could ever find someone like him to spend my life with.

When the car stops, I close my eyes and try to push it all out of my head. I want one hour, just one, for myself. One that doesn't involve him. Jonah slides his hand in mine with a smile, giving it a reassuring squeeze.

I get out and they grab a cart, allowing me to jump in because they have to be nice to me. I let them parade me around the store, and we collect far more than what we came for. By the time we get to the snack aisle, my savings have withered away.

We each pick a candy and a chocolate for balance and then go to the chip aisle for some salt. Jonah decides that having just snacks won't be enough and that we need to order food on top of it.

I chuck Gouda's new bedding at him. "Weren't you the one calling everyone fat like an hour ago?"

He bends down to pick it up, then places the bedding back into my lap. "This is skinny! If we order pizza, we complete all health goals for the day. Vegetables, grains, dairy, protein."

Eliana skips into the aisle, dropping energy drinks into the cart. "Yes! We haven't had pizza in so long. It's been all healthy cooking because Sean-"

Jonah covers my ears with his hands, and I shoot him a glare. "Relax. I'm not five. I can hear his name without losing it. Let's just check out, I'm starving."

His eyes narrow. "I thought you weren't hungry?"

"Oh, that was a lie. I just wanted you to leave me alone."

* * *

We sit on the floor of Eliana's room, which is completely Sean-free. We tried to start a new movie, but it ended up being background noise since we couldn't go ten minutes without talking.

"All I'm saying," Jonah pauses, shoving another bite of pizza into his mouth before continuing, "is that we're all doing too much. Humans all have cancer and depression because we were meant to just hang around an island and eat fruit all day. There's too much responsibility now, it's all so serious."

I raise my hand. "As someone who has been living on that island for three weeks, it's not all that it's cracked up to be."

He snaps his fingers. "That's because you didn't eat fruit, you ate stale cereal for half of it. And, there's a certain energy change at the beach, which you also weren't at. No one is depressed when there's sunshine on their face and hot lifeguards to stare at."

"I second it." Eliana lies on her back, hands bracing her stomach. "Let's move out of the city, discover an island, and live amongst ourselves."

We end up talking for the rest of the night, the two of them falling asleep on the hard carpet, no blanket in sight. Although it was a clear distraction, it was nice to feel normal again, to feel like myself.

I grab my phone and scroll through our old messages, something that's become a calming mechanism for me. I even go as far as to listen to a voicemail he left, just so that I can hear him again. It's borderline creepy, but I haven't texted him, so I call it a win.

When I go to open the app, I see a new one at the top from my mother that I missed somehow. I click on it, curious as to what she wants.

"Hi, Summer. I know I said I would give you space, but I think I gave you a little too much freedom with that. I think if I don't make the first move, you won't ever be ready to talk again, not that I'm blaming you. I'll be in town this week, and I thought we could maybe grab lunch? Or something smaller, whatever works for you. Anyway, I'm rambling. Just shoot me a text so that I know you're okay. Bye."

I feel a little guilty at her tone of voice, nervous, and clearly a little rejected. I don't owe her anything, I know that, but it doesn't make icing her out any easier. Before I can think against it, I text her, just to say I'm open to meeting up. It's a start.

I plug my phone in and shut it off, then look at my friends snoring away, noticing a contentment settling in. I can live like this. Surrounded by friends, doing what makes me happy and nothing more. I don't need an island, I just need them.

And maybe a job.

Forty

Sean

I wipe the sweat off my brow, leaning my head against the brick wall behind me. I snatch a water bottle from the cooler, letting the smooth liquid glide down my throat.

"All good boss?"

I look over at Caleb, one of the guys on my crew. I like everyone here, but him the best. He's real, never tried to suck up or get me to like him. He's been honest with me from day one, and his work ethic only makes him better.

"Yeah, let's call it. Good work today. Let the guys know."

He backs away, throwing his walkie in my direction, and I catch it swiftly. I walk back to my truck and throw my gear in the bed, then hop into the driver's seat. I shove the key in and twist, letting the engine hum to life.

Instead of driving off, I rest my head against the steering wheel, giving myself a second of grace. It feels weird. Being the one in charge.

Back home, I never had a crew that was entirely my own.

They always had Ethan as their true boss, but here, he gives me full reign. He stayed for the initial start-up a few weeks ago, just to make sure I knew what to do, but left when he knew I was comfortable.

Since I've been here, all I've done is work. I do all the paperwork and any managing jobs in the evening or early morning. Then, during the day, I let myself work on site. It allows me to feel like I'm changing something with my own two hands, where I get to watch the projects grow from the ground up. It may not be traditional, but it's all I have.

I jolt at the sound of pounding and turn to see Caleb placing his face against my window. I roll it down, cocking a brow at him. "Yes?"

"Look, man," he places his arms inside the vehicle and I slap them away. "You gotta get out. All you do is work, then go back to whatever hole you live in, then work some more. This isn't a life. We're going out for drinks tonight, come with us."

I sigh. "I don't really think the guys want to hang out with their boss during their free time."

He clicks his tongue. "Honestly, Sean, you don't really have the boss vibe going on, so I'm sure they'd be cool with it."

"Watch it."

"I'm watching it." He throws his hands up in surrender. "Bar down the road, go clean up, then come back to meet us. I'm sure you could use a drink at the very least."

He's not entirely wrong. The only social interaction I've had outside of work is a few phone calls with Eliana, but even those were short and curt. Not that I deserve anything more.

"Fine."

He chuckles and slaps a hand on the truck, beckoning me away. I throw him a warning glare and roll the window back up, speeding away before he decides to say anything more.

I pull into the driveway of the small condo I'm renting, temporarily, like everything I have at the moment. Because of how fast I dropped everything and came, I haven't had time to actually settle. I signed a contract for the place the day I got here, then went out to rent a work truck.

I step inside to total emptiness. It's a metaphor, really. Ever since I left Summer alone in her bed, that's all I've been feeling. Numb. Empty. Nothing at all.

But I had to do it. I couldn't stay there, not with the way she was looking at me, not with everything that I wanted to say so close to slipping out. I got too attached. I found myself thinking about her at every waking moment.

I let it get too far. If I had stayed any longer, she would've had me as a constant in her life. I know myself. I know that I can't be that for anyone. For as long as I can remember, I've been the flakey one. The one that left and barely came back, barely called, barely tried.

If anything were to happen to me, I couldn't let her feel the way my mom felt, or live the way she lives. If I let her go now, she has time to find someone else, even if it means I can't have her. So I'll buy a truck. And a house. And I'll live in this boring ass state if it means she can have the life that she deserves.

I jump in the shower and wash myself off, then throw on a pair of jeans and a black T-shirt. I spray some cologne and head out, praying the night passes quickly. Or that they serve decent scotch at the very least.

Everyone's already there when I walk into the bar, and Caleb spots me immediately. He waves me over, pulling out a stool next to him. I make my way over and pat him on the shoulder in thanks, sitting down.

The other guys turn towards me. "Hey boss, I didn't know you were coming out tonight."

I tip my head at him. "No need to call me boss here, Andy. My name is Sean. You can use it."

He salutes me. "You got it, boss. Sean. Sorry."

Caleb cackles at his awkwardness, giving his chair a kick. "Bro, relax. He's not your boss here. He won't fire you for acting the way you normally do."

"I might."

Andy gulps. The bartender comes over to me, asking if I want to order. I look around the table, seeing that everyone has beers. Oh, this is like a hangout. Not an excuse to get drunk. Got it.

"Just a Bud Light, thanks."

They continue talking, and I let myself fade into the background. It's amusing, seeing a group of men that spend every day together interact. I can tell that they have each other's backs no matter what, which is why they tolerate any changes I throw at them. They're just happy they got to stay together.

"So Sean," Caleb starts, tipping his beer at me, "I thought Ethan was gonna run the show here for a while. What made you want to move to Oklahoma?"

I give him a closed-lip smile. "Just needed a change of scenery, I guess."

He lets out a breathy laugh. "Oh, I get it."

"Get what?" I ask, before taking a swig of my beer that has just arrived. I let the starchy drink glide into my stomach, ignoring the disappointment when it doesn't burn my throat. I miss hard liquor.

He points at me. "Who's the girl?"

I set my beer down and cross an arm over my chest, feeling defensive. "I don't know what you mean."

Some of the other guys chuckle. Caleb throws an arm around my shoulders. "The only reason anyone has to pack up and ditch their life is that they're running from something or someone. And based on your reaction just now, I'm going with the latter."

I shrug him off of me. "There's no girl." I grit out, the lie feeling metallic on my tongue.

"Is she hot?" Josh, one of the younger guys, asks.

I slam a palm on the counter. "Enough with the girl talk already. Aren't you supposed to be talking about fucking concrete or something?"

He stares back at me, mouth wide open, before snapping his jaw shut and giving me a sly smirk. "She's totally hot."

I slip out of my chair, slamming a $50 on the counter, and stomp out of the bar, no longer feeling very social.

Forty-One

Summer

I stand outside of the restaurant we agreed upon, regret starting to pile up. I'm not ready. At least I don't think I am. She expects me to change overnight. She's pushy, that's where I get it from. But it's not fair. Not after everything.

I take one last look at the door, then start to turn away when she spots me. There, on the patio, is my mother, waving her arms dramatically at me. Shit.

I wince and spin on my heels, heading into the direction of her table. I pull a chair out, and it gives an ear-curdling screech. *Accurate.*

"Hi, Mom." I grab the napkin and unroll it, placing my silverware on the table. I set it over my lap and cross my legs, automatically feeling classier in her presence.

"Summer! I'm so glad you texted." She grabs the water pitcher and fills up two mason jars, then passes me one.

I give her a close-lipped smile. "Sure. You just seemed very insistent on it."

"I wasn't trying to push, I swear. I just was afraid that if I didn't reach out, you would think I forgot about you, or didn't care. Which I do. Care, that is."

"Right." We sit there, staring at each other. I clear my throat and take a long gulp of water, just to get her eyes off me. I set it down and wipe my mouth, looking back at her.

We stay like that, averting each other's eyes and making comments about the weather. Just when I'm about to call it, she bursts up from her chair, running her hands down her sides. "This is weird, right? It feels weird. Formal."

I nod. She reaches into her purse and drops $20 on the table, then steps away. "Let's do something not as awkward. Maybe it'll feel less pressured. It's a beautiful day. How about a walk?"

I let out a breath I didn't know I was holding. "Please."

She smiles and takes my arm, maneuvering us onto the sidewalk. We spot a park nearby and decide to walk the trails.

"So, how have you been? Work is good?"

I let out a nervous laugh. "I quit actually."

Her eyebrows shoot up, and her step falters. I can see her fight against whatever she's thinking, trying not to let her old ways take over. "Oh! Well, where are you working instead?"

I sigh. "The past few weeks haven't been great for me. I was trying to give myself a second to breathe before I get a new job. But it's time for me to get my life back together. I'll start looking soon."

She nods. "Of course, don't put too much on your plate."

I bite my lip. Why does her being nice piss me off? It's like she's trying to be the mother I always wanted, but it isn't fitting. If it's this easy for her to act like a decent human being, then what the hell took so long?

She pulls me towards a bench, motioning for me to sit. She settles beside me, tapping her knee. "What's made the past few weeks so bad?"

I look away. "We don't have to do that."

"Do what?"

I jut my chin out. "Pretend like this is normal. Like you actually care what's going on in my life."

She slumps in her seat. "I understand where you're coming from. I do. I haven't given you a reason to trust me. But if I didn't care, then why would I be here? Seriously, Summer, what could I possibly gain from asking you about your life?"

"I don't know, okay? It's just weird."

"Fine." She crosses her legs. "Then we'll just sit here. And stare at these ugly birds, and wait for enough time to pass, and then politely go our separate ways."

"Fine."

About a minute passes, and she's unable to contain herself. "Did I ever tell you about my parents?"

I eye her curiously. "No. I assumed they were dead."

"My father isn't," she admits. "Although sometimes I think my life would've been a whole lot easier if that were true."

"Why?" I try not to pry too much, but I can't help myself. She's never shared anything about her childhood with me, not willingly, at least. I won't lie and say I'm not a little intrigued.

She looks towards the sky, replaying memories in her head. "My father was a drunk. He was successful, inherited a real estate business from his parents, but a drunk nonetheless. He was obsessed with his wealth, flaunted it as much as he could."

She places her hands under her legs to stop them from fidgeting. "Their relationship never made sense to me. My mother was warm and humble. She always told me he was different when they met. But his old self fizzled away with every piece of power that he gained."

"That sounds familiar." I tort.

"Don't be silly, your father has always been the way that he is." She rolls her eyes playfully. She looks different in the sunlight, more youthful. "Before my mother died, dad had an alcohol problem, but it was nothing like the one he had after. The first thing he did was marry me off to your father, and I was grieving too much to object."

"You were close?" I ask.

She smiles warmly. "She was my best friend. You act just like her, look like her too. Our favorite thing to do together was playing in the lake near our house. Summer was her favorite season, it's what I named you after."

"Really?" It excites me a little, knowing that I'm connected to what seems like is the only normal person in my family. I don't understand how my mother can be so opposite of her own.

"Really. It was the only thing I fought your father on."

The mention of him darkens the mood, and awkwardness passes over us again. "So what happened after that? Did you see your dad again?"

She shrugs. "Here and there. He became messy, a joke in the circles we ran in. I saw him at a party a few years ago, drunk off his ass, screaming at the help. Haven't seen him since."

"Do you ever feel guilty?" Her brows knit together. "That you never tried to help him?"

"Men like our fathers don't want help. They want power, and control, and attention, but never help. Nor was I willing to give it. I owed him nothing, and the positions he puts himself in are his own fault."

"Right." I don't know how I expected our outing to go, but it wasn't like this. I've seen a different side of her today, and I might as well confide in her in return.

"I'm having boy problems." She chortles, and I shoot her a scowl. "It's not funny!"

She places a hand on my shoulder. "I'm sorry, I know it's not. I just never thought I'd see you so worked up over a man."

"What, because I'm unlikable to the species?"

She shoves me playfully. "No. Because you are the most stubborn person I have ever met. You'd die before you let someone else's actions mess with your head. So what did he do?"

I kick a rock into the grass. It hits a bump and flies a little, splashing into a pocket of mud. "How do you know that it wasn't me that screwed it up?"

"Because I saw the way that boy looked at you. And the way that he stood up for you in front of your father. He cares about you, and he hates that he does. I could see it in his eyes."

I meet her stare. "How'd you know it was him?"

"Psh, with a man that looks like that in your life? There isn't anyone else."

A giggle bubbles out of me. "Maybe it's all for the best. I can't help but think that I accidentally caught feelings for someone like him." A beat passes. "Dad, I mean."

This time, a full laugh falls out of her mouth. It's a weird noise to hear coming from my mother, one that I never thought I would encounter. She sounds like me. "He is nothing like your father. I don't know what went on between you too, but your father would never have stood up for me like Sean did for you. He would've never carried me home when my feet were tired. And he wouldn't look at me with the tenderness that I saw Sean have. The only thing your father has in his eyes is ice. But Sean? No, that boy is pure warmth."

I feel a tear forming and I curse internally. I'm just so tired. Tired of caring more than he clearly did. Tired of being so affected by the choices of someone else. Tired of the fact that she's right. He's nothing like my father, I know that. But it would be so much easier if he were.

I lean my head against her shoulder, letting myself experience the motherly affection that I've never had. My movement startles her, but she recovers quickly, and wraps an arm around me, letting me mold into her.

We let the silence take over, but it's comfortable this time, natural. We stay like that, savoring the change of pace within our relationship. After a while, she gives my back one last rub and then rises.

"I have to go. I'm starting a new therapy group today."

I ignore the memories that the words spark and give her a curt nod. "Good luck then."

She hesitates, but begins to step away. She shoots me one last look over her shoulder, and I jump to my feet, causing her to stop in her tracks. "Wait."

She twists fully around to face me. "I'll call this time. For real."

She beams. "I'll answer."

Sean

I lean my head against the window frame I'm working on, letting the cold metal chill my forehead. I wait for the ache in my chest to dull every day, but if anything, it gets stronger. Every minute that I'm away from her, it feels like the string between us is getting more and more tense. Like I'm staying in one spot, but she's pulling away, taking the best parts of me with her.

I can hear Caleb's footsteps behind me, his tool belt making a loud clanking sound with every step. "Hey, sorry to interrupt the moment you're having currently, but I was wondering if I could head out an hour early today?"

I eye his hopeful expression, not caring enough to say no. "Sure."

His face lights up and he snaps his belt off, slinging it over his shoulder. "Are you gonna ask what for?"

I shrug. "No."

His smile falters a little, making him look like a sad puppy. I hold back a sigh. "Would you like to tell me, Caleb?"

The grin returns, and he nods eagerly. "I'm asking my girlfriend to marry me."

That catches my attention, and I stand up straight, patting him on the back. "Congrats, man, that's a big step."

He leans against the wall beside me. "I know. I can't wait. I mean, I've always known that she was it for me. That there wouldn't be anyone else. It's just a feeling you get. Like every time you're away from them, you can't think of anything else. You count down the seconds until you see them again, and then when you do, you savor it even more than the last."

He places a hand over his mouth and looks down, replaying a memory in his head. "I remember this one time, she got so pissed at me for forgetting to run the dishwasher. She stood there, stomping her foot with her face all scrunched up. Even angry, she looked so fucking cute. I just thought to myself, even if I spent the rest of my life with her mad at me, I'd be the happiest man alive. Anyway, I'm rambling."

I feel a lump in my throat at his words. "No no, you're fine."

He runs a hand through his hair. "I just don't know what I'll do if she says no. I'm selfish around her. I don't think I'd be able to let her go. If I ever lost her, I think I'd feel empty. Since I met her, it's like life is so much brighter. It would be like if the world lost its color. But I would still die happy today, as long as it meant I got to be hers for even a little while."

I'm an idiot. I'm such a fucking idiot! What the hell was I thinking? I had her, all of her, right in front of me, and I walked away. I was scared, and I let it take over me again, and now everything is colorless and dull and what is wrong with this state? Why does everyone wear jeans all the time? They're so fucking uncomfortable and I'm an idiot.

A snap brings me out of my thoughts and Caleb's standing there, a concerned look on his face. "Did I lose you there?"

I barely process his words and slide past him. "Yeah, yeah good luck man."

I saunter out of the house, picking up the pace when I see my truck. I can't live like this, I want to be selfish. I want her to yell at me for forgetting to start the dishwasher, I want to count down the seconds before I see her, I fucking need her. More than I've ever needed anything, more than I need air.

And I'll spend my life fighting to get her back if it means that I tried everything. But the way I'm living right now? It's not the person I want to be. So I shoot Ethan a text asking if he can come out to cover me for a little while, and I book the first flight back home.

Because that's what she feels like. Home.

Forty-Two

Summer

I give another pound to Eliana's door, hoping it'll get her to finally answer. She still doesn't respond, but I hear rustling in the room. "Alright, enough. I'm coming in!"

I barge through the door, cringing at the look of her. She's wrapped in multiple blankets, balled up in her bed. There's a trash can beside her and she looks a little pale, not to mention the weird groaning that sounds like a dying animal.

"Jesus. You look like shit."

She chucks a dirty tissue at me. "I feel like it. I don't think I can go."

"Damn." I pull my phone out, ready to call Shelly and reschedule. "Okay, I'll cancel our class. Maybe we can try next week."

"No!" She jerks up, hand raised to stop me. "You can't! I already tried. We'll lose the money, and it seems like such a waste. You go, and I'll just join a class a little later to finish mine."

I drop beside her in bed, careful not to touch her. "No way. I can't do an entire class with Pam without you as a buffer. Shelly will understand. Let me work with her a little."

"Apparently it's the owner, not Shelly. She can't break policy, it'll be fine! Maybe ask for a silent session and just listen to music. I'm sure she would agree to that."

"Ughhh." I flop back, covering my face with my hands. "Fine. But you owe me big time."

She shrivels back into her cocoon, and I stomp out, grabbing my keys. The only reason I have fun at these is because we get to do it together. Messing with Pam is just an added bonus.

I call in an order to our favorite Chinese place on the way, and deliver some hot and sour soup for Eliana. When I get to the studio, I jump straight out of the car, not allowing myself to fume. Shelly waves as I walk in, motioning for me to step up to her desk.

"Hi, honey! You should probably go straight in today. No time for chitchat." I eye her weirdly, never guessing that those words would come out of her mouth. I mean seriously, the queen of talking isn't in the mood today? *Weird.*

"Sure." I bypass her and go to the room, laughing evilly at the concept. A whole hour with just me and Pam in a room. She's gonna die.

Still laughing at my ingenuity, I push the door open, stopping in my tracks when a pair of green eyes meet mine. "What the fuck?"

He leaps out of his chair and steps towards me, hands up in defense. "Please, sunshine. Just hear me out."

"Sunshine? SUNSHINE?" *Damn it, Eliana.* I throw my hands into my hair, stepping back away from him. "What gives you any right to call me that? To call me anything? No.

I'm not gonna stand here and listen to your shitty apology so that you can feel less guilty about what you did. Fuck this."

I start to walk out of the room when I slam into someone, making me falter. Pam places her hands on her hips, tipping her head at him. "I should've known from day one that you wouldn't make my life easy. You paid for this session and I'm required to teach it. Take a seat."

My jaw clenches. "Hell no. I'm leaving, teach your class to him."

She rolls her eyes. "Always so dramatic. Sit your ass down." My eyebrows shoot up at her language. "You heard me. Now."

My body takes control and suddenly I'm sitting with my pieces in front of me. I spot the toolbox and slyfully set it on the floor, out of his sight. I can feel his stare at the side of my face, sending heat in its path. I ignore him completely. She can make me stay, but she can't make me talk to him.

I put on the apron and hold back a laugh when she hands him a pink one that has sparkles on it. He puts it on without hesitation, and it barely covers his chest. At least I know she's on my side.

"All the paint I have is placed at your table, so I give you creative freedom. There's nothing more for me to teach you, not that you would listen, anyway." She says, eyeing me. "I'll leave you to it. I'll be at the front if you need me."

I snatch her arm, pulling her close to me. "Don't leave me with him!" I whisper-shout.

She steps out of my grasp. "Hear the man out. He's here. That's a start."

Then she's walking out, snapping the door shut behind her. I take a deep breath, feeling the weight occupying the air between us. It's not fair. He gets to walk out on me without an explanation, then comes back looking better than before.

His jaw is covered in short scruff, and his skin is tanner than before. I can tell he's been on the job because of how his figure has grown slightly, his muscles looking even bigger than before. Meanwhile, I haven't washed my hair in a week and my mascara is two days old. I hate men.

I stare at the pieces in front of him, a pot, a plate, and something else that I can't see. He notices my look and holds one of them up. "I called in yesterday, asking if I could make some pieces. I did a private session, and she used this dryer thing so that they'd be ready in time for today. It was so hard, not coming to you the second my plane landed. But I wanted to be in a place that you felt comfortable in, and I thought it might be awkward if I was just sitting here watching."

I scoff. "I'm so sure. You left without a word for a month, but one day away from me was so hard. Bullshit."

He rubs the back of his neck. "I know I haven't given you a reason to believe a word I say, but I made a mistake. I didn't want to admit it, but it's true, and I knew that if I didn't fix it, I would never forgive myself."

"Great." I give him a fake smile. "Then don't."

I grab some of the paint that Pam set out, squirting it onto a palette. I won't let his presence ruin this for me. Somewhere along the way I actually started liking pottery, and I'm not leaving without my artwork completed.

I do my mug first, making the inside light blue and the outside white. He follows my lead and starts painting his own. I try not to be annoyed at how perfect his looks, but I can't help but feel like it's a competition.

I paint small blue flowers on the outside, with little green leaves. He looks at my concentration and smiles. "I remember the first time I saw you this concentrated. You were fifteen and had to take PE for a graduation requirement. In order to pass the class, you had to be able to score a free throw. You spent hours in our driveway, trying again and again, with no success. It got to a point where I couldn't watch anymore, so I came out and showed you how to hold a ball. I remember feeling your heartbeat pick up, your breathing getting heavy. I thought it was weird how easily winded you got playing a sport."

The memory jogs my mind, and my hand goes limp, causing one of my flowers to look deformed. I curse lowly, then dip my brush into some white so that I can clean it up.

He sets his finished pot down, bright yellow, with an orange sun on the front of it. "It wasn't the basketball though, was it? I know because it's the feeling I get every time you're around me. It's like my body can sense your presence before I can. My skin heats up, my heart skips a beat, and my breathing quickens. Even just a flip of your hair sends me into a spiral. I'm going crazy over here, sunshine."

I ignore him, not wanting to give in, even if every bone in my body is fighting me on it. I pick up my jewelry stand next and choose neon paint this time. My hand reaches for pink, green, and orange, then adds a healthy amount onto my palate. I start with a swirly design, wanting it to look abstract.

Sean moves his plate so that it's in front of him and grabs some colors to start working with. "I never actually hated you, y'know? I mean, I think that much is obvious. But when I first got here, you didn't annoy me at all. I liked having someone constantly nagging me, testing me, not letting me get away with my usual shit.

"You kept me in line, and that was one of the first things that made me so attracted to you. I would piss you off just so that I could hear you yell at me, because then I would finally get some honesty from someone. And I couldn't help but notice how cute you looked when you got all flustered."

He lets out a small laugh. "Your face would get so red, and your nose would scrunch up. Even angry, you could steal the attention of every man in the room. Anytime I saw another guy around you, it would make my blood boil. I almost killed Jonah that night you brought him over. I knew exactly what was happening, but it still got to me. Everything you do affects me."

"I want you to stop."

He looks away from his plate and studies my face. "No."

I drop my paintbrush. "What do you mean 'no'?"

"No." He tilts his head to the side. "I'm not going to stop. I've already fucked this up once and it was the biggest mistake I've ever made. I'll keep bugging you until the day I die, if that's what it takes. Because I'm selfish. I'm selfish when it comes to you, Summer. And I thought that if you found a guy that could give you something I can't then I'd want you to be happy. But that's a lie. Because I'm giving you everything I have. I'm giving you all of me, and I won't stop until I've put it all on the line."

I move my jewelry holder to the side, satisfied with how it looks. I can't help myself, so I look at what he painted. This time, his plate is gray, and has a small white mouse on it. I instantly recognize it as Gouda and have to pull my lips into my mouth to stop from smiling.

"Well, I'm done now, so time is up. Goodbye, Sean."

I stand to leave, but he reaches an arm out, softly setting me back down in my chair. "Wait! What about your third piece?"

I make a popping noise with my mouth. "Don't have one."

His brows knit together. "I know you do. Pam told me about it. Wouldn't say what it is, but talked about how much she loved it."

I gesture helplessly. "Must've been thinking of someone else."

He grins slyly, knowing what's happening. "Fine. I'll just have to show you mine."

He pulls out a wired-shaped ceramic and hands it to me, making me gasp when I see what it is.

"Eliana told me that you quit, but I know this isn't the end of the road for you. I thought you should have something to remind you of that."

I stare down at the piece. It's a stethoscope that has the hose wrapped into a heart shape. On the bell, there's a small heart engraved with a little sun inside of it. I feel sick to my stomach.

My head is reeling, my thoughts conflicted. I'm not sure what to do anymore. I was fully convinced that if I ever saw him again, I would tell him to shove it and leave. But with the way he's looking at me right now? It makes it so much harder.

I don't want to be that girl. The one that keeps going back to her dickhead boyfriend because he can talk her into anything. But I know he isn't like that. He makes mistakes because he's hurting. I just don't know if I can be the one that has to heal him.

I hand it back to him, letting him paint it how he likes. I grab the toolbox but keep it out of his sight. "I'm going to finish it, but I don't want you to see it. So don't look over here. You owe me that much."

He dips his head. "Got it."

I use orange and black for all the tools, knowing it's the color scheme of his actual set. I start with the outside and keep peeking up at him to make sure he's not looking, but he stays focused on his own work, following my command.

"I know I fucked up," he says hoarsely. "I was a coward, and scared, and I didn't even say goodbye because I couldn't bear to see the look on your face when I left. The hurt. I stayed up for most of that night, savoring the feeling of you in my arms. I didn't want to sleep because it felt like a waste of time. And I had already wasted so much.

"From the minute I left that apartment, it's like there's been a weight attached to me, getting heavier every day I spent without you. Then, when you walked through those doors today, it was all lifted. Because that's what you do for me. You make me feel lighter."

He sets the stethoscope down and stands, staring at my face, pleading. "From the day I met you, my world got brighter. All of my feelings are tied to you, and I'd be heartbroken forever if it meant that you made me that way. Because I worship the ground you walk on, sunshine. You see me more than anyone in my life ever has. You make me feel like I can be vulnerable, like I can show my true emotions after hiding them for so long."

I push the toolbox away. "I don't want your emotions to revolve around me. I need you to be your own person, can't you get that?"

He shakes his head. "No. I'm sorry but I can't. Every emotion, every feeling, that I have is attached to you. Because I love you. I love everything about you. I love the way you interact with people, how raw and honest you are with them. I love how you can make the wittiest comments without a second thought. I love the smell of your perfume, and the way you ball your fists up every time you get angry.

"I love the face you make when something confuses you, and the smile you give me when you know something I don't. I love how strong and resilient and positively human you are. You're something real, Summer Rhodes. Something special. How could I not love you?"

He swipes away a tear that I didn't know had fallen. He grabs my face in his hands, stepping into my space. He bows his head so that our lips are an inch apart. But he stops.

He's letting me make the choice. I stare at his lips and feel mine moving closer without my instruction. I want to stay mad at him. I want to yell and scream and kick him out. But I can't. Because he loves me.

He's stubborn, and grumpy, and infuriating, and moody, and the absolute opposite of perfect. But he's also affectionate, and caring, and devoted, and tender. He's the kind of man that would scrape the snow off my car in the morning, and say nothing about it, not expecting a reward.

He would buy me "just because" flowers and keep one so that he knows when they're dead. He would use gifts as surprises, and words as apologies. He would fix the wobble in my table the second he noticed it, and he would listen to me rant, just to hear the sound of my voice.

He made a mistake. A big, colossal mistake. But he's here now. And he's begging for one more chance, just one, to show me that he won't make another. So who am I to say no?

I close the distance between us and he reacts instantly, groaning at the connection. I can feel his grin against my lips, and the way his body melts at my simple touch. He loves me.

He pulls me to my feet, wrapping his arms around me. He places one hand on the small of my back, arching me into him. The other wraps into my hair, twirling and flattening it. This asshole actually loves me.

He pulls away, smiling brightly. "What'd you make me?"

I drop my head, suddenly feeling self-conscious about the gift. I eye it, silently allowing him to look. He steps closer to the table and carefully picks up each piece one by one, examining them closely. He only touches the dry parts, making sure the paint doesn't smudge.

When he realizes what the dates are, he turns back to me, beaming. He grabs my face again, slamming his lips onto mine. He places a kiss on my forehead, then each cheek, then a soft one on my nose. "You love me."

I roll my eyes. "Shut up."

He wiggles his eyebrows cheekily. "You love me. Admit it."

I huff. "Yeah, whatever, I love you. Don't make it weird." He laughs loudly and I follow. He then picks me up off the ground and spins us.

Pam walks back in at that moment, trying to look annoyed at our antics. "So I see you're just as persistent as she is."

He smiles at her, slowly lowering me back to my feet. "If I could be half the person she is, then I'd be a saint."

Pam cocks a brow. "I wouldn't go that far."

He turns back to me, connecting our foreheads. I sigh contently, finally feeling like I can breathe again. "Let's go home."

He interlocks our fingers. "I'm already there."

Epilogue

Summer

9 months later.

"I think if room five hits his call light one more time, I'm ripping it out of the wall and taking it." I shut it off on the monitor, my tech graciously volunteering to go in.

Kaydee laughs, plopping into the seat next to me. "He's lonely and thinks you're pretty."

"He calls me baby girl."

She cringes. "Yikes. No matter where you go, there will always be creeps that follow."

"Preach it, sister." I grab an alcohol wipe and start cleaning my belongings. I end with my badge, decorated with my newly awarded DAISY pin.

After everything that happened last year, getting a new job was inevitable. I wanted to give nursing one last shot, mostly because Sean forced me into not giving up just yet. And thank God that he did.

A few weeks after I stopped working at my old hospital, I messaged Kaydee from the conference I spoke at and asked if she wanted to get coffee. I thought it would be nice to be friends with a more positive nurse, based on the fact that me and Jonah tend to complain too much.

I thought that if anyone could get me back into it, it would be her, and I was right. She was a nice change of pace from my other friends and she ended up telling me about a spot that was opening up on her unit, and asked if I wanted to pick up a short contract just to try it. I said yes, and she became my new work bestie, not that Jonah could be replaced.

He ended up staying at my old unit up until recently, where he decided that travel nursing would work out better. Shockingly, he kept his abstinence strong, and has even tried dating. It's not going well, but it's the thought that counts.

As much as I miss being on the unit with him, I love my new job. Working in oncology was never something I expected to love, but it made so much sense once I tried it. The patients are there for a longer period of time, so I got to have consistency and bond with them on a much deeper level than before. Their families are usually incredibly kind and helpful. They do everything in their power to make the patient feel at home, and I end up getting to bond with them as well.

Not to mention the feeling I get when someone rings the bell, signaling that they beat the cancer. All the staff and other patients gather around to celebrate their success, and it's the most heartwarming thing that a nurse can see. It also makes me feel a little more connected to Sean's father, even if I never met him.

When I told Sean that I was taking the position, he was so excited for me. All he wanted was for me to use the potential that he saw, and the fact that I could help people like his dad just made it better.

I lounge with Kaydee for the last few minutes of our shift, waiting until it's not too early to clock out. When the time hits 7:23 AM, we leap from our chairs, heading towards the exit. Don't get me wrong, I love my job, but twelve hours is pushing it.

I click the down arrow on the elevator and wait for it to come. When the doors open, I see a familiar set of green eyes. I step inside, throwing my arms around him, and he leans into my hold.

He kisses my hair, then tilts my head up to land one on my lips. "I missed you."

I mold into his side, keeping an arm wrapped around his waist, while his hooks around my shoulders. "I missed you too. I thought you weren't coming back until tomorrow?"

He shrugs, smiling softly. "Caught an earlier flight."

I grin up at him, knowing he didn't want to stay away for another night. After he came back almost a year ago, we decided that it would make sense for us to try long-distance. He still had a lease to finish back in Oklahoma, and he couldn't leave Ethan to figure out a plan after he made a commitment.

I also thought it'd be best for us to have some distance, so that we could work on our issues separately. It's no secret that both of us had some trauma going on, and we knew that starting a relationship by piling it on top of each other was a bad idea.

He started therapy over there and worked through his PTSD and grief. I continued to work on my relationship with my mother, and let myself truly feel the absence of a parent, even if he was a shitty father.

Even though I had written them both out of my life, I hadn't truly processed it or gotten any closure until they came back. It made me lose any hope that one day, he would change. But with the official loss of him, I gained a true mother figure in my life, which is something I never thought I could say.

We walk out of the hospital, still connected, and he opens the door for me when we reach the car. Like always, he buckles me in, then gives me a quick peck on the lips. He rounds the car and we drive back to our new apartment, parking in our designated spot.

It's still completely empty, being that we brought no furniture with us. Sean has none, since the place he rented in Oklahoma was already furnished. We also thought that starting fresh with things that we could pick out together was a better idea than leaving Eliana with nothing at the old apartment.

We found this one about a week ago and immediately signed the papers. We had been looking for one for about a month, checking a few out every time he was in town. This one just had everything we were looking for.

Beautiful big windows, a good distance between both of our jobs, a large master bedroom with a nice kitchen, and a guest room for Eliana or Caroline to stay in. It's a big upgrade from what I had before, mostly because my new job pays a lot better, and Sean's management position came with a big raise.

Now, with him running the Chicago branch, and Ethan moving to Oklahoma, he still gets to keep a big role. I felt guilty, taking him away from the crew that he bonded with, but he claims that he'd trade them in for me any day.

For a while, we were nervous to tell Eliana that we were

looking at places, but she ended up being more excited than we were. Apparently she has a bunch of savings from her new career as an author, so rent wouldn't be a problem. I also know that having the apartment to herself would make it easier to have her boyfriend over whenever, but I don't point that out to Sean.

So here we sit. On the floor of our new apartment, boxes scattered around us, Gouda in his cage next to me, sprinting on his wheel like usual. I never expected to like a quieter life. My biggest fear used to be settling down with some boring guy, buying a suburban house, and birthing kid after kid.

But with Sean? Nothing could ever be boring. I could sit in a silent room with him and still be grateful for every second. He made me feel alive again, when for a while, I was just coasting.

It was hard in the beginning, having someone relying on me. But we learned and grew together, and he was more patient with me than I deserved. If anyone would have told me I'd end up falling for Sean Jacobs, I would have laughed in their face. But now that I have? I wouldn't trade this feeling for the world.

Author's Note

Now's the time for me to make a confession. I had never planned on writing a book, let alone publishing one, but here we are. I have always been a lover of books. I was the person whose backpack weighed 40 pounds because I needed to have one with me. I also have fallen victim to countless slumps, time and time again.

I remember being in such a long reading slump, over six months, and couldn't look at a book and gain interest. Then I got some inspiration from my life, and thought to myself, "This would make a great novel, I should sell the idea." I wrote it down in a locked note, banishing it from my brain.

Then one day, I found it. I read through the concept, and decided if I couldn't read a book, maybe I should write one. So I did.

My first draft was atrocious. I didn't know how much planning and thought really went into every book I've read, even just the silly romances. My grammar was awful. I kept rewriting scenes and was never happy.

Eventually, I looked at it and realized that it was never going to be perfect by my standards. As someone who has read

294

millions of rom-coms, I could find things in even my five-star reads that I didn't like, or would have written differently. At the end of the day, this is the first of many. So no, it's not perfect. But it's something, and that's enough for me.

About The Author

Want to Know More?
If you found yourself particularly attached to the characters,
specifically a certain raven-haired flight attendant, updates
will be posted across all platforms!
Facebook- Stella Forelove
Tiktok- @stella.forelove
Instagram- @stella.forelove
Liked the book?
Post a review! Or reach out to let me know ;)
Email- stella.forelove.fans@gmail.com

www.ingramcontent.com/pod-product-compliance
Lightning Source LLC
Chambersburg PA
CBHW071537110726
47908CB00007B/1925